Shakespeare & Creative Criticism

Shakespeare &

Series Editors:
Graham Holderness, *University of Hertfordshire*
Bryan Loughrey

Volume 5
Shakespeare & the Ethics of War
Edited by Patrick Gray

Volume 4
Shakespeare & Creative Criticism
Edited by Rob Conkie and Scott Maisano

Volume 3
Shakespeare & the Arab World
Edited by Katherine Hennessey and Margaret Litvin

Volume 2
Shakespeare & Commemoration
Edited by Clara Calvo and Ton Hoenselaars

Volume 1
Shakespeare & Stratford
Edited by Katherine Scheil

Shakespeare & Creative Criticism

Edited by
Rob Conkie
&
Scott Maisano

berghahn
NEW YORK • OXFORD
www.berghahnbooks.com

Published in 2019 by
Berghahn Books
www.berghahnbooks.com

© 2019 Berghahn Books

Originally published as a special issue
of *Critical Survey*, volume 28, number 2.

All rights reserved. Except for the quotation of short passages
for the purposes of criticism and review, no part of this book
may be reproduced in any form or by any means, electronic or
mechanical, including photocopying, recording, or any information
storage and retrieval system now known or to be invented,
without written permission of the publisher.

Library of Congress Cataloging-in-Publication Data

Names: Conkie, Rob, editor. | Maisano, Scott, editor.
Title: Shakespeare and creative criticism / edited by Rob Conkie and Scott
    Maisano.
Description: New York : Berghahn Books, 2019. | Series: Shakespeare and ;
    volume 4 | Includes bibliographical references and index.
Identifiers: LCCN 2019003846 (print) | LCCN 2019009465 (ebook) | ISBN
    9781789202519 (ebook) | ISBN 9781789202496 (hardback : alk. paper) |
    ISBN 9781789202502 (paperback : alk. paper)
Subjects: LCSH: Shakespeare, William, 1564–1616—Criticism and
    interpretation. | Creative writing.
Classification: LCC PR2976 (ebook) | LCC PR2976.S3337 2019 (print) |
    DDC 822.3/3—dc23
LC record available at https://lccn.loc.gov/2019003846

British Library Cataloguing in Publication Data

A catalogue record for this book is available from the British Library

ISBN 978-1-78920-249-6 hardback
ISBN 978-1-78920-250-2 paperback
ISBN 978-1-78920-251-9 ebook

Contents

List of Illustrations	vii
Introduction *Creative Critical Shakespeares* Rob Conkie and Scott Maisano	1
Chapter 1 **Responses to Responses to Shakespeare's Sonnets** *More Sonnets* Matthew Zarnowiecki	21
Chapter 2 **Exit, pursued by a fan** *Shakespeare, Fandom, and the Lure of the Alternate Universe* Kavita Mudan Finn and Jessica McCall	38
Chapter 3 **A Merry Midsummer Labor Merchant's Tempest in King Beatrice's Verona** Jessica McCall	54
Chapter 4 **Pickled Red Herring** Kavita Mudan Finn	61
Chapter 5 **Enter Nurse, or Love's Labour's Won** Scott Maisano	101
Chapter 6 **Echo and Narcissus, or Man O Man!** Mary Baine Campbell	119

Chapter 7
The Fair Maid of Alexandria, or The Glass Tower
Dan Moss

128

Chapter 8
A Tragedy of the Plantation of Virginia
David Nicol

146

Chapter 9
***Othello*, Original Practices**
A Photographic Essay
Rob Conkie

165

Index

181

Illustrations

0.1.	Falstaff's fat suit.	14
0.2.	An alacrity in sinking.	14
0.3.	A poor old woman.	15
1.1.	Detail of vol. 2, p. 2126 of *Le Grand Robert de La Langue Française*.	35
1.2.	Detail of Sonnet 80, line 5.	35
2.1.	Tumblr post from NicoDreams.	47
3.1.	"One-Acts!"	58
4.1.	CSI: *Richard III*.	62
9.1.	Doubling.	166
9.2.	Damien Millar as the Herald.	168
9.3.	A goblet unmoved.	169
9.4.	Tom Considine as Othello.	169

9.5.	Andre Jewson as Desdemona.	169
9.6.	Roderigo (Bob Pavlich) and Iago (Trent Baker) sitting on a step in the stage.	170
9.7.	A long, narrow thrust with audience on three sides.	170
9.8.	The difficulties of fighting with scripts.	170
9.9.	An unholy alliance.	170
9.10.	The kiss, the clown.	171
9.11.	Emilia's fabric management.	173
9.12.	Desdemona asleep.	174
9.13.	'Think on thy sins.'	174
9.14.	'Out strumpet! Weep'st thou for him to my face?'	175
9.15.	'Down, strumpet.'	175
9.16.	'What did thy song bode, lady?'	176
9.17.	I've not witnessed a more emotionally wrought Othello than Tom Considine's.	176
9.18.	It was very confronting to see this act so close up.	177
9.19.	Audience feedback.	178

Introduction
Creative Critical Shakespeares

Rob Conkie and Scott Maisano

Here is a beginning of *Shakespeare and Creative Criticism*:
> The range of creative responses to Shakespeare has expanded recently to include critical writing that is evocative, affective, and performative. This seminar invites papers—on any Shakespeare-related topic—that integrate creative and critical modes of writing. The aim is to examine how creative modes of writing might facilitate new or different types of critical engagement with Shakespeare. What kinds of critical insights are made possible only or especially via creative strategies? And, indeed, how do critical perspectives impel creative (re) engagement with Shakespeare?

I (Rob) say *a* beginning because there are multiple origin stories to this overall story. To begin (I hesitate) with, the abstract (above) for the seminar I convened at the 2014 Shakespeare Association of America conference in St Louis, went through several drafts. The Trustees, perhaps quite sensibly, didn't quite trust that there were enough scholars out there quite as out there as I was. They wanted me to run a seminar which included critical accounts of creative

Notes for this section begin on page 19.

work and not necessarily the integrated/both kinds of approaches I was hoping to solicit. After considerable back and forth they relented and the seminar papers responding to the call above perhaps both confirmed and dispelled the Trustees' initial uncertainty. Some contributors wrote fine critical essays about creative responses to Shakespeare (they are not included here). Some planned very interesting creative critical pieces but were thwarted by the creative practice – through failure to obtain theatre performance rights and through the non-running of a creative writing graduate class – they were depending upon not, at last, materialising (also not included). But some answered the call I made in ways that still delight and intrigue me (more on them below).

One of those seminarians was me (Scott) and I eventually contributed what I called a 'fragment from a fictional future Arden edition.' But it took some time to get from my initial impulse to that final idea. I'd long been mulling over Elizabeth King's account of how the sixteenth-century Court Clock Master to the Holy Roman Emperor engraved his astronomical clock with an inscription reading: 'QVI. SIM. SCIES. SI. PAR. OPVS. FACERE. CONABERIS.' (or in King's translation 'You will know who I am if you try and make this')[1] and wondering how that challenge might apply to our scholarly attempts to understand and appreciate Shakespeare. For Rob's seminar, I first proposed getting to know Shakespeare by 'writing Shakespeare' (as distinct from 'writing *about* Shakespeare') and making bold to produce one or two scenes that he 'could have' – which is not to say 'would have' or 'should have' – written. I started writing my first scene about a middle-aged nurse *cum* nun in an early modern hospital *cum* monastery. Quickly, I realized that I knew precious little about nurses or hospitals in Shakespeare's time. I wondered whether Shakespeare himself knew any more than I did. When did the word 'nurse' become associated with today's modern medical profession? Consulting the *Oxford English Dictionary*, I was a bit surprised (and a bit sceptical) to find Shakespeare credited with the first use of 'nurse' in this sense. What about the word 'hospital'? How often – and in what contexts – did Shakespeare use it? That was when I realized that Shakespeare concluded *Love's Labour's Lost* with Berowne agreeing to 'jest a twelvemonth in an hospital.' Here was something Shakespeare *could have* written: *Enter Nurse*, the long-lost sequel to *Love's Labour's Lost* and, as it turned out, the porny but poignant prequel to *Romeo and Juliet*.

Following Rob's lead, I proposed my own seminar, 'Shakespearean Scene-Writing,' for SAA 2015, which met with universal euphoria from that year's Trustees, with one caveat: I was advised 'this should probably be a workshop because the things produced are not standard scholarly product.' Here's a description of the workshop – newly imprinted and enlarged to almost as much againe as it was, according to the true and perfect coppie – as it appeared in the June 2014 Bulletin:

> Are there limits – and alternatives – to what criticism and commentary can teach us about Shakespeare? What if knowing *why* Shakespeare made use of adaptations, allusions, asides, backstory, characters, costume, cued parts, dancing, dialogue, disguise, duels, dumbshows, eavesdropping, ekphrasis, entrances and exits, flora and fauna, foreshadowing, ghosts, hendiadyes, insults, irony, letters & messengers, midline switches, music, noise, pacing, parody, plays-within-plays, plots, props, prose, proverbs, short lines, silence (or implied pauses), songs, time schemes, even lacunae and cruces as he did depended on learning *how* (or at least trying) to do it ourselves? Drawing on humanist methods of *imitatio* and early modern 'maker's knowledge traditions,' this workshop will require participants to create new 'Shakespearean' scenes with period-specific diction, grammar, and iambic pentameter. Finally since Shakespeare wrote in collaboration with other playwrights, participants should feel free either to write alone or to form groups of two or more 'hands.' Responses may include scholarly notes, readings, performances.

What I got in response to this call for papers were indeed 'not standard scholarly product,' but instead an embarrassment of riches, the most creative set of abstracts I had seen in my dozen years of attending the SAA.

This was creative writing informed by literary criticism – *literary creaticism?* – and the possibilities got me very excited. I doubted that any members of the workshop would be interested in writing more than a scene or two – after all, we all had 'real work' to do – but I decided to share with them my ultimate fantasy: I imagined having a team of twelve scholars (and/or playwrights) agree to write three plays each – a comedy, a history, and a tragedy – over the course of the next several years so that we would have 36 new plays, a new Folio, to be published in 2023 to mark the 400th anniversary of the First Folio. Imagine that: Shakespeare scholarship producing a monumental tome that is not of an age but for all time...

So Scott, now that our Special Issue, *Creative Critical Shakespeare* is being tweaked and republished as *Shakespeare and Creative Criticism*, I figure we need to flesh out this Introduction somewhat. How about a conversation in which we reflect on some of what we have learned since that publication and on how the fantasies are playing out? I'm interested, for example, in what you have learned through the process of writing *Enter Nurse*... going back to the clock inscription – 'You will know who I am if you try and make this' – I am struck (no pun intended) by a few thoughts. One, there is a warning that the attempt will prove fiendishly difficult, perhaps impossible. But two, it's the attempt at making and not necessarily its successful completion, that will lead to understanding. Some questions for you, then, in no particular order: what have you learned about Shakespeare (that you might not have been able to learn via traditional modes of scholarship) through the process of attempting to imitate him? What have you learned about creative labour? How fiendishly difficult has it been and how do you judge your success thus far?

NOSOPONUS: Rob, I like what you've done here. The conversation, I mean. But as long as we're having a conversation could we frame it as a dialogue? A fiction? Like this: you will note I've adopted a persona as well as a speech prefix. For some odd reason, I've lately been reading from Erasmus's *Ciceronianus* (1528), in which Bulephorus, a fictional spokesperson for Erasmus himself, engages in conversation with Nosoponus, a pedant who, after seven years vainly spent trying to master the style of Cicero, has physically wasted away, his complexion gone sallow. He has contracted the disease of Ciceronianism. Bulephorus, taking pity on this scholar whose studies have taken such a toll on him, intends to heal his old friend by pretending to have the same disease, that is, an overzealous reverence for – and a corresponding compulsion to imitate – the writings of Cicero. Then in a Socratic tour de force, Bulephorus peppers poor Nosoponus with questions that encourage the latter to divulge how for seven whole years he has read nothing but Cicero, read and reread to the point of memorizing every word Cicero wrote, compiled those words in a two-volume alphabetical lexicon, in which the entry for each word spans several pages (because Nosoponus diligently records where it occurred in a given work, and whether it appears at the beginning, middle, or end of a sentence), hung portraits of Cicero all around his residence, worn a pendant of Cicero about his neck, forgone a wife, children, friends, civic commitments, and anything else that might intrude on his cherished communion with the Latin god of eloquence. Only then does Bulephorus point out that, of course, Cicero did none of these things. Cicero had a life. He wrote about the world as it existed, using words which were current, in his own time. Anyone fool enough to imitate the style of Cicero (or, I might add, Shakespeare) centuries after that style – and the world that gave rise to it – has crumbled to oblivion will find they have imitated a finished product but, in doing so, have neglected the vital, rapid, unconscious, and inimitable processes of living, loving, and thinking that make inventive and imaginative writing possible, and desirable, in the first place. It took me a while but I *think* I've heeded that lesson. For a long time, I'd try Nosoponus-like to write even my roughest of rough drafts in Elizabethan English and iambic pentameter. Eventually I realized that not only does that result in very slow composition but also in a relatively lifeless imitation: the verse often lacked ellipsis and surprise (*viz.* a certain comic flight and errancy). It was lyric to the point of lacking action. Admittedly, of what appears in this book, which is what appeared in the journal a couple of years ago, one could say, as Dover Wilson said of *The Murder of Gonzago* in Hamlet, 'It is not a play; it is not even a scene; it is a piece of a scene [or in my case pieces of scenes], terminated… at the very moment when the only action which occurs in it is about to take place.'[2]

More recently, I've started writing earlier in the mornings, when I am barely conscious, and in 'plain-everyday-unvarnished English.' In the classes I teach, I'm constantly asking my students to give me their best approximation of what a Shakespearean character says in this kind of language [1. Sorry to interrupt, mate, but I feel like Salanio waiting for his 'my bond' cue in *The Merchant of Venice* 3.3.4–19;[3] I don't want to interrupt so I'm just going to insert these internal notes that will, from now on, appear at the end of your oration. Carry on]. Now, for my play, I'm just doing the reverse. I'm getting an abundance of half-thoughts, nascent ideas, and instinctive language on paper first and only then taking the time to experiment until I find the nearest Shakespearean approximation. There's action now and scenes. Soon there will be a whole play – and for me that's exciting, even if no one cares to read or stage it [2].

What I've learned about creative labour (can we call that 'play'?) is that it makes one feel alive. And based on how alive I've felt every hour spent working on this play – and on the fact that I've spent more hours working on it than I care to imagine, let alone admit – I'd call it the greatest success I've ever known. We wrote a bit in the Introduction to the special issue, which is now going to follow this bit, about how important pleasure is to creative critical work; equally important, perhaps, is pain. That is, I think what Renaissance rhetoricians called 'energia' and what William Hazlitt dubbed 'gusto' in any kind of writing comes from the stuff that gets you out of bed in the morning and the stuff that keeps you awake at night. There's an element of the personal, the private, the unconscious and the subjective in writing that leaps off the page and captures our attention. It may not be explicit – more likely, it is implicit, folded into the writing until it's barely noticeable, even to the author – but it is there nonetheless. The approach Nosoponus takes to imitation in Erasmus's *Ciceronianus* (he effectively amputates his personal life and sees any peculiarities from his private thoughts as distractions from or intrusions upon an objective ideal of Ciceronian style) precludes this vital element from entering into and animating his imitations. Some approaches to Shakespeare criticism have sought (in vain) to eliminate it too.

Indeed, what I find interesting about your request to 'judge [my] success,' especially in light of how our title has been tweaked, from *Creative Critical Shakespeare* to *Shakespeare and Creative Criticism*, is the reminder that historically 'criticism' has not been aligned with creativity but, instead, with judgement. Exactly 100 years ago, in 1919, T.S. Eliot began his essay 'Hamlet and His Problems' with a warning about 'that most dangerous type of critic: the critic with a mind which is naturally of the creative order, but which through some weakness in creative power exercises itself in criticism instead.' Eliot warns of 'Goethe, who made of Hamlet a Werther' and 'Coleridge, who made of Hamlet a Coleridge.'[4] What makes their creative criticism 'dangerous' is twofold: first, they remake Shakespeare's character in their own image; second, the writing they produce persuades readers to see the character that way too. Now, obviously, what makes Shakespeare's characters unique is that he writes them in such a way as to invite, if not demand, readers, actors, directors, and, yes, critics to inhabit them. Stephen Greenblatt writes about 'the excision of motive' – that is, how Shakespeare does not explain or make explicit why, for example, Hamlet has to 'put an antic disposition on' – which leaves audiences to speculate, guess, imagine and infer their own motives.[5] But I digress: the point is that Eliot, in his role as critic, 'judges' *Hamlet*. '*Qua* work of art,' Eliot writes, 'the work of art cannot be interpreted; there is nothing to interpret; we can only criticize it according to standards, in comparison to other works of art.' In his criticism of *Hamlet*, Eliot pulls no punches: 'there are unexplained scenes – the Polonius-Laertes and the Polonius-Reynaldo scenes – for which there is little excuse... So far from being Shakespeare's masterpiece, the play is most certainly an artistic failure.'[6] Unlike Goethe and Coleridge before him, Eliot refuses to fill in the gaps of Hamlet's psyche; nor will he exercise his own imagination in an attempt to explain – make sense of – the play's unexplained scenes. The hardest thing to imitate in Shakespeare, I've found, is precisely this ability to leave room for readers, actors, and audience members to become collaborators in the fiction. Some readers, like T.S. Eliot, dismiss this ability as mere inscrutability; others, like Keats, celebrate it as Shakespeare's 'negative capability.'[7]

Now, having divorced creativity from slavish imitation – and aligned myself with humanists, like Erasmus, and Romantics, like Keats – let me say a few words in favour of imitation at its most slavish: transcription. I have made a habit of writing a thousand words a day but there are days when I'm stuck and cannot seem to get any of my own words onto the page. On those days, I transcribe scenes from Shakespeare. Typing every single word, including speech prefixes and stage directions, of a scene not only gives one the sense of creating Shakespeare effortlessly, without ever blotting a line [3], but also slows each scene down [4], allowing one to notice things that might have been overlooked in even the closest of close readings. For example, this morning I was transcribing Act 2, Scene 1 of *Troilus and Cressida* which begins with Ajax apparently trying to get his servant Thersites' attention. But what is Thersites doing in the meantime?

AJAX
  Thersites.
THERSITES
  Agamemnon—how if he had boils, full, all over, generally?
AJAX
  Thersites.
THERSITES
  And those boils did run? Say so, did not the General run then? Were not that a botchy core?
AJAX
  Dog.
THERSITES
  Then there would come some matter from him. I see none now.

At this point Ajax, having failed to snap Thersites from his reverie, resorts to striking him. Websites created to help students make sense of what is happening in Shakespeare's plays prove pretty unhelpful in this case. According to Sparknotes, 'Ajax summons his slave, Thersites, and orders him to find out the nature of the proclamation that has just been posted.'[8] This makes it sound as though Ajax entered first and then called for Thersites who entered in answer to his master's summons. Clearly, that's not the case. Shmoop, as usual, offers a better summary than Sparknotes: 'Ajax yells at his slave Thersites, who ignores him and talks smack about what it would be like if Agamemnon had a bunch of nasty, oozing boils and skin ulcers.'[9] This answers the question: Thersites does talk smack about Agamemnon. But why? And more importantly, to whom? Agamemnon is not present; Ajax is not listening; that leaves only Thersites himself and perhaps an imagined audience [5]. Thersites, moreover, is rapt, completely immersed in the jokes he makes about Agamemnon, to the point that he does not notice Ajax. Thersites here is not unlike Hamlet, who, in his most famous soliloquy, fails to see (or pretends to fail to see), until the end, that Ophelia is onstage. But Hamlet was either weighing the pros and cons of suicide or else performing suicidal ideation for two more onstage (though concealed) characters, Claudius and Polonius; either of these activities would seem more intense and important than Thersites' roasting of Agamemnon. Unless, of course, Thersites is rehearsing material, going over potential jokes, sifting ideas and playing with phrasing, in anticipation of a future performance. We know from Ulysses that Patroclus 'pageants' and parodies both Agamemnon and Nestor for the private entertainment of Achilles (but how does Ulysses know this? Has he been in attendance at a performance? He never says). Perhaps Thersites is working on a bit. Jerry Seinfeld in an interview with *The New York Times* says 'comedy writing is something you don't see people doing; it's a secretive thing,' adding that he takes anywhere from two days to two years working on a single bit. Not only does Seinfeld consider each word in a joke but, as he puts it, 'you'll shave letters off of words, you'll count syllables, you know, to get it just – it's more like songwriting.' Of the punchline to a bit, Seinfeld explains: 'that [line] took a long time. I know it sounds like nothing.'[10] Thersites, like Seinfeld (or like Shakespeare), is *absolutely* working on a bit. Indeed, a few lines later, Thersites insults Ajax by saying 'I think thy horse will sooner con an oration than thou learn a prayer without a book.' Who better to make this otherwise odd, if not inexplicable, insult than someone who has just been working on his own oration of sorts, a standup routine, and conning his lines, that is, committing them to memory, before being interrupted by a 'beef-witted lord' oblivious to how difficult comedy writing can be?

Sorry. That was a long example [7]. And, for a dialogue, I'm not giving you much chance to speak [8]. Perhaps readers have begun to wonder what your character is doing during my interminable monologue. But I can see what you've done, Rob, and am choosing to ignore it [9]. That Thersites labours in advance over quips that in performance probably look improvised reminds me of transcribing a couple of Shakespeare's own one-liners. While typing Hamlet's final soliloquy, well the final soliloquy in Q2 (it gets cut from the Folio), I paused at Hamlet's asking himself 'Why yet I live to say "This thing's to do;" / Sith [Since] I have cause and will and strength and means / To do't.' As you might have guessed, the line that got me wondering is the one with three 'ands,' an excess of conjunctions that Greek rhetoricians called *polysyndeton*. Does Shakespeare not know about commas? Of course he does. Just a few lines later, Hamlet describes Fortinbras and his soldiers as 'Exposing what is mortal and unsure / To all that fortune, death and danger dare.' So what keeps Hamlet (or Shakespeare) from using a couple of commas – e.g. 'Since I have cause, will, strength, and means to do't' – to achieve a satisfyingly end-stopped, albeit metrically irregular, line? The answer comes proleptically in the preceding sentence, which thus far I've only quoted the tail end of:

...Now, whether it be
Bestial oblivion, or some craven scruple
Of thinking too precisely on the event,
A thought which, quarter'd, hath but one part wisdom
And ever three parts coward, I do not know
Why yet I live to say 'This thing's to do;'

Hamlet wonders if his delay is due to not thinking enough about his revenge, a kind of forgetfulness about his father, which is what he accuses his mother of in Act 1 ('...a beast, that wants discourse of reason, / Would have mourn'd longer'), or if, to the contrary, he is 'thinking too precisely' on his revenge, in a way that leads to each thought being 'quarter'd,' as in 'drawn and quartered,' and broken down into its constituent parts. What the use of *polysyndeton* in that puzzling line does – beyond maintaining an iambic rhythm and not coming to a firm conclusion or full-stop till the next line, where it creates an awkward caesura or hesitation – is to *show* us Hamlet dividing his thought into quarters: 'cause and will and strength and means.' Most people are not going to catch this irony in performance; most readers are not going to make the connection even if they study this speech in isolation; nor can Hamlet be aware of it. Like Seinfeld, Shakespeare had to 'shave letters off of words [and] count syllables' to get that line just right: it must have taken a long time even though in the end it sounds like nothing (again, the Folio omits it).

The other example of a one-liner that comes to mind when I think of Thersites laboring in advance over his seemingly spontaneous quips is King Lear's perfectly iambic, albeit with feminine ending, pentameter line: 'I am a man more sinn'd against than sinning.' I recently saw Ian McKellen as Lear in the National Theatre Live broadcast and, although I was completely immersed in the fiction, when he spoke this line I thought to myself, 'What an amazing stand-alone line. I wonder if it emerged organically as part of this speech or if Shakespeare had it and finally found a place to use it.' In other words, I couldn't help but think to myself that Shakespeare while writing, especially in blank verse, must have had moments, away from the page, when a line of blank verse would come to him and, not knowing what to do with it but not wanting to forget it, he would jot it down. That line, in particular, feels as though it could be spoken by any number of characters (men or women in disguise as men) in this play or a number of others. One great thing about having a free-floating, detachable line of blank verse is that it enables the writer to experiment: if Shakespeare always intended the line to be Lear's, he might have played around with where (which speech? at what point in the drama? spoken to whom?) to place it. Or, if the line came to him without a character or situation firmly attached, then he might have experimented with a variety of characters, situations, and even plays: seeing what would happen to the line itself and to the character speaking it as a result. I guess what I'm saying is that an individual line of blank verse, in this case one that is end-stopped, implies a speaker and a scenario. You might hold onto the line until a scene demands it or you might build a speech, a speaker, and eventually an entire scene around it. As it turns out, most modern editions of *King Lear*, following the Folio, split what I keep referring to as a singular and perfect pentameter line across two lines, the second of which forms the first half of a shared line with Kent. Seeing that, I was dumbfounded and thought maybe I'd only heard the line as a discrete unit when in fact it was always just the natural conclusion to that speech. Curious, I went and looked at the Quarto editions on the British Library's website: there, as I suspected, the line was neither split nor shared but intact and complete unto itself, the culmination of a speech that is every bit as coherent, if not as cogent, without it.

But as you can see I'm still talking about lines, lines, lines. What is missing from everything I've said thus far is theatre, the stage itself. Shakespeare knew the actors who would play his characters and speak his lines, knew them intimately; he wrote with them in mind. His characters, I am certain, are conceived from first to last with particular bodies, voices, faces, and mannerisms in mind. This is an essential – probably the essential – element of Shakespeare's style and of his own original practices, which brings me to '*Othello*, Original Practices: A Photographic Essay.' You focus on roughness as an antidote to 'orthodox practices of Shakespearean production which enshrine polish, precision, and psychological nuance.' And roughness is another indispensable quality of Shakespeare's style. Your essay also references an Ian McKellen performance, in Trevor Nunn's 1989 RSC *Othello*, where, as you note, McKellen attends to the accident of dropping a bunch of matches on stage by picking them up *in character* as Iago. This points up an obvious oversight in my own thinking above: even if we allow for Thersites as a sort of standup comedian working on his shtick with all the obsessiveness of Jerry Seinfeld, Shakespeare knew he would not be performing or giving life to his own lines. Again, I think it helped that he knew the actors who would be portraying his characters almost as if they were extensions of himself but, even so, once a play had made it to the stage Shakespeare would have found himself in your position: a helpless bystander witnessing the inevitable 'cock-ups' and yet thinking all the while 'This falls out better than I could devise.' I must say your written account of the performance bristles with what must be the same energy that was in the room that night. Each time I read it, I'm a little anxious and on edge. There is also the added thrill of *ekphrasis*, capturing the sights, sounds, smells, and sensations of live theatre not only in words but in photos. There is one moment in the essay, however, where, for me, as a reader, one photo goes off script, as it were, and seems not to perform its role as written: I'm thinking

thinking of Illustration 9.10. The essay tells us 'Othello, with one especially marked smudge right on his nose, looked like a clown,' adding 'The audience laughed a lot.' I think it's the expression on Tom Considine's face at the moment the photo was taken – or it may be something as simple as a loss of digital resolution in the printing of the photo – but the photo makes me wince. I do see a clown but it reminds me of Emil Jannings at the end of *The Blue Angel* (1930): abject, pathetic, and humiliated. I'm wondering 'is it just me?' Or can you, unhearing the laughter of that night, look at the photo and see it this way too? [10] I'm also wondering whether you've done more with original practices – and/or with photographic essays – since the journal's publication [11]. If so, what else have you learned about either or both in the interim? Oh and one more thing: what I love about the roughness of your original practices performance is that it perfectly combines the creative and the critical. As you explain, leaving inconsistencies of tone in place not only approximates an early modern experience but serves to 'critique' the smooth as silk productions audiences have come to expect and to hold up as standards. That kind of critique can then lead to the creation of new standards, new expectations, or, better yet, no expectations, which is tremendously exciting. And long overdue.

Well played, sir, well played. You have taken the ball and run with it, right out of the stadium, and then kicked it into the trees. Don't worry, I have fetched it back with these notes.

[1] I was first prompted to interrupt on the notion of paraphrasing, of you asking your students to give [you] their best approximation of what a Shakespearean character says in plain unvarnished English. Lucy Bailey, director of multiple productions at Shakespeare's Globe and the Royal Shakespeare Company, does 'a lot of paraphrasing as an exercise in rehearsal'[11] so I figure if it's good enough for the RSC I shouldn't begrudge my students the occasional use, and critical creation, of parallel editions (the use of which you return to).

[2] I have promised you to stage the finished play.

[3] I wonder if this exercise would offer a different quality if you handwrote those transcriptions, especially as you refer to not blotting a line. When I write with my LAMY Joy™ I feel like I

understand Hélène Cixous's notion that 'It is in the contact with the sheet of paper that sentences emerge.'[12]

[4] Writes Harry Berger Jr. of slowing a scene down through 'imaginary audition': 'Decelerated microanalysis thus enlarges and emblematically fixes features not discernible in the normal rhythm of communication.'[13] I think this is what you are doing.

[5] An imagined audience? But there is an audience. You make me reach for Bridget Escolme's *Talking to the Audience: Shakespeare, performance, self.* Her chapter on *Troilus and Cressida* is entitled 'Bits and Bitterness'. And she has much to say on Thersites:

> There is no sense in which he has to 'come out of character' to talk to us; he appears not to know which is the world of the fiction, which the world of the play... he can get carried away with this duality, forgetting there is a plot to get on with in his desire to make us laugh. Thersites has this meta-theatrical job in *Troilus and Cressida*.[14]

None of this invalidates your argument, of course. I just think it means that Thersites perhaps refines – spoiler alert – his comic routine in conjunction with his actual auditors.

[7] That was a great example.

[8] It's ok, I've found this way to chip in.

[9] I'm choosing to subvert you deliberately ignoring me. I've been reading (and writing) about collaborative writing. In one 17-author article I read, one particular seventeenth of the authorship suggests that 'friendship as a basis for working together recovers writing from the ambit of work, from conventions, from the obligation of a certain type of outcome, from the critical self-consciousness that informs the attitude that one gives to a good performance, to a career.'[15] You find it very difficult, I think, to suspend 'critical self-consciousness', but I love the way your writing has obliged an outcome I couldn't have foreseen (and there's more of that below). And, our friendship, and others formed with contributors here, has been perhaps the most valuable part of the project.

[10] Yes. I can absolutely see/read the photograph like that.

[11] And Yes. I have done more with illustrated essays (and original-ish and other practices).

Glad you asked (we didn't plan this).

In 2017 I directed King Lear with students in the middle of winter in an outdoors, promenade production. An essay on that production has just come out in a special issue of *Shakespeare Bulletin* on Eco-Shakespeare in Performance and I'm sending off a brief film for Katie Brocaw's eco-Shakespeare panel discussion at the 2019 Shakespeare Theatre Association (STA) conference in Prague. You've also prompted me to re-visit my 2014 production of *Bartholomew Fair*, also outdoors, and beautifully photographed. But in 2016 I directed *The Merry Wives of Windsor* with trained actors, and Bernard Caleo, with whom I collaborated on 'Graphic Shakespeare', sketched during the rehearsals. You think Tom Considine looks abject, pathetic, and humiliated as Othello? He does, but look at these Falstaff drawings.

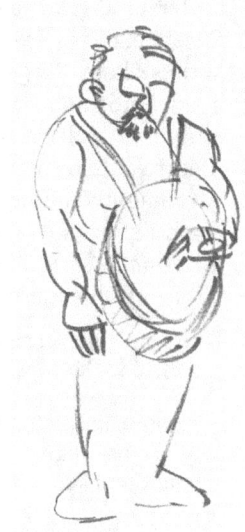

Illustration 0.1: Falstaff's fat suit. © Bernard Caleo.

I call this series, and there are lots more (for another publication), Falstaff Down Under. He's an Australian Falstaff, of course, and the earliest evidence we have for a production of Shakespeare in Australia is a playbill from 1800 for *Henry IV, Part 1*.[16] This first image is of down under the costume, with the fat suit on display, but I think you can already see, in the downward glance, the melancholy that exists down under this particular Falstaff. The next one is more metaphorical. Falstaff is falling down under the Thames – sans buckbasket – but the waters towards which he plummets are more like hellish flames.

Illustration 0.2: An alacrity in sinking. © Bernard Caleo.

Illustration 0.3: A poor old woman.
© Bernard Caleo.

But what about this last Willy Loman image? From down under the disguise of the Mad Woman of Brainford and the retributive blows administered by Ford's cricket bat, Falstaff returns as if suffering PTSD. And yet, this comment was typical of the reviews of the production: 'Considine is a barrelling and bright-eyed force of nature. He plays the deluded knight as a rutting stag with a baggie of blue pills in his shirt pocket. He's gruff, explosive and thrilling to watch.'[17] We were lucky, I think, that Philippa Kelly saw the production in an early run and offered me the note that Falstaff should bounce up like a rubber ball from his every trouncing. The beauty of a fine actor embodying Shakespeare, their form of creative criticism, is that they can balance and play with the abject and the explosive almost simultaneously. What beauty, too, and equally subtle creative criticism, Bernard's images offer: of the play; of the character; of acting; of what is down under (Falstaff, drawn and quartered).

In what ways, then, are the Shakespeare-inspired creative essays, stories and plays contained in this volume also critical? And what kinds of critique do they offer? Another way of approaching these questions is to imagine alternative titles for this collection. Almost all of the contributions here might, for example, be gathered under the more general heading of 'Shakespeare and Adaptation'. All of the contributions consider, with varying degrees of depth or 'fidelity', a Shakespearean source and adapt it into a new form. Like Djanet Sears's *Harlem Duet* and Paula Vogel's *Desdemona: A Play About a Handkerchief*, both included in Daniel Fischlin and Mark Fortier's *Adaptations of Shakespeare*,[18] the subheading of which is *A critical anthology of plays from the seventeenth century to the present* (emphasis added), and both of which offer trenchant creative critiques of *Othello* and its afterlives, adaptations here offer similar ripostes to cultural constructions of identity propped up by Shakespeare's dated universalism. Jessica McCall and Kavita Mudan Finn, for example, who co-author an introduction to their respective fanfic pieces, aim their critical creative sights at normative representations of mainly sexuality and gender, but also of dis/ability and race.

'Shakespeare and Fanfiction' is another viable alternative title for this book. Not just these prose pieces just mentioned, set respectively in an American high school and in a CSI-like New York City, but also in the four dramatic contributions to the volume. With a fervour equal to that early fanfic author, Maurice Morgann, but with perhaps greater self-reflexivity, each of these play fragments draws much closer, assuming their hitherto separation, the worlds of fanfiction and academia. Peter Holland writes of these converging worlds:

> Fan studies are often concerned to distinguish between the fan and the academic. But Henry Jenkins, a principal figure in the study of fans and of convergence culture, describes himself as an 'Aca-fan', 'a hybrid creature which is part fan and part academic', and sees his own writing ... as an attempt to bridge the two ... If the distinguishing features of fandom include attending conventions and accumulating souvenir materials, often, in the high-brow fan, materials that are offered as ironic commentary on the subject, then almost all Shakespeare scholars must be fans as well as academics, with the strict proviso that ... we do not dress up as characters in our beloved works.[19]

Beloved characters are dressed up in and through the dramatic fanfiction offered here, the creation of which generates its own souvenir material, lost and re-discovered fragments from an alternative Shakespearean universe.

A special critique these fanfic plays make is of the academy itself, of the seriousness with which it conducts, monitors and regulates itself, and particularly in terms of the demands of publication. Both Scott Maisano (this is Rob writing) and David Nicol take very funny and well-aimed sling shots at the Shakespearean editing Goliath: their pieces do not just re-create (and re-critique) Shakespearean drama, they also offer editorial, Arden 3-like, notes, and often to hilarious effect. Indeed, the former's *Enter Nurse, or Love's Labour's Won*, contains a glossarial explication of its dramatis personae almost as long as the dramatic verse that follows it, and the latter's *A Tragedy of the Plantation of Virginia* (1623) is prefaced by an Eco-like introduction to its elusive textual status and the inclusion, in the marginalia, of disapproving and corrective notes from the Master of the Revels. These writings, and those by Mary Baine Campbell and Dan Moss, are funny. They are, we hope, a pleasure to read, even as they were a pleasure to write: and this writing-pleasure, we think, offers its own critique of academic endeavour, in particular, of publishing.

In the first (closest example to a conventional) chapter in this volume, 'Responses to Responses to Shakespeare's Sonnets: More Sonnets', Matthew Zarnowiecki describes his encounter with *The Sonnets: Translating and Rewriting Shakespeare*, 154 separate (broadly-defined) poetic replies to Shakespeare's *Sonnets* thus: 'the effect, in terms of my own reading activity, is double-booked'. Further, the effect of the double-booked effect, of having both books open and going back and forth between them, is that 'They both go both ways: each one deepens the other'. The contributions to this volume repeatedly offer the pleasures and rewards of double-booking: 'Pickled Red Herring' made me (Rob) wide-eyed with admiration for the economy of its (and Shakespeare's) plotting and structure and for its commentary on *Richard III*, its various histories – 1480s, 1590s, 2010s – and on the processes of literary adaptation. And the other submissions herein invite the reader into immersive, creative critical, and double-booked engagement with new Shakespearean worlds: ancient Egypt; Jacobean London; Greek myth mashed with fairy tale; and perhaps that most dangerous and foreign of all worlds, junior high.

In Mary Baine Campbell's *Echo and Narcissus*, Little Red, like the pair(s?) of lover(s?) she comments on, is at once 'a child "on the brink of adulthood"' and an archetype predating any proper author. Her interrogative 'Bow-wow' echoes Echo's ' – Ow-ow', with a reverb distortion effect that reminds us (as Echo does time and again) how easily semantics can slip off to reveal bare sound. In Dan Moss's *The Fair Maid*, 'The Persons of the Play' are nearly all notorious figures who bring their own 'instant backstory' to the drama. One can hardly wait to see what Shakespeare would do with Herodotus, Solon, Hermes Trismegistus, Callimachus, and Nefertiti. Will they fulfil or subvert an audience's expectations? The notes included in David Nicol's *A Tragedy of the Plantation of Virginia*, like Will Summers' running commentary throughout *Summer's Last Will and Testament*, serve to (1) anticipate and forestall some of the audiences' or readers' questions and/or objections; (2) supply a refreshingly modern counterpoint to the early modern rhetorical fireworks; (3) meet the audience halfway between the fictional and real worlds; and (4) compete for attention with the play they alternately elucidate and obfuscate. These faux-Shakespearean dramas play games with history, with time-travel and anachronism, and so the last contribution, Rob Conkie's '*Othello*, Original Practices: a photo-essay', corresponds with Henry Jackson and with the 1610 Oxford production of *Othello* he describes.

We do not wish to suggest that here is the beginning of Shakespeare and Creative Critcism – it has multiple origin stories, too. We follow in the footsteps of series like Shakespeare Now!, we seek creative collisions and try to tell tales from Shakespeare like Graham Holderness,[20] and we aim to write performatively,[21] with passion and with purpose. We continue the work in volume 25.3 of *Critical Survey*, which was intent on 'dismantling barriers ... between intellectual enquiry and imaginative recreation'[22] and we look forward to future work in this playful field of Shakespeare and Creative Criticism.

Rob Conkie is Senior Lecturer in Theatre at La Trobe University. His teaching and research integrates practical and theoretical approaches to Shakespeare in performance. He is the author of *Writing Performative Shakespeares: New Forms for Performance Criticism* (Cambridge University Press, 2016), *The Globe Theatre Project: Shakespeare and Authenticity* (Edwin Mellen, 2006), and numerous journal articles and book chapters. He has twice (2013, 2016) been appointed Associate Investigator of the Australian Research Council Centre of Excellence for the History of Emotions, for which he has produced theatre productions and workshops and related symposia. He has directed about a third of the Shakespeare canon for the stage.

Scott Maisano is Associate Professor of English Literature at the University of Massachusetts Boston. His work on Shakespeare has been featured in *Lapham's Quarterly*, *Smithsonian Magazine*, *Scientific American*, *The Telegraph*, *Ideas with Paul Kennedy* (CBC Radio), and *The Science Show* (Australian Broadcasting Company). His publications include 'Shakespeare's Revolution: The Tempest as Scientific Romance,' about Prospero and particle physics in *The Tempest: A Critical Guide* (Bloomsbury Arden Shakespeare); 'Now,' about Einsteinian spacetime in *The Winter's Tale*, for *Early Modern Theatricality* (Oxford University Press); and 'Rise of the Poet of the Apes,' about intelligent apes and monkeys in plays from the beginning to the end of Shakespeare's career, for *Shakespeare Studies*. He is coeditor of *Renaissance Posthumanism* (Fordham University Press) and is currently completing a new Shakespearean comedy entitled *Enter Nurse, or Love's Labour's Won*.

Notes

1. Elizabeth King, 'Perpetual Devotion: A Sixteenth-Century Machine That Prays', in *Genesis Redux: Essays in the History and Philosophy of Artificial Life*, ed. Jessica Riskin (Chicago: University of Chicago Press, 2007), 274.
2. John Dover Wilson, *What Happens in Hamlet*, 1935, Cambridge UK: Cambridge University Press, 2009, 145.
3. Simon Palfrey and Tiffany Stern, *Shakespeare in Parts* (Oxford: Oxford University Press, 2005), 200–204.
4. T. S. Eliot, 'Hamlet and His Problems,' Bartleby.com, https://www.bartleby.com/200/sw9.html, Accessed December 17, 2018.
5. Stephen Greenblatt, 'The Death of Hamnet and the Making of *Hamlet*,' *The New York Review of Books*, October 21, 2004, https://www.nybooks.com/articles/2004/10/21/the-death-of-hamnet-and-the-making-of- hamlet/
6. Eliot, 'Hamlet and His Problems.'
7. John Keats, *Complete Poems and Selected Letters*, ed. Edward Hirsch (New York: The Modern Library, 2001), 492.
8. SparkNotes Editors. 'SparkNote on *Troilus and Cressida*.' SparkNotes.com. SparkNotes LLC. n.d.. Web. 17 Dec. 2018.
9. Shmoop Editorial Team. '*Troilus and Cressida* Act 2, Scene 1 Summary.' *Shmoop*. Shmoop University, Inc., 11 Nov. 2008. Web. 17 Dec. 2018.
10. Jerry Seinfeld, 'Jerry Seinfeld Interview: How to Write a Joke,' *The New York Times*, YouTube, December 20, 2012, https://www.youtube.com/watch?v=itWxXyCfW5s.
11. Abigail Rokison-Woodall, 'Interviews with theatre practitioners about texts for performance', Shakespeare Bulletin 34.1 (2016), 47–68 (60).

12. Cited in Verena Andermatt Conley, 'making Sense from the Singular and Collective Touches', *SubStance*, 40.3 (2011), 79–88 (80). Conley goes on to write that 'Cixous claims to draw the sentences from her unconcious' (p. 80), another notion that resonates closely with those you have expressed.
13. Harry Berger, Jr., *Imaginary Audition: Shakespeare on Stage and Page* (Berkeley: University of California Press, 1989), 148.
14. Bridget Escolme, *Talking to the Audience: Shakespeare, performance, self* (Abingdon: Routledge, 2006), p. 39.
15. Petar Jandrić, et al, 'Collective Writing: An Inquiry into Praxis', *Knowledge Cultures* 5.1 (2017), 85–109 (93).
16. John Golder and Richard Madelaine, '"To dote thus on such luggage": Appropriating Shakespeare in Australia', *O Brave New World: Two Centuries of Shakespeare on the Australian Stage* (Strawberry Hills: Currency Press, 2001), 1–16 (14).
17. Chris Boyd, 'Considine's Falstaff ensures a jolly knight', *The Australian*, 25 April 2016, Arts, 12.
18. Daniel Fischlin and Mark Fortier (eds), *Adaptations of Shakespeare: A critical anthology of plays from the seventeenth century to the present* (London: Routledge, 2000).
19. Peter Holland, 'Spinach and Tobacco: Making Shakespearian Unoriginals', *Shakespeare Survey* 68 (Cambridge: Cambridge University Press, 2015), 197–209 (206).
20. Graham Holderness, *Tales from Shakespeare: Creative Collisions* (Cambridge: Cambridge University Press, 2014).
21. Rob Conkie, *Writing Performative Shakespeares: New Forms for Performance Criticism* (Cambridge: Cambridge University Press, 2016).
22. Graham Holderness, 'Introduction', *Critical Survey* 25.3 (2013), 1–3 (3).

Chapter 1
Responses to Responses to Shakespeare's Sonnets
More Sonnets

Matthew Zarnowiecki

This chapter is an exploration of recent engagements with Shakespeare's sonnets, primarily in the form of adaptations, appropriations, and responses, but also in the form of dramatizations and filmed recitations. It comes after long thought and a long chapter on the sonnets as they appeared in their early printed editions.[1] In this present chapter, an outgrowth of that previous work, I am interested in what we now do with the sonnets, other than the traditional things. These traditional things can be divided into two categories: we read them, and often do close readings of individual sonnets, whatever that means any more; we make new editions of the whole sonnet collection; and we sometimes make claims about what the collection means as a whole book. In addition to these, there are also a set of new engagements with the sonnets: responses, adaptations, and mutations. In reading the sonnets, and teaching students to read the sonnets, we produce talk or text about what we think they mean. Or we read silently. Editing the sonnets means making more sonnets, on paper or on screens, that bear some resemblance to the first edition of *Shake-speares Sonnets* (1609).[2] Usually this involves lots of glossing and detailed choices about different ways of presenting, or rather re-presenting, this book. These choices inevitably accrue into an overall understanding of the poems, presented to the reader explicitly in the introduction or other accompanying text, and foisted onto the reader implicitly in the form of the edition itself. Just think of Stephen Booth's edition, or Helen Vendler's, or more recently, Carl Atkins's or Don Paterson's or Paul Hammond's.[3]

My interest in creative critical responses to Shakespeare's sonnets stems from an experience with a now lost website, called Linkerature, which I first noticed and briefly discussed at a Shakespeare Association of America (SAA) session years ago, on electronic Shakespeares. At the time, I was excited about the possibilities afforded by the Internet, and particularly by hypertextuality, for reconceiving not only the book of Shakespeare's sonnets, but also the ways we read, interpret, and respond to them. After searching through the available online editions, I was mostly disappointed by what I found. But Linkerature was an exception, and I responded enthusiastically to it at the time; it seemed to be at the forefront of interactive, social, and hypertextual creative commentary on Shakespearean texts. There have been other online editions of Shakespeare's sonnets since then, but they are all rather unimaginative. They reproduce traditional interactions with the sonnets. Sonnets appear one by one or in a scrolling text, with either footnotes or links to glosses and images. They tell you what the sonnets mean in the ways you might expect: strange words get demystified, cruxes get conjectured about, patterns get recognized. Nothing very interesting happens to or with the sonnets (though I don't want to downplay the value of Internet-based accessibility to the sonnets for first-time readers).

While I was getting more and more frustrated with these online versions, I was also noticing that more creative responses to Shakespeare's sonnets have been happening all through their critical history. And in the years since that prior SAA session and now, I have come across at least two creative responses that I find quite admirable, and one that I find fascinatingly and distressingly subservient to an imagined version of Shakespeare's mood. So in what follows, I briefly sketch an important pattern in the critical history of the sonnets, then discuss these three creative responses. Finally, I give my own creative critical sonnet response a try.

I ~ OUT OF ORDER

The order of Shakespeare's sonnets is a problem that comes and goes in alternating currents. At first there is no problem at all: the 1599 *Passionate Pilgrime* prints two sonnets, some songs from *Love's Labour's Lost*, and some other poems, attributing them all to Shakespeare, in a nice little miscellaneous volume.[4] The 1609 quarto first edition of the sonnets (commonly referred to as 'Q') prints them with numbers, though not on separate pages. That is, the sonnets are adjacent to one another, and break across the pages. Also, *A Lover's Complaint*, a 329-line narrative poem in rhyme royal, follows the last sonnets and comprises gatherings K and L (about 18 per cent of the total page count of this slim volume). Then in 1640, John Benson prints the sonnets in an entirely different format: he groups multiple sonnets together into larger poems, and gives these descriptive titles. He completely ignores the order of the 1609 quarto, and he includes other material. Shakespeare, deified as a playwright in the 1623 Folio, is miscellaneified in Benson's *Poems. VVritten By Wil. Shakespeare. Gent.*[5] Contrary to the judgement of a whole generation of early textual critics, Benson's creative meddlings with the sonnets and other poems are not particularly untoward adaptations.[6] They conform to expectations of poetic circulation at the time, and thus they constitute an act of creative criticism, but not one that would have seemed unexpected or inappropriate.

Benson's edition rode its tide for almost a hundred years. The rise of eighteenth-century critical editing practices restored the 1609 quarto sonnet order. But then, the tide changed again, when many editors and commentators strived to change the order of the sonnets from their order in the quarto to a different order that would 'solve' all interpretive difficulties. This new creative critical tide lasted from about the mid-1800s until the resurrection of critical editing of Shakespeare's poetry and plays. This is an interesting time in creative Shakespeare commentary. Lots of editors profess that they have, through careful reading and arrangement, arrived at The Answer. They feel much freer with the text than eighteenth-century editors, much closer to Benson, though perhaps for different reasons. In the words of one, perhaps representative rearranger, 'it is not only our privilege to reconstruct the order of the Sonnets, but, if this will aid us in the appreciation of them, our duty to do so.'[7]

In his *Variorum* edition of Shakespeare's sonnets, Hyder R. Rollins, the prolific, early twentieth-century critical editor of early modern miscellanies and poetry, compiles the efforts of the sonnet rearrangers into a table showing which editions put which sonnets in which positions. The effect of the table, as well as his often snide commentary on other sonnet commentators, is not only to belittle the whole rearrangement endeavour, but also, somewhat paradoxically, to cast doubt on the order of the sonnets as they appear in the 1609 quarto.[8] Shakespeare's order (if he had one) seems anyone's guess. The guesses came fast and furious from the mid-1800s to the early 1900s, but they all assumed, with Wordsworth, that 'with this key / Shakespeare unlocked his heart' and that with the proper key, they could unlock the secret identities of the Dark Lady, the Young Man, and the Rival Poet, and therefore chart the undiscovered country of Shakespeare's real biographical, psychological, and romantic story.[9]

This goal – knowing the author's life from his work – has long since become critically unfashionable, or even entirely unviable. With the rise of material historicism, the ability of editors or responders to reimagine the sonnets outside of the Q box has reached its low-water mark. Critical editions like Rollins's and his heirs' operate under well-established editorial principles, most importantly that of the 'copy text'. For Shakespeare's Sonnets, Q is the copy text, and any edition starts with it, is based on it, and really has no right to deviate from it, except glossingly, non-substantively, and certainly not creatively.[10] As well, with the rise of 'unedited' texts via *Early English Books Online* (*EEBO*), we have the (false) spectre of unmediated access to The Original. Online editions labour under these principles, probably most often by taking a modern edition as their own copy text. Any brief search for Shakespeare's sonnets online will lead to many, many online editions following Q's order, and either none, or few, with any other order.[11]

Perhaps we need not worry very much that no one is meddling with the order of Shakespeare's sonnets these days, since the re-ordering efforts were so entangled with an associated desire to untangle Shakespeare: to unlock the key to his heart, and to plot out the story of his creative and amatory life. Yet it is a source of vexation to me that there can now be no reordering for other reasons. Shakespeare's sonnets, freed somewhat in the nineteenth and early twentieth centuries, have become for us a re-bounded book, comprised of 154 sonnets (and maybe 'A Lover's Complaint' too) in a certain order. This re-bounding changes and refocuses both the critical questions we ask of these poems and, potentially, the creative responses that are possible to envision. That is to say, if we 'know' the sonnets are this one thing, this bounded and ordered book, then adaptations of them, creative responses to them, and even basic readings of them must originate with that one thing. As a way of specifying this observation, I turn now to three recent creative responses to the sonnets. The first is a theatrical performance, the second is a book of 'translations and adaptations' published in 2012, and the third is a set of videos being released on the Internet under the title *The Sonnet Project*.

II ~ 'LOVE IS MY SIN'

This is the title of a production of selected sonnets that premiered in Paris at the Bouffes du Nord in April 2009. Directed by Peter Brook, and featuring Michael Pennington and Natasha Perry, it was characterized by Brook's minimalistic staging aesthetic, and also employed sparse music. It lasted just under an hour, and was thus somewhere between a recitation and a play.

As expressed in the notes to this piece, Brook's professed goal is to find a 'dramatic continuity ... in a relationship between two people', and he separates the performance into four sections. These he calls 'Devouring Time', 'Separation', 'Jealousy', and 'Time Defied'. Although these seem to be thematic in nature, it is clear from Brook's commentary that he sees the dramatic task as essentially narrative:

> At first, Shakespeare evokes a shared tranquility, but little by little the pains of love appear: there is separation, then infidelity and treachery which lead to a disgust of the body and flesh. But in a final phrase, Shakespeare affirms the reality of a love that can transcend all barriers that is even more powerful than age or death.[12]

In searching for both thematically connected sonnets and a narrative arc that makes romantic sense, Brook naturally culls and carves the sonnets best fit for these purposes. He chooses thirty-one in total, and orders them as he sees fit. Brook therefore abandons any pretence of dramatizing a supposed narrative told in the complete,

Q version of the sonnets.[13] The love affair, in this production, is between a man and a woman. It is also between an older man and an older woman, so the emphasis is more on their shared experience of ageing than on the differing concerns of youth and age.

Brook's primary creative response to the sonnets is this condensed narrative, and of course, the moving tableaux he creates with actors, music, and physical and vocal directions. However, by the very act of textually simplifying and reducing Q, taking 154 sonnets on diverse subjects with at least three main figures and reducing them to 31, with two figures, Brook also makes possible some particularly interesting creative critical rereadings of individual sonnets or sets of sonnets. Perhaps the most illuminating moment of the performance is the combination of 'Alas 'tis true' (Q's 110, spoken by Pennington) followed by 'Th'expense of spirit' (Q's 129, spoken by Parry). The infamous sonnet 129 becomes, in this performance, a sonnet of disgusted rebuke. First, in 110, the wandering male speaker admits in a cavalier way that he has been unfaithful, and then, in 129, the female speaker takes him to task for giving in to the lusts of the body. Brook's version modifies the disgust and bitterness this sonnet usually achieves, when we assume it is spoken by a male regarding the horrors of sexual contact with women. Changing the sonnet's voicing and addressee confronts the male speaker with both infidelity and his own ageing body's failures. So, Brook's initial gambit, which reduces the queerness of Shakespeare's sonnets by denying the young man his place and by smoothing over the misogyny of the last sonnets, nevertheless questions or even reverses the bleak misogyny of sonnet 129 by revoicing it and complicating its narrative moment.

Despite this brilliant reinterpretation, there is much that Brook gets wrong about Shakespeare's sonnets. He assumes, with the nineteenth- and twentieth-century critics, that the sonnets represent 'Shakespeare's own, most secret life' and provide us with 'his private diary'.[14] But as a dramatist, whose production unfolds sequentially in time, Brook does provide his answers to questions that some of the sonnets pose: How do we survive through time? Who is the 'we' of the sonnets? What happens to statements of permanence when that 'we' is itself subject to time and change?

III ~ SONNET TRANSLATION: A MISCELLANY

If Brook condenses the sonnets, and tightens them into a single narrative composed of four neat phases, then Cohen and Legault's *The Sonnets: Translating and Rewriting Shakespeare* (2012) does nearly exactly the opposite: it explodes the sonnet collection into its 154 component parts, and in the process unencumbers them from narrative, from author, and often even from the original texts themselves and the sonnet form. This book reinvigorates a long tradition of adaptations of Shakespeare's sonnets by being unfaithful to the original, irreverent to the Bard, and yet at the same time somehow even more indebted and reverent (or, for some of the adaptations, derivative) than projects merely designed to perform or reprint Shakespeare's supposed original intentions.

The book was edited and put together by the founding editors of a translation studies journal. Their avowed intent, in inviting poets to provide English-to-English 'translations' of the sonnets, is for the poets to 'approach the original texts from their multitude of vantage points, that they would board the ship, loot and pillage, break things down, and reconstruct it all in a fashion that would allow us to view multiple dimensions of the original work in a new light, as a new structure'.[15] Although the editors have an oversimplified view of the 1609 quarto and 1640 *Poems* printings of the sonnets (they call them simply 'thefts'), the spirit of this project is admirable, and its execution is largely successful, if the aim is to create something new that nevertheless has deep connections to the original pattern.

Cohen and Legault's book of adaptations is a printed, bound paperback. This is not a trivial observation; it crucially defines their project as originating from one printed paper book (though Q would probably have been sold as unbound sheets) and moving to another. Its jacket design visually emphasizes the connection: it is modelled on the title page of the 1609 Q, with virtually the same printer's device at the top border. Their title occupies the space in which 'SHAKE-SPEARES | SONNETS | Neuer before Imprinted' appears on the 1609 Q's title page (in the middle), and the editors' names appear at the bottom of their title page, where the original publication information is in Q. More importantly, in the sonnets proper, the editors follow the Q order, and they assign one sonnet to each of the 154 authors. So the correspondence is one to one, the sonnets are numbered 1 to 154, and each author takes on the translation or adaptation in her or his own way, but with his or her contribution only extending to the assigned sonnet.

The poems are, not surprisingly, quite diverse. Some of them are rather lifeless adaptations into modern English; sonnets 129 and 130, by Terese Svoboda and Harryette Mullen, are particularly disappointingly derivative, given the notoriety of the one sonnet and the popularity and ubiquity of the other. Sonnet 116, the most famous of all, beginning 'Let me not to the marriage of true minds', fares better in June Jordan's hilarious and vervy 'Shakespeare's 116th Sonnet in Black English Translation'. A fair number of poets offer adaptations inspired by the L=A=N=G=U=A=G=E poets and by concrete poems, as well as by the found-poetry movement. For example, Gregory Betts's poem looks like a soup of letters, until you realize that the soup is exactly fourteen lines tall, and then further realize that he has started with the full text of sonnet 128 ('How oft when thou my music music play'st'), taken out all but a letter here and a letter there, and then called the thing 'Shakespeare's Alphabet'. A somewhat surprising number of them have fourteen lines, though there are several prose poems of multiple pages, and a few that involve visual processes, database processes, or Google Translate. Some, like Uljana Wolf's '(who's watching)' (sonnet 61), Pierre Joris's 'Shakespeare's sonnet #71, re-Englished after Paul Celan's German version without consulting the original even once:', and Thom Donovan's (sonnet 64), take translation as a subject in itself, and the sonnet as a means of exploring this subject. These entries are very much in the spirit of the publishers, but also, I would argue, in the spirit of a lively tradition in which Shakespeare sonnets, from the start, were fungible poetry, able to be manipulated for the purpose of the author or publisher. In the act of manipulation and adaptation, here more than in perhaps any other reproduction, the authors create a textual object that is shared between them and Shakespeare, and that spans the gulf of time between 1609 and today. This spanning and sharing seems very much in the spirit of a collection of sonnets that repeatedly asserts, in the continual lyric present, that 'this gives life to thee' (sonnet 18.14).

This is not meant to be a full review of the book. I like some of its poems and dislike others. I think a few of them are brilliant, and a few are downright doltish. But a few aspects of the book are relevant here. First, as a reading experience, there is no point in doing anything but dipping in and out. Everything changes, one poem to the next: form, style, mood – all the basic parameters of poetry. 'You' and 'I', those basic questions of lyric, also shift with every poem, because each sonnet adaptation takes on its own voice and its own position with respect to Shakespeare's original 'you' and 'I'. Second, it seems best to read the one book alongside the other book: I read the new poem and then, to try to figure out what the poet has done, I read Shakespeare's sonnet. Sometimes the design is obvious, and sometimes not. But the effect, in terms of my own reading activity, is double-booked. The two books are inseparably companionate volumes. They also go both ways: each one deepens the other. You could read the new book without knowing the old one, or without keeping them in such close contact. But I do think this new book of sonnet adaptations and translations helps us to disrupt the primacy of *Shake-speares Sonnets*, helps us to remember that from the beginning they really were messed with and messed about, and that we are heirs to that process as well as to the long tradition of sonnet explication codified in *Variorum* editions, Arden and Oxford editions, and now in Internet editions.

IV ~ SONNETS IN THE CLOUD, FROM THE CROWD

My final examination of Shakespeare's sonnets in an adaptive context is from a collection entitled *The Sonnet Project* (TSP). The project's aim is to produce 154 short films, one for each sonnet. Each sonnet is filmed by a different director, at a different location in one of the five boroughs of New York City. There are parameters to which each short film has to conform, including a four-minute limit and the assignment by TSP of a primary actor for each film. Each director must apply to the project and must provide his or her own equipment and extras. According to its executive producer, Ross Williams, TSP is many things, including 'a tapestry of cinematic art that infuses the poetry of William Shakespeare into the poetry of New York City', a way to 'demystify his work and connect it to our own culture', and 'a sprawling, barely controllable, ever-growing, ever-changing tribute to Shakespeare's art, New York City, and the artists that live here'.[16]

This project shares some of the concerns and artistic desires expressed by Cohen and Legault's *Translating and Rewriting Shakespeare* collection. Most significantly, each project apportions single sonnets to single adapters, so that the resultant work, insofar as it is a single work, is the combination of 154 individual artistic visions of the 154 individual sonnets. Narrative coherence, such as that emphasized by Brook's dramatic production or the earlier attempts to reorder the sonnets, is not emphasized in either collection. In fact, both seem designed to eschew coherence itself; the closest Williams comes to emphasizing coherence is calling TSP a 'tapestry'. Cohen and Legault go even further: variation, non sequitur, and contradiction between approaches all seem to be the logical result of a project design that assigns different sonnets to different authors who have different poetic goals and methods.

Despite a shared basic methodology, TSP differs from Cohen and Legault's collection in a number of ways. First, TSP is entirely a twenty-first century text; it is a version of Shakespeare's sonnets that would not have been envisioned even as recently as the early 2000s. It is both crowd-sourced and web-based. It began as a Kickstarter campaign (its funding coming from a set of donations made via a Web-based appeal to the masses), and continues toward fruition as one by one, volunteer directors complete their online applications to direct a sonnet, work in tandem with the project, submit their finished work to the project director, and have their completed videos uploaded to the master website.[17] Second, TSP is not a book, of course. But neither can we call it simply a film, or a website. On TSP's website, one can read about the project, apply to direct a sonnet film, and also view the films that have been released.[18] But TSP does not reside solely at this website. One can also navigate to TSP sonnet films from their group on Facebook, from the website Globeplayer (a repository of films sponsored by the Globe Theatre in London and the Shakespeare Globe Trust), from TSP's channel on YouTube, and probably from many other websites both personal and professional. More importantly, TSP also exists as an app. This version of the project largely replicates what is available on the website, but with an important difference: it includes a map of all the sonnet films across the New York City landscape, with pins for each individual film's location, and with a blue dot indicating the reader-viewer's location in this landscape.

This feature of TSP encapsulates its novelty in the field of Shakespearean adaptations. Cohen and Legault's collection and TSP both rely on individual adaptations. They both contain intentional diversions from Shakespeare's sonnets right alongside attempts to reproduce or perform Shakespeare's supposed intentions or meaning faithfully, though in a different form. But TSP's emphasis on location means that the five New York City boroughs become as much the subject and the through line of this project as Shakespeare. Not only that, but the topocentric emphasis brings the reader-viewer into the project's landscape. One witnesses the places and spaces of the films' locations first as virtual pins stuck into a map on one's phone or screen, then as the set of the brief film. The resulting landscape, sonnet films plotted onto a map, invites a different kind of participation, neither solely spectatorial nor solely readerly. As I write this sentence, my own blue dot holds steady at Fifth Avenue and 42nd Street, at the central New York Public Library, the Stephen A. Schwarzman Building. There is a pin right here: sonnet 17 (beginning 'Who will believe my verse in time to come') was directed by Marco Ricci and Jason Whitaker on 2 April 2013. Carey Van Driest recites the poem, on the steps of the building, at the pedestal of one its famous lions (not in frame), and at one of its doorways. So here I am, at the scene of this sonnet in this adaptation. A dozen more are within a short walk: two at Grand Central Station, one at the Algonquin Hotel, one at the New Amsterdam Theatre, and more than ten in Central Park. Predictably, Manhattan is crowded with sonnet pins, while large swathes of the other boroughs languish sonnet-less.

Yet of course I am no more at the scene of this sonnet than anyone else: that time is past and gone, even if the building remains more or less intact. A few of the sonnets play upon this persistent theme in Shakespeare's sonnets: what lasts, what decays, and whether to indulge in the illusion of permanence. Perhaps the best answer is the film of sonnet 64 (beginning 'When I have seen by Time's fell hand defaced'), directed by Jeff Barry, and set in Trinity Church Cemetery in lower Manhattan. At the third line of this sonnet, 'When sometime lofty towers I see down razed', the actor (Julian Elfer) gazes up at 'The Freedom Tower', One World Trade Center, which was built near the site of the 'sometime lofty' World Trade Center towers. (The director of the film of sonnet 55, the more famous 'Not marble, nor the gilded monuments', sets it at the 9/11 memorial, which preserves the twin towers as voids, rather than monuments.) These sonnet films take on decay, ruin, and the passage of time explicitly in their images, but behind the whole project is the spectre of impermanence: the actors, their settings, and whoever we can say the 'I' and 'you' of each film is – these all come within the compass of Time's bending sickle.

Although at the time of writing, not all 154 films of Shakespeare's sonnets have been produced, TSP's project will eventually come to its completion. One final significant difference between this adaptation of the sonnets and any other is that it might potentially have no ending, unlike a bound book or a performance in a theatre. The project's director has decided that there is to be one film per sonnet, but a quick glance at YouTube will provide a host of amateur videos for just about any given Shakespeare sonnet. (Typing 'Sonnet Project' into YouTube's search engine reveals this problem of disambiguation: many of TSP's videos appear alongside amateur and student videos.) We might thus consider TSP as itself taking part in a larger, much more organic and unsupervised project: the twenty-first century explosion of personally produced videos made available instantly to anyone with an Internet connection. TSP's set of videos is curated, monitored, and controlled, and indeed most of the videos look and sound a certain way. They will also, when the project is completed, have documented the look and feel of many spots in New York between the years of 2013 and 2016. But as Shakespearean video adaptations of the sonnets, they ought to be enfolded into a much larger set of productions, so that if indeed 'from fairest creatures we desire increase', the fair creatures of these sonnets have in the past few years increased and multiplied beyond all expectation.

V ~ I TAKE MY CHANCES

It seems either unfair or ill-advised to write so much about adaptations, translations, performances, and responses to Shakespeare's sonnets without offering my own attempt. Without time or (yet) inclination to create responses to all or even a subset of Shakespeare's sonnets, my method of choosing was to rely heavily on chance, combined with my own specific surrounding circumstances. (The 'Notes on Method' below explain this.) As is usual for me, those circumstances were a library on successive afternoons, and the outcome (detailed in the poem below and its notes) combines a line from a sonnet with a bit of text from one of the books in the reading room in which I wrote. The chance-determined sonnet is number 80:

80

O how I faint when I of you do write,
Knowing a better spirit doth use your name,
And in the praise thereof spends all his might,
To make me tongue-tied speaking of your fame.
But, since your worth, wide as the ocean is,
The humble as the proudest sail doth bear,
My saucy bark, inferior far to his,
On your broad main doth wilfully appear.
Your shallowest help will hold me up afloat,
Whilst he upon your soundless deep doth ride;
Or, being wracked, I am a worthless boat,
He of tall building and of goodly pride.
    Then, if he thrive and I be cast away,
    The worst was this: my love was my decay.[19]

I'd not thought it would come so close to sense.
What but endurance? Love time poetry change age identity do we really need to go on
to go on?
    The poem writes itself,
and a puff of breath lasts way more foreverer than
you name it: marble,
              steel,
                        or a million half-lives.

But the ocean.
The poor ocean has come a long way.
It may not be able to take us much longer.
It may begin being beyond compare. ~ :: ~ Ocean – a sad little interim –
                                        ~ :: ~ Ocean – hungry –
                                        ~ :: ~ Ocean – wide –
How much longer will you hold me,
Poisonous as I am?
Clearly I don't want you implacable; I want hurricanes.
I don't want you patient; I want a rise.
I am so small.
                That I define you breaks us both apart.

Matthew Zarnowiecki is Associate Professor and Chair of the Department of Languages and Literature at Touro College's Lander College for Women and Lander College for Men, New York. His research interests are in early modern literary studies, Shakespeare, print and manuscript history, and lyric poetry and song. His monograph, *Fair Copies: Reproducing the English Lyric from Tottel to Shakespeare* (University of Toronto Press, 2014) examines the production and reproduction of poetry in printed collections. His articles have appeared in *Critical Survey*, *Spenser Studies*, *The Sidney Journal*, and *EMLS*, among other places; an article on Thomas Ravenscroft is forthcoming in *New Ways of Looking at Old Texts*. His current book project is (for now) called *Part Song: Polyphonic Songbooks and Literary Participation in Renaissance England*.

NOTES ON METHOD

(1) Here are some numbers. 114 → street I am on; 5 → floor I am on; 10027; 37 → shelves around me in a square; 6 → shelves per shelf; 5:25 3-13-2014 = start hour minute day month year. Latitude longitude? Distance from sea? [half a mile tops] 11:39 3-14 = finish hour minute day ... rest the same.

(2) Four walls surround like a clock. There's a future-telling method involving random pointing at random pages and lines of the *Iliad*. Or Cerutti's Italian Grammar. Bibliomancy. People are under the impression that it's by chance that any of us are born to any one place.[20] Less so any one time. The lottery. The choice to constrict. There's only one ending; there are all endings. Where is one? From the top or from the bottom? From the left or from the right? What do I do at sundown? Tails is the beginning?

(3) Result #1: 11/37; 3/6; 2/17; 2126/2230 = in the determined book,[21] either '*endurcissement*' or '*endurer*'; Coin flip: tails; 1/8 usage explanations (see Illustration 1.1).

(4) PAIRING: 80/154, 'Oh how I faint when I of you do write'; 5/14, 'But since your worth, wide as the ocean is'; 8/9: 'ocean' (see Illustration 1.2).

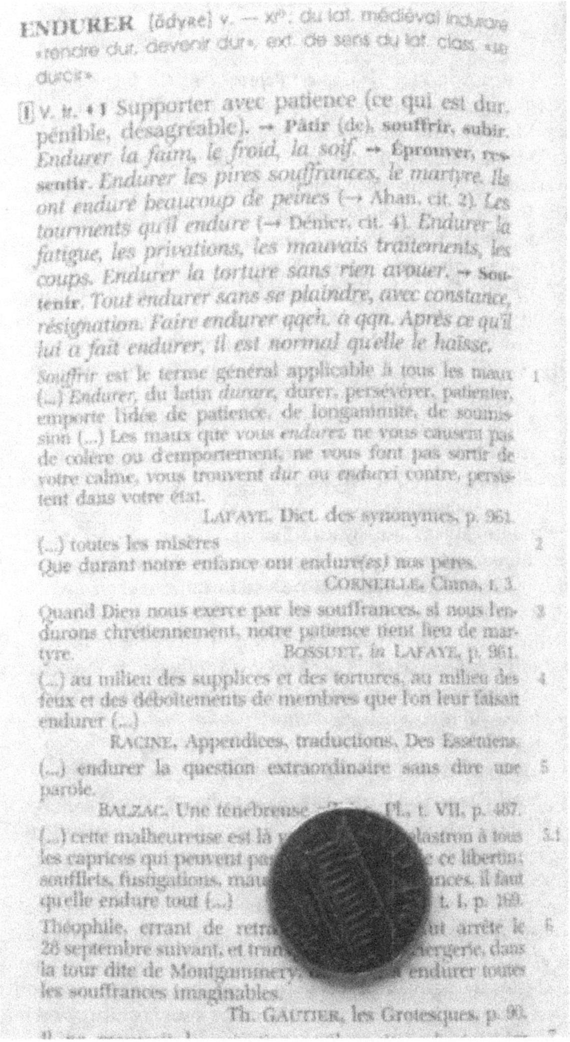

Illustration 1.1: Detail of vol. 2, p. 2126 of *Le Grand Robert de La Langue Française* (see note 21). My photograph, with addition.

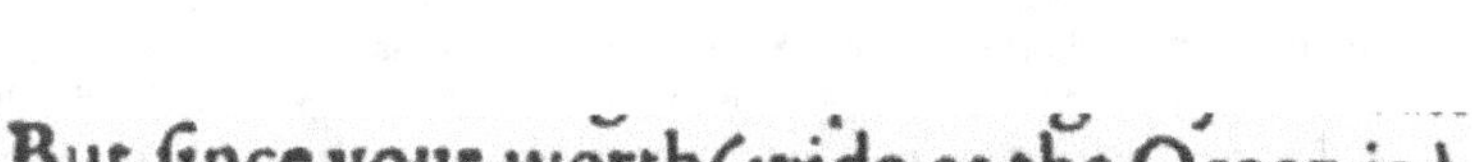

But since your worth(wide as the Ocean is)

Illustration 1.2: Detail of Sonnet 80, line 5 (EEBO, STC 22353, 2nd ed.).

Notes

1. Matthew Zarnowiecki, *Fair Copies: Reproducing the English Lyric from Tottel to Shakespeare* (Toronto: University of Toronto Press, 2014), chap. 5.
2. William Shakespeare, *Shake-speares Sonnets. Neuer before Imprinted* (At London: By G. Eld for T[homas] T[horpe] and are to be solde by William Aspley, 1609).
3. There are, of course, hoards of editions, far too many to list. Here are the editions referred to above: Stephen Booth, ed., *Shakespeare's Sonnets* (New Haven: Yale Nota Bene, 2000); Helen Vendler, *The Art of Shakespeare's Sonnets* (Cambridge, MA: Harvard University Press, 1997); Carl D. Atkins, *Shakespeare's Sonnets: With Three Hundred Years of Commentary* (Madison, NJ: Fairleigh Dickinson University Press, 2007); Don Paterson, *Reading Shakespeare's Sonnets: A New Commentary* (London: Faber and Faber, 2010); Paul Hammond, *Shakespeare's Sonnets: An Original-Spelling Text* (Oxford: Oxford University Press, 2012). It looks like Atkins and Hammond had the same idea at about the same time: a critical edition using original spelling. Paterson's edition employs a much more personalized and informal commentary.
4. William Shakespeare, *The Passionate Pilgrime. By W. Shakespeare* (At London: Printed [by T. Judson] for W. Iaggard, and are to be sold by W. Leake, at the Greyhound in Paules Churchyard, 1599).
5. William Shakespeare, *Poems: VVritten by Wil. Shake-Speare. Gent* (Printed at London: By Tho. Cotes, and are to be sold by Iohn Benson, dwelling in St. Dunstans Church-yard, 1640).
6. Debate has raged, and Benson has been called a pirate and a rogue. But so has the first printer, Thomas Thorpe. A good introduction to the debate is Arthur F. Marotti, 'Shakespeare's Sonnets as Literary Property', in *Soliciting Interpretation: Literary Theory and Seventeenth-Century English Poetry*, ed. Elizabeth D. Harvey and Katharine Eisaman Maus (Chicago: University of Chicago Press, 1990), 143–73.
7. Henry David Gray, 'The Arrangement and the Date of Shakespeare's Sonnets', *PMLA* 30, 3 (1915), 631. This is also the view of Clara Longworth de Chambrun, in *The Sonnets of William Shakespeare: New Light and Old Evidence* (New York: G.P. Putnam's Sons, 1913).
8. For example, Rollins says that the rearrangers 'do no harm', and that they 'amuse themselves as with a jig-saw puzzle'. Hyder Edward Rollins, ed., *A New Variorum Edition of Shakespeare: The Sonnets* (Philadelphia & London: J.B. Lippincott, 1944), vol. 2, 212. At the same time, he reminds us that 'by far the majority of editors have printed the sonnets exactly in Thorpe's order, which, by a mere show of editorial hands, has an enormous vote in its favor; but, even so, many follow Thorpe, not because they think his sequence correct, but because they despair of producing any that will be better, or merely because they conform to tradition' (ibid.).
9. Charles Armitage Brown in his 1838 edition declares that seeing the sonnets as not individual poems, but long poems in sonnet stanzas 'unlocks every difficulty, and we have nothing but pure uninterrupted biography' (qtd in Rollins, *A New Variorum Edition*, vol. 2, 76).

10. See W.W. Greg, 'The Rationale of Copy-Text', *Studies in Bibliography: Papers of the Bibliographical Society of the University of Virginia* 3 (1950), 19–36.
11. Checking this assertion, I did find one reordered version available online: Gerald Massey, 'The Secret Drama of Shakespeare's Sonnets, by Gerald Massey (1888 edition)', *Minor Victorian Poets and Authors*, accessed 15 February 2016, http://gerald-massey.org.uk/massey/cpr_shakspeare_index.htm. Massey's essay, 'Shakespeare and His Sonnets', is also reproduced on this site, and it gives an indication of what he was searching for and what his aims were in this edition.
12. 'Playbill, The Duke on 42nd Street: Love is My Sin', *Playbill Incorporated*, April 2010.
13. Here, if it is not already apparent, I should unequivocally state my position: there is no such thing as 'the story of Shakespeare's sonnets', except in the protestations and asseverations of each commentator and editor who declares that there is, and that he or she has found it.
14. 'Playbill, The Duke on 42nd Street'.
15. Sharmila Cohen and Paul Legault, eds, *The Sonnets: Translating and Rewriting Shakespeare* (Brooklyn: Telephone Books, 2012), i.
16. 'The Sonnet Project', *New York Shakespeare Exchange*, 2013, accessed 8 February 2016, http://sonnetprojectnyc.com.
17. At the time of writing, 36 sonnets have not yet been released on the site, and nine of these have not yet been assigned to directors. 118 sonnets are available on the site, or its corresponding app, to be viewed.
18. 'The Sonnet Project', http://sonnetprojectnyc.com.
19. I use Stephen Booth's slightly modernized text: see Booth, *Shakespeare's Sonnets*.
20. Martha C. Nussbaum, *Cultivating Humanity: A Classical Defense of Reform in Liberal Education* (Cambridge, MA: Harvard University Press, 1997), 62.
21. Paul Robert and Alain Rey, eds, *Le Grand Robert de La Langue Française*, Nouvelle édition augmentée (Paris: Dictionnaires Le Robert, 2001), vol. 2, 2126.

Chapter 2
Exit, pursued by a fan
Shakespeare, Fandom, and the Lure of the Alternate Universe

Jessica McCall and Kavita Mudan Finn

Amongst fans and the academics who study them, it is generally accepted (perhaps even a truth universally acknowledged) that a good portion of what we consider canonical literature – including Shakespeare – also fits the broadest definition of fanfiction, in that it is clearly written in response to or adapting a specific source text.[1] Although it is difficult to reconcile any category that comfortably includes both Shakespeare's plays and E.L. James' *Fifty Shades of Grey* – 89 per cent of which had already appeared on the Internet as a piece of *Twilight* fanfiction entitled 'Master of the Universe' – some have argued that this juxtaposition is the very point of fanfiction. However one feels about it as literature, transformative fiction (known as *fanfiction, fanfic,* or *fic*) also offers an alternative form of both close reading and contextual *criticism* when applied to premodern writers, just as it does for contemporary media properties.

Notes for this section begin on page 51.

In a world of undead authors and readers unsure of their own critical authority, fanfiction provides a unique opportunity to undercut the positivism of traditional approaches to interpretation. Even subversive theoretical lenses like gender studies, queer theory, and presentism are trapped (for reasons both necessary and infuriating) by standards and restrictions that are meant to ensure strong academic rigour but nonetheless silence more radical discourses. Scholars in gender and race studies in particular have pushed back against some of these restrictions; Sara Ahmed, for instance, argues that it is incumbent upon academics to 'bring theory back to life' rather than allow it to exist only in abstraction.[2] Fanfiction eschews these restrictions altogether because it exists in the limen between genre and generative narrative, or 'myth', and provides unique opportunities for rewritings by the amateur, the marginalized, and the academic alike. Where academic discourse is built on the politics of exclusion – specialized vocabulary and hierarchical epistemologies to name two – the semiotics of fanfiction offers a different avenue towards dialectical critical interpretation. Fandom values qualities more often dismissed in traditional academic circles, such as emotion (or, in academic parlance, affect), self-insertion, and subjectivity. These qualities have been historically derided as feminized – and thus less critical – approaches to texts. Furthermore, prizing these qualities places a premium in fandom on rewritings that are grounded in a reader's subjective response to a text and encourages remythologisation of historically enforced readings of those texts. Our goal here is therefore not to 'translate' fanworks back into the critical idiom – which would, indeed, reinscribe them into the very framework they are resisting – but to offer a critical introduction to two examples of transformative fanworks based on Shakespeare's plays that may then speak for themselves.

By always already being 'out of bounds', fanfiction offers a staging ground for radical and terrible readings and rewritings alike. Fanfiction has no formal peer review system in place; a fundamental characteristic of fanfiction is its openness and availability to all contributors no matter how illogical the interpretation or rewriting. *Beta* or *beta-reader* is a catch-all term for a fellow member of the fandom who acts as anything from a copy editor (correcting spelling, grammar, and punctuation) to a coauthor or informal critic who offers suggestions on plot, characterization, and style. This process mimics that of academic peer review by subjecting individual interpretation and discursive contribution to a larger community of educated peers. Unlike a peer reviewer, however, the beta is not a position of administrative power; they cannot dictate whether or not a piece of fanfiction is posted and read. Whatever power a beta holds is granted through community participation and the high value placed on interpretation as a result of discussion. This dissolution of central authority amongst the larger community of fans fundamentally alters the interpretative logic of close-reading, and thus demands from academics an awareness of the hierarchical and restricted vocabulary of literary criticism when analysing fanfiction and fandom more generally. Imposing the restrictive discourse of academia onto criticism of fannish texts stops remythologisation and, thus, stymies the power of fandom itself.

Pedagogically speaking, the amateur nature of fanfiction undercuts the authority of 'Shakespeare' and empowers students to make meaning out of Shakespeare through a method that requires they translate the text for themselves rather than rely on commercially published 'translations', such as *No Fear Shakespeare*, approved through capitalist-driven corporations. Ann Berthoff states,

> When we read critically, we are reading for meaning – and that is not the same thing as reading for 'message'. Meanings are not things, and finding them is not like going on an Easter egg hunt. Meanings are relationships: they are unstable, shifting, dynamic; they do not stay still nor can we prove the authenticity or the validity of one or another meaning that we find.[3]

Fanfiction makes no pretence of changing meaning. Shannon Farley calls written fanfiction (as opposed to vids, vlogs, or fanart) a form of 'intralingual translation' or 'the transfer of source text from one sign system to another, but within the same language', though, in the case of Shakespeare, it is closer to the kind of interpretation often seen in performance.[4] We could even go so far as to argue fanfiction is the beginning of a new kind of criticism, as it allows students and readers to make their own meaning from Shakespeare rather than have a predetermined message thrust upon them. Reading and writing fanfiction can preserve the multiplicity and complexity of meaning in the text rather than replacing it; it also offers a radical and safe space for students and amateur Shakespeareans alike to stretch their wings through a ridiculousness that only exists, and can only exist, in the unmonitored marginalia of academia. Louise Geddes' study of the fandom devoted to Mercutio in *Romeo and*

Juliet offers a glimpse of this kind of engagement, complete with references to teachers who, at least in the fans' view, fundamentally misunderstand the point of the play.[5]

As a pedagogical exercise, fanfiction has countless applications – asking students to write their own fanfiction or to read and interpret select fanfiction alongside traditional texts is the most obvious starting place.[6] While the critical muscles being exercised in these kinds of activities and assignments are not identical to those in traditional literary analysis, students are still engaging in close-reading of primary (and potentially secondary) texts and coming up with interpretations of those texts. Students, particularly in the United States, are often afraid of Shakespeare, or believe that they should be afraid of him. Positioning Shakespeare as the be-all and end-all of literature and falling back on bardolatry as the reason why we study his works is an exercise in intimidation. This explains the often frustrating reliance on *No Fear Shakespeare* or SparkNotes; from the students' perspective, Shakespeare is not even in English, let alone relevant to their lives. One of the refreshing and truly enjoyable things about the fandom devoted to Shakespeare's plays is that they are making Shakespeare relevant and interesting while preserving the complexity and ambiguity of the plays themselves.

As Anna Wilson explains, the writing of fanfiction is above all things rooted in love of the source text.

> The most fundamental lack at the heart of all texts is their finite quantity; most readers can identify with the hollow feeling that comes with the end of a book one has enjoyed. Fan communities have created a space where this desire becomes generative, the community's own efforts going towards feeding its own desire for more.[7]

A fan author looks at a Shakespeare play and sees not just a self-contained text, but a series of generative potentialities.

Elizabethan and Jacobean dramatists worked within a strict framework defined and circumscribed by staging practices, casting choices (e.g. all-male theatrical companies), and – like media creators today – perceptions of what their audience desired. Thus, fan authors and readers of fanfiction approach Shakespeare not necessarily because they find his works lacking – although this is a factor in some cases – but because his plays, and those of his contemporaries, are rife with potential for expansion, revision, and transformation. Some authors draw on specific productions or interpretations; for example, a fan author who was particularly struck by Julie Taymor's film version of *The Tempest* might write a story where Prospero is, in fact, a woman. In some cases, these fan interpretations (production-based or otherwise) gain a footing within some enclave of the fandom as a whole. These are called *headcanons* – ideas so well received that their rewritings become accepted as 'canon' within larger fandom discourse communities.[8]

Fandom, as Karen Hellekson and Tisha Turk have both argued, functions as a large-scale gift economy: 'gifts within fandom are not simply given but distributed – and potentially, via links and reblogs, redistributed, sometimes well beyond the corner of fandom in which they first appeared. Fandom gifting is not just one-to-one but one-to-many'.[9] Similarly, working within medieval and early modern patronage systems, writers were almost always writing for both specific persons and general audiences, negotiating the requests and desires of both. In the contemporary fannish gift economy, fans provide prompts, usually focused on a scene, set of characters, or point of interpretation, and, more often than not, one or several other fans will fill that prompt. The resulting works range from drabbles (five hundred words or less) to novel-length stories, and represent an equally large spectrum of characters, genres, and tropes.

One of the most popular genres to request for Shakespeare's plays is the 'alternate universe' (AU), a genre that, on the surface, radically alters the source text, but is in fact intended to illustrate the flexibility and adaptability of that source text to different contexts. There are two broad categories of AU stories and an endless variety of subgenres. The first, which Douglas Lanier calls the 'revisionary narrative' and known within the fandom as *canon divergence*, 'begins with the characters and the situation of the source but changes the plot'.[10] This type of story usually picks up at the point of divergence and explores what might have happened had the plot taken a different turn. A version of *Othello* where Emilia discovers Iago's plot in Act IV and saves Desdemona's life or a *Romeo and Juliet* where Friar Laurence's letter doesn't go astray before it reaches Romeo would both qualify as canon divergence AUs – and, indeed, one could argue that Shakespeare himself wrote that version of *Othello*, doubled the clowns, added a bear, and called it *The Winter's Tale*.

The other major category of AU fanfiction preserves the characters and plotline of the source text while transposing the action to a different time period and/or location. It begins with a commonplace in modern productions of Shakespeare (an alternative setting) and goes one step further: instead of a setting for a pre-existing text, in an AU fanfiction, the setting becomes the text, and as a result, needs to possess some kind of internal logic. Nobody gets married, for instance, at the end of the 1999 film *10 Things I Hate about You*, an adaptation of *The Taming of the Shrew*, because the internal logic of a twentieth-century American high school setting does not allow for it.[11] Authors need to consider not just the original text and its concerns, but how those concerns translate out of Shakespeare's world and into the alternate setting. Along with the challenges of the AU setting, however, comes the potential for readings that are not possible in the original setting, particularly with regard to issues of gender, sexuality, race, and disability, which remain some of the most pressing and complicated areas of cultural theory and lived experience.

Our ability to theorize and critically discuss these issues is tied to our ability to explore them through fictionalized representations (in short, #RepresentationMatters). The continued significance of Shakespeare's text and the possibility for critical conversation remain limited by the discursive boundaries bordering imaginative possibilities and then perpetuated through mythic discourse. If we are able to break away from historical attempts that provide positivist definitions of myth (creation myth, hero myth, apocalypse myth) and focus instead on myth as generative narrative, fandom is clearly a driving cultural force and author of myths and re-myths. There is no question that 'Shakespeare' has taken on mythic status in modern Western society. As Ayanna Thompson observes, 'Shakespeare is often used to mean his now-canonical body of work: a synecdoche of sorts in which the name Shakespeare stands in for his entire creative output. But the name is also employed to signify a mythical fantasy about the author as a symbol for artistic genius, or as a symbol for the difficulty of the work created by that genius'.[12] AU stories require a reader to reconsider the discursive boundaries of Shakespeare and how those boundaries limit interpretation. Functioning as revisionist myth-making of Shakespeare, the AU quietly rewrites the rules of what Shakespeare's texts are or can be. Sujata Iyengar argues,

> We cannot 'adapt' Shakespeare in a genetic sense: we lack access to its unmodified DNA, and moreover Shakespeare is (if we are going to stretch this metaphor) epigenetic. Or maybe Shakespeare is more of a *chimera*, a half-human hybrid that bears its manifestation in the world (in its material and textual forms) traces of other forms that

it did not 'inherit' in a straightforward manner, a creature that has inherited two or more distinct and identifiable lineages or that has mutated during the process of growth or reproduction.[13]

Fandom and fanfiction take the stories of Shakespeare – much as Shakespeare borrowed from chronicles, classical mythology, and other writers who came before him – and transform those stories for the modern fan community.

Furthermore, fandom is overwhelmingly driven by marginalized readers: women, members of the LGBTQIA+ community, and readers of colour who are actively agitating against white patriarchal epistemologies that have historically defined which texts have cultural value and how those texts should be interpreted. While these different groups do not always sit harmoniously alongside one another, and some voices are louder than others, the diversity within fandom as a whole offers a stark contrast to the overwhelming whiteness of literary fiction and literary studies.[14] To take one recent example, although the authors who have published thus far in Random House's Hogarth Shakespeare novel series do well in terms of gender parity (5 women, 3 men), only one of these authors is not white.[15] While fan communities have a variety of issues concerning race and representation – one need only look up 'racefail' on Tumblr or Fanlore – alternate universes often offer the chance to draw attention to racial or gender representation in ways not necessarily permissible within the original canon. The act of revisionist myth-making, or remythologising, shifts interpretations and conversations from what once seemed impossible to a space that is not only feasible but also carries revolutionary possibilities. How does *The Taming of the Shrew* fit into the twenty-first century and, if modern audiences prefer a revisionist work like *10 Things I Hate About You*, is that a sign of immaturity, or the rejection of a disturbingly violent and misogynistic text still taught, staged, and marketed as a comedy? Similarly, if audiences and readers reject the comic ending to *The Merchant of Venice* and seek to subvert the play's anti-Semitism, not to mention its questionable depictions of gender and sexuality, how do we as teachers and scholars find more productive ways to engage with it? The answers to these questions are important ones, not simply in regards to the future of Shakespeare, but also to larger conversations critiquing and making visible hegemonic power structures.

Shakespeare and Shakespeare's fandom are not simply working and reworking myths of history, gender, and magic; fanfiction also reworks the myth of 'Shakespeare' that took shape in the eighteenth century and haunts classrooms to this day. The authoritative notion of Shakespeare as author-god, someone who so completely captured the 'human condition' that we can only humbly read his words and hope to glean enlightenment, plagues secondary and collegiate classrooms. It is also simply untrue. Approaching the language of Shakespeare as an opportunity for imagination, creativity, and curiosity changes the difficulty of a dated text from something insurmountable and out-of-reach into something to be enjoyed, played with, and reconsidered.

The critical discourse about Shakespeare, fandom, adaptation, and appropriation has evolved since the initial publication of this chapter and we the authors wish to address some of these developments directly. Adaptation studies writ large has seen a flood of new scholarship, ranging across different media from stage and film adaptation to print to the infinite variety of online and digital platforms. Collections such as *Shakespearean Echoes* (2015) and *The Shakespeare User* (2017) offer a range of perspectives on these topics, while the journal *Borrowers and Lenders* specializes in adaptation and appropriation of Shakespeare.

With regard to Shakespeare and fan studies more specifically, two parallel branches of critical discourse have formed with the distinguishing difference being the framing of the fan in relationship to the fanwork.[16] One branch builds on adaptation studies within Shakespeare criticism and presents fans in a quasi-ethnographic manner, as inadvertent subverters of academic tradition operating within a 'Shakespeare Multiverse'.[17] While there is much value in this larger concept – where contemporary transformative fanworks exist alongside early quartos or adapted performances like Nahum Tate's alternate ending to *King Lear* – we do take issue with the treatment of fans themselves. Positioning fans as inadvertent subverters robs fans of their agency and elevates the scholar at the expense of the fan. Valerie Fazel has approached this topic with regard to Shakespeare videos on YouTube, which she describes as 'dynamic sources that are difficult to separate from their producers and creators precisely because of the interactive medium employed'.[18] She chose to contact the producers of the videos she analysed, but allowed that other researchers might decline to do so.

In the case of fanfiction, which usually if not always appears under some sort of pseudonym, these questions are thornier. Some scholars operate on the assumption that anything posted in an open archive, such as the Organization for Transformative Works' Archive of Our Own, is automatically in the public domain. While that is certainly legal and accords with academic study of modern fiction, film, and television, the fact that fanfiction is produced for and within a specific community and that fan authors are writing without financial recompense, suggests that the polite choice is to make them aware that their work has become part of scholarly research. Contacting authors, furthermore, allows them to provide commentary that may illuminate aspects of their works, particularly with regard to positionality. Authors belonging to marginalized groups may make certain interpretative choices for different reasons than the stereotypical white cis female fan. It may well be 'typical' that 'with fannish production, the hierarchy and timeline of influence are at best convoluted, and work is littered with partial citations and incorrect references, making apparent the messy circulation of influence', but allowing fan authors to contextualise their work offers opportunities for us as critics to untangle some of those influences.[19] As Rukmini Pande has argued, 'nonwhite fans are seen to interrupt normative operations of such structures only in specific contexts when they make themselves visible'.[20] This trend echoes what Ayanna Thompson has observed in Shakespeare performance and Shakespeare studies – the prevalence of 'race-blind' or 'gender-blind' casting, rather than addressing racial disparities, results in the erasure of non-white perspectives while allowing existing power structures to stand unquestioned.[21] Given the convergence of these issues between fan studies and Shakespeare studies, our goal in studying fans and fanworks is to adhere to the rules and norms within the community and to credit them for the interpretations and meaning they produce, rather than reinterpreting it through an unnecessarily theoretical lens. Our contribution to this volume, therefore, combines traditional criticism with two different pieces of Shakespeare-based fanfiction in order to illustrate the potential and versatility of this type of textual engagement. Both pieces fall under the category of AU, but follow two very different trajectories.

* * *

KAVITA

Jess, you wrote your piece in response to a post you saw on Tumblr, reproduced here.[22]

> yemite:
>
> > sarah531:
> >
> > > The other day I had a really good idea for a story:
> > >
> > > A high school Shakespeare club angrily splits into two groups when they can't agree on the correct interpretation of *Romeo and Juliet*. One group thinks it's a cautionary tale about the stupidity of youth and shallow lust; the other group think it's a beautiful tragedy about poisonous hatred conquered by love. Reconciliation seems impossible–
> > >
> > > –then *a person from one group falls in love with a person from the other*
> >
> > #it would be better if somehow EVERY OTHER SHAKESPEARE WAS HAPPENING AT ONCE#like you got a benedict and beatice b-story#and then somebody see's their dad's ghost#and there's cross-dressing#and three upperclassmen tell macbeth he will be drama club president

Illustration 2.1: Tumblr post from NicoDreams, 'The other day I had a really good idea for a story', *All About That Space*, Tumblr, 8 March 2014.

If we assume, as we've discussed above, that fans are playing with Shakespeare's texts as a form of criticism as well as just for fun, what kinds of critical lenses are at work in this exercise?

JESS

Certainly presentism, but it intersects with traditional approaches of close reading as well. Rather than only asking for a creative misreading of Shakespeare's plays, a fanfiction that provides imagined interiority or backstory for the characters, this prompt asked that a Shakespeare AU simultaneously wrestle with competing interpretations of Shakespeare. Do we feel sympathy for Romeo and Juliet or dismiss them? Does it matter if, ultimately, the majority of the audience still desires a love story above all else? And the prompt itself acknowledges and explicitly demands that this fanfiction discuss, through creative writing, the impossibility of positivism as an act of literary interpretation by changing the primary conflict from one of class and nation into one of textual authority. I was intrigued by this prompt because it isn't only asking for fanfiction based on Shakespeare, but for fanfiction of Shakespeare criticism as well.

KAVITA

Now, looking at the story itself, you incorporated some but not all of the elements in the prompt. What was your rationale for which elements you chose and which you left out?

JESS

The choice to include romance, betrayal, and dates to prom was conscious on my part; aside from being obvious Shakespearean themes, the date to prom substituting for marriage here, a focus on romance is also a key characteristic of fandom where 'OTPs' and 'shipping' are driving forces of discourse.[23] Furthermore, romance has come to be seen as the purview of femininity (despite its constant hypocritical appearance in action movies as a clear marker of heteronormative masculine dominance) and fandom has re-legitimized the validity of loving love as a particularly feminist and subversive act. This subversion is further complicated by the emphasis on slash ships[24] – something I attempted a nod at with the queering of 'Romy and Julie'.

One thing I really loved about your fanfiction, Kavita, was the decision to make Meg Stanley the primary point-of-view character. This demonstrates the point about the power of AUs to provide alternate readings that aren't possible with the original canon. What drove you to make that decision?

KAVITA

The story's protagonist, Detective Meg Stanley, is a conflation of Shakespeare's Lord Stanley and the historical Stanley's wife, Margaret Beaufort, mother of the future Henry VII. Margaret Beaufort does not appear at all in *Richard III* despite her prominent role in actual conspiracies against Richard III in 1483; Shakespeare gives that role to Lord Stanley and reduces Margaret to a few snide references in speeches by other characters. Lord Stanley is one of the few characters in the play who is legitimately caught on both sides of the conflict, as he is initially made by circumstance to support Richard but works from within to destroy Richard's regime. The alternate setting not only foregrounds the role a woman could play in Richard's downfall but calls attention to those elements within the play (the alliances between the mourning queens, for instance) that are more subversive than they first appear to be. In this particular story, I also chose to change the character of Buckingham to a woman, which is a choice I've seen in one or two productions since there's nothing about the character (other than a perhaps misplaced sense of historical accuracy – misplaced, given how much licence Shakespeare himself is taking with history) that requires him to be a man. In fact, many of the characters in *Richard III*, including Richard himself,[25] could easily be gender-swapped with potentially interesting consequences, but the prevailing trend I've noticed in performance is the excision of the few female roles that *are* in the play, particularly the interaction between the mourning queens in Act 4, Scene 4 that is frequently cut because it's perceived (by male directors and scholars) to be repetitive and tedious.

JESS

How do you see the choice to foreground the role a woman could play as currently relevant in critical conversations about culture?

KAVITA

An alternate setting, much like gender-swapped casting in modern productions, allows the play's female characters greater freedom of action than was permissible in either late fifteenth-century London or on the Elizabethan stage, where they were not present at all. It also provides an interesting test case when considering our present predicaments with women's insufficient and unsatisfactory representation in popular media. This is slowly beginning to change, but it's still not at all surprising to encounter a contemporary media property (whether in film, on television, or in popular books) where most of the main characters are male and the one or two female characters are barely more than sketches, intended to serve as a prize for the male protagonist or, just as frequently, hurt or killed to advance a male character's plotline. Female bodies simply did not exist on the Elizabethan stage, nor were Shakespeare's female characters initially written to be played by women, but part of why his works are perceived as universal is that they transcend their original staging practices. According to a fan author interviewed by Sheenagh Pugh, 'people wrote fanfic because they wanted either "more of" their source material or "more from" it',[26] and Shakespeare is no exception: just as scholars and critics delve into Shakespeare's works partly to unpack characterization, fan authors try to explain what makes these characters tick. And especially in the case of female characters, who are sometimes frustratingly underwritten – Ophelia in *Hamlet* and Lady Anne in *Richard III* both come to mind – fanfiction offers a chance to make sense of them.

* * *

There is no easy solution to the questions 'What is fanfiction?' and 'What place, if any, does fanfiction hold in literary studies?' Part of the problem is the distinct lack of a theory of fanfiction. For many, we know it when we see it, but the particular characteristics, applications, and contributions of fandom and fanfiction remain a slippery landscape of exciting possibility and outright chaos. Furthermore, bringing fanfiction into the classroom undercuts the necessary subversive and anonymous nature of fanfiction, arguably perverting it and rendering it useless. The discourse of fanfiction operates opposite the authoritative discourse of academia and the moment a student writes fanfiction for their teacher instead of themselves it arguably loses some of its revolutionary power, but perhaps it retains the possibility of meaning-making. Perhaps fanfiction can only exist in the limen but even that presents a radical question: if fanfiction cannot come to academia, can academia realistically find its way to fanfiction? It is worth considering fanfiction as a potential critical language for premodern texts, alongside performance studies and the more traditional apparatus of close reading and contextual analysis. What sets not-for-profit fanfiction apart from many of its published counterparts is less about innate quality and perhaps rooted more strongly in the expectations of and the assumptions made about audiences and readers. For fan authors and readers, Shakespeare becomes just another sandpit to play in – and perhaps that's just what he should be.

Jessica McCall is an Associate Professor of English at Delaware Valley University in Doylestown, Pennsylvania. She focuses on intersections of myth and gender in warrior women from Spenser's Radigund through DC Comic's Wonder Woman. She is the author of several articles focusing on both Shakespeare and modern popular culture.

Kavita Mudan Finn is an independent scholar who has published widely on medieval and early modern literature, Shakespeare, and fan studies. She has taught literature, history, and gender studies at Georgetown University, George Washington University, the University of Maryland at College Park, and most recently at Simmons College. In her (sadly minimal) spare time, she writes fanfiction. She credits this hobby for the successful completion of her D.Phil. thesis and many of her subsequent academic works.

Notes

1. For an overview of these debates, see Abigail Derecho, 'Archontic Literature: A Definition, a History, and Several Theories of Fan Fiction', in *Fan Fiction and Fan Communities in the Age of the Internet*, ed. Karen Hellekson and Kristina Busse (New York: McFarland, 2006), 61–78; also Anne Jamison, *Fic: Why Fanfiction is Taking Over the World* (Dallas: BenBella, 2013), 27–36; Catherine Tosenberger, 'Potterotics: Harry Potter Fanfiction on the Internet', unpublished PhD thesis (University of Florida, 2007), 14–26; and Cait Coker, 'Problems of Literary History and Fandom', unpublished conference paper, 2016.
2. Sara Ahmed, *Living a Feminist Life* (Durham, NC: Duke University Press, 2017), 10.
3. Ann Berthoff, *The Making of Meaning* (Upper Montclair, NJ: Boynton/Cook Publishers, 1981), 42.
4. Shannon K. Farley. 'Translation, Interpretation, Fanfiction: A Continuum of Meaning Production', *Transformative Works and Cultures* 14 (2013), 2.2. http://dx.doi.org/10.3983/twc.2013.0517. Accessed 27 Nov 2018.
5. Louise Geddes, 'Unlearning Shakespeare Studies: Speculative Criticism and the Place of Fan Activism', *Shakespeare Survey* 71 (2018), esp. 213–18.
6. See Anna Wilson's two-part essay on the blog *In the Medieval Middle* for an example of how this assignment has worked in a medieval literature class: 'Part I: Margery Kempe IN SPACE' and 'Part II: A Fanfiction Assignment'. 10–11 August 2018. http://www.inthemedievalmiddle.com/2018/08/part-1-margery-kempe-in-space.html.
7. Anna Wilson, 'Immature Pleasures: Affective Reading in Margery Kempe, Petrarch, Chaucer, and Modern Fan Communities' (Ph.D. Thesis, University of Toronto, 2015), 26.

8. Sometimes headcanons already prevalent in the fandom later appear in high-profile productions, rather than vice versa. For example, the fanon of Richard II as bisexual existed in fanfiction well in advance of Ben Whishaw's 2012 performance or David Tennant's in 2013, and developed from source texts and queer criticism of the play. See Kavita Mudan Finn, 'History Play: critical and creative engagement with Shakespeare's tetralogies in transformative fanworks', *Shakespeare* 13.3 (2017), 210–25.
9. Tisha Turk, 'Fan Work: Labor, Worth, and Participation in Fandom's Gift Economy', *Transformative Works and Cultures* 15 (2014), n.p. http://dx.doi.org/10.3983/twc.2014.0518. Accessed 31 January 2014. Turk draws on Karen Hellekson's formulation in 'A Fannish Field of Value: Online Fan Gift Culture', *Cinema Journal* 48, 4 (2009), 113–18.
10. Douglas Lanier, *Shakespeare and Modern Popular Culture* (Oxford: Oxford University Press, 2002), 83.
11. Amy Heckerling's 1995 film *Clueless*, an update of Jane Austen's *Emma* often credited with starting the craze for adaptations of classic works in high-school settings, lampshades this choice by having the narrator Cher remark at the end of the film that she is sixteen and 'this is California, not Kentucky'.
12. Ayanna Thompson, *Passing Strange: Shakespeare, Race, and Contemporary America* (Oxford: Oxford University Press, 2011), 4.
13. Sujata Iyengar, 'Shakespeare Transformed: Copyright, Copyleft, and Shakespeare after Shakespeare', *Actes des congrès de la Société française Shakespeare*, 35 (2017), 12.
14. See Rebecca Wanzo, "African-American Acafandom and Other Strangers: New Genealogies in Fan Studies," *Transformative Works & Cultures* 20 (2015); Rukmini Pande, *Squee from the Margins: Fandom and Race* (Iowa City: University of Iowa Press, 2018); Ebony Elizabeth Thomas, *The Dark Fantastic: Race and the Imagination from Harry Potter to the Hunger Games* (New York: NYU Press, forthcoming 2019).
15. These include Jeanette Winterston (*The Winter's Tale*), Howard Jacobson (*Merchant of Venice*), Anne Tyler (*Taming of the Shrew*), Margaret Atwood (*The Tempest*), Jo Nesbø (*Macbeth*), Tracy Chevalier (*Othello*), Edward St. Aubyn (*King Lear*), and Gillian Flynn (*Hamlet*). Howard Jacobson is Jewish and his novel is deeply concerned with Jewish identity. Moreover, Tracy Chevalier's *New Boy*, her retelling of *Othello*, has come under considerable criticism for its treatment of race and sexuality.
16. The field of fan studies has expanded considerably since the pioneering studies of Henry Jenkins (1992) and Camille Bacon-Smith (1991), and questions about research ethics provoke a range of responses. See Adrienne Evans and Mafalda Stasi, 'Desperately seeking methodology: New directions in fan studies research', *Participations* 11.2 (2014), 4–23; EJ Nielsen, 'Dear Researcher: Rethinking engagement with fan authors', *Journal of Fandom Studies* 4.3 (2016), 233–49. Issue 4.3 of *The Journal of Fandom Studies* (2016) is a special issue devoted to ethical debates in fan studies.
17. See the work of Louise Geddes and Valerie Fazel, especially '"Give me your hands if we be friends": Collaborative authority in Shakespeare fan fiction', *Shakespeare* 12.3 (2016), 274–86, and their introduction to *The Shakespeare User* (New York: Palgrave, 2017); also Geddes, 'Unlearning Shakespeare'.

18. Valerie Fazel, "Researching YouTube Shakespeare: Literary Scholars and the Ethical Challenges of Social Media," *Borrowers and Lenders* 10.1 (2016), n.p. http://www.borrowers.uga.edu/1755/show
19. Geddes, 'Unlearning Shakespeare', 214.
20. Pande, *Squee from the Margins*, 6.
21. Ayanna Thompson, "Shakespeare, Race, and Performance," Lecture at Wellesley College, Wellesley, MA. 12 April 2018.
22. NicoDreams, 'The other day I had a really good idea for a story', *All About That Space*, Tumblr, 8 March 2014, http://nicodreams.tumblr.com/post/79000959862/yemite-sarah531-the-other-day-i-had-a-really.
23. 'Shipping' refers to the practice of interpreting two characters as romantically entwined (regardless of canon) and goes hand-in-hand with favoured pairings, also known as 'OTPs' (One True Pairings).
24. 'Slash' refers to same-sex pairings, but is almost always in reference to specifically male/male pairings (female/female pairings are typically called 'femslash'). 'Ships' is derived from 'shipping' (see previous note).
25. Several productions in the last ten years have cast Richard as a woman, including *The War of the Roses* in 2009, where Cate Blanchett played Richard II and Pamela Rabe played Richard III, and Peter Evans' 2018 stand-alone production for Bell Shakespeare with Kate Mulvaney in the title role. There are also several fanworks on Archive of Our Own that feature a genderswapped Richard.
26. Sheenagh Pugh, 'The Democratic Genre: Fan Fiction in a Literary Context', *Refractory: A Journal of Entertainment Media* 5 (2004), n.p. http://refractory.unimelb.edu.au/2004/02/03/the-democratic-genre-fan-fiction-in-a-literary-context-sheenagh-pugh. Accessed 31 January 2014.

Chapter 3

A Merry Midsummer Labor Merchant's Tempest In King Beatrice's Verona

Jessica McCall

Act VI Part II

Beatrice hated Mr. Lear. In fact the only person she hated more than Mr. Lear was Benedict and that was only because she hated everything about Benedict – especially his face. Her current rage, however, was because Mr. Lear had turned their spring play – the jewel of the drama club – into two one-acts. Mr. Lear insisted *Romeo and Juliet* was a play about the 'titanic struggle of love and family' and Benedict had agreed with him like the snake-in-the-grass suck up he was. Beatrice had helpfully pointed out Romeo and Juliet were thirteen and choosing an outfit was a titanic struggle for thirteen-year-olds, but Mr. Lear had been less than amused and thus her chance to perform the leading role in a Shakespearean tragedy had been ripped from her grasp. Everyone knew Mr. Lear punished you if you didn't tell him how awesome he was.

One-acts. He wanted to reduce *Shakespeare* to *one-acts*. It was preposterous.

The only hope Beatrice had left was to stage a one-act so perfect, so glorious in its totality that it left no doubt who was the superior dramatist at this school. She crafted a modern reinterpretation that focused on Juliet's possible queerness through a postmodern feminist lens; if one act was all she had then she intended to perform a scathing critique of the patriarchal cage that had left Juliet powerless and historicized that powerlessness as true love for the past four hundred years. Now if her classmates would just stop being stupid.

'Julie I swear if you cannot remember your lines I will cut you from this play!' Beatrice warned.

'Then who will be the Nurse?' Julie shot back. A boy-crazy freshman who was habitually late to rehearsals, Julie seemed fundamentally incapable of higher reasoning.

'I need a break!' Beatrice huffed. 'Everybody take ten.'

She stormed off to the green room, desperately in need of Tums for this never-ending heartburn. Lord save her from the suffocating confines of high school.

'You shouldn't be so hard on her.' Beth was Beatrice's second-in-command and her most trusted friend.

'She's hopeless,' Beatrice moaned.

'She's also sneaking off to Ben's practices,' Beth offered nonchalantly.

'*WHAT?*'

'Just thought you might want to know,' she shrugged. Beatrice stormed off and Beth chuckled, anticipating the next big Beatrice vs. Benedict blowout. 'In the words of Mumford and Sons,' she said, '"Stars hide your fires!"'

'Well if it isn't Beth McBethy-beth,' said a snide voice behind her. She spun, not bothering to hide her sneer.

'Well if it isn't the three weird girls. What do you want?'

'We wanted to talk to you about Beatrice,' Regan said.

'Not everyone's happy with how she split the drama club apart,' Goneril added.

'Some people want to elect a new President,' finished Tamora.

'I don't like you, remember?' Beth sighed. 'Go away.'

'*You* should be Drama Club President,' Regan said.

'I'm out of here,' Beth pushed past them. 'This conversation is ridiculous. Go shave your beards.' She stormed out, pissed at the girls but pissed at herself for listening to them. Beth had stood by Beatrice through elections and the unexpected betrayal of their other best friend, Hero, cheating with Beatrice's then boyfriend Benedict. It was all a mess. Maybe they would be better off with less drama? No! She would never betray Beatrice too.

'Oof!' She'd been so distracted she ran straight into Hamlet.

'Watch it sophomore!' she snapped. 'God, what are you even doing here? You're so freaking emo.'

Hamlet watched Beth storm off with a petulant look on his face. He was used to bullies, but Beth Macintosh wasn't usually one of them. Looking back down at his sketchbook he saw his drawing of a skull had been smeared when she ran into it.

'I hate high school!' he shouted, throwing the sketchbook against the wall. 'What's even the point of this stupid place? I'm never getting out of here, and even if I do it doesn't matter. The pretty ones are the worst. Girls are all crazy, two-faced who—'

'*Hamlet...*'

Hamlet froze. The fluorescent lights flickered over his head and he shivered in the inexplicable cold. 'Who's there?'

'*Hamlet...*'

A door opened and shut. Something rattled the lockers at the end of hall, the metal echoing over empty tiles. The rattling moved closer.

'*Hamlet, girls don't like you,*' a disembodied voice said.

'Who are you?!' Hamlet shouted. 'This isn't funny! I'm not scared!'

'*They don't like you because you're sexist.*'

'That's not true!' Hamlet screamed. 'Girls are crazy! They're all crazy!'

'*We're watching you, Hamlet. We're watching to make sure you treat women like people.*'

'This isn't funny!' he whined. 'My dad's the principal! I'll...'

'*Don't you mean your uncle?*'

'Leave me alone!' Hamlet yelled. 'Just leave me alone!' Grabbing his sketchbook, he ran through the doors crying. He never heard the giggling behind him.

'Oh man, that was great!' Andrew said, throwing Toby a high five.

'We didn't go too far did we?' Maria asked.

'Nah,' Toby shrugged. 'He was a total tool to Ophelia. He deserved it.'

'You guys are mean,' Julie interrupted them. 'You shouldn't do that to someone.'

'You're no fun,' Andrew brushed her off, but the three walked away subdued.

'It's so cool how you stand up for people.' Julie spun, a smile lighting her features for Romy.

'Hi Romy,' she blushed, playing with her hair.

'Hi Julie,' Romy smiled back. 'Aren't you supposed to be in rehearsal with Beatrice?'

Julie shrugged, unconcerned. 'I messed up my lines on purpose so she'd storm off. I missed you.'

'I know,' Romy said, reaching out and grabbing Julie's hand. 'You know, I – I only joined Drama Club so I could spend time with you. Hey, did you know when you stand right there the light through the door makes you look like the sun?'

'You say the sweetest things!' Julie giggled. 'Why didn't you text me back?'

'Well...', Romy trailed off.

'What?' Julie pleaded. 'What aren't you telling me?'

'Do you promise not to freak out?'

'I swear,' Julie said.

'Julie.' Romy stopped and took a big breath. 'Ilikeyouasmorethanafriend.'

'What?' Julie whispered.

'I *like* you, like you.' Romy finally met her eyes then, looking prepared for the worst. 'I'm a girl who likes girls, okay? I'm a ... *lesbian.*'

Julie stared at her for a long time, her eyes tracing her face as if seeing her for the first time and then she stepped forward slowly, tenderly, her hand reaching out to brush gently across her hair. 'So?'

'So?' Romy asked. 'SO?! What do you mean so?'

Julie leaned in slowly, so slowly, and gently kissed Romy on the lips. 'What's in a name?'

'What?' Romy whispered.

'I don't care,' Julie said again, stronger. 'I love you. I meant it. I love *you.*'

'What a bunch of star-crossed lovers,' Benedict interrupted them.

'Leave them alone,' Hero sighed. 'If freshmen be the food of love, right on.'

Illustration 3.1: "One-Acts!" Artwork by Rocco Russo ©.

'Well isn't that just adorable?' Beatrice sneered from behind Hero.
'I'mgoingtogopracticemylines,' Julie blurted out, face beet red.
'Yeah,' Romy agreed. 'Me too.'
Awkward tension filled the hallway as Beatrice faced off against Benedict and Hero.
'Once more unto the breech,' Beatrice said, '*dear* friends'.
'How about no?' Hero said.
'Excuse me?'
'I said no.'
'There's no taming this shrew,' Benedict said. 'She won't listen.'

'She will,' Hero replied, not releasing Beatrice's gaze. 'I'll make her. I didn't cheat with Benedict.'

'Seriously?' Beatrice laughed. 'That's the best you've got? Well then, if you say so! I don't know what I was so worried about!'

'How can you believe Iago over us?' Benedict cried. 'You aren't even friends with him. You know exactly what kind of guy he is but he feeds you some line about Hero and me and you just believe him? What even is that?! Who seriously gets that jealous?'

'What, I'm just supposed to believe you when you say you didn't cheat?!'

'Yes!'

'This isn't on us,' Hero pushed. 'We were studying Chem and you stormed in like you expected to find us making the beast with two backs! I was crying because I was failing Chemistry and Benedict was trying to tutor me. How is that cheating?!'

'You were alone with *my* boyfriend!'

'You never trusted me!' Benedict shouted.

'How could I?' Beatrice asked. 'You're the most popular guy in school. You go through girls like tissue paper. I was just your latest conquest. You never loved me.'

'Is that what Iago told you?' Hero countered.

Beatrice threw her hands up. 'Yes! No! I don't know!'

'Beatrice,' Benedict said, grabbing her hands and pulling her to him. 'You were never a conquest. You know that. If you ever loved me you know that.'

'Do I?' Beatrice asked him. 'Are you honest? Are you fair?'

'The course of true love never did run smooth,' Benedict replied.

'But Iago–'

'Iago's an asshole!' Hero screamed.

All three of them froze, shocked by her outburst – sweet, gentle Hero liked everybody. Then slowly, so slowly it was merely a trickle at first, laughter burst from them. A beautiful, healing laughter that washed away the poison of Iago's words.

'Oh God, Hero,' Beatrice said, reaching out and grabbing one of Hero's hands.

'I know,' Hero agreed, tears in her eyes. 'Me too.'

Beatrice hugged Hero for all she was worth, suddenly ashamed of herself for the last six weeks. How had she ever doubted her friend? How could she believe someone like Iago over the girl she'd loved since junior high? With one last squeeze Hero let her go and Beatrice saw her mouth 'Fix this!' at Benedict on her way back into the auditorium.

'So,' Benedict started.

'So,' Beatrice said.

'I, uh, that is,' he stammered. 'Would you go to prom with me?'

'I'd love to.'

When he kissed her it felt like coming home.

Fin

Jessica McCall is an Associate Professor of English at Delaware Valley University in Doylestown, Pennsylvania. She focuses on intersections of myth and gender in warrior women from Spenser's Radigund through DC Comic's Wonder Woman. She is the author of several articles focusing on both Shakespeare and modern popular culture.

Chapter 4
Pickled Red Herring

Kavita Mudan Finn

Title: Pickled Red Herring; or, CSI: *Richard III*
Play: *Richard III*
Characters / Pairings: Stanley, Hastings, Elizabeth, Richard, Buckingham, Mistress Shore, Lady Anne, the Duchess of York, and the corpse that was formerly George
Rating: PG13
Warnings: Violence, profanity, references to drug use, references to prostitution, descriptions of murder scenes, canonical ableism, shady economics, infidelity, bad life choices, Epic Legal Fail, POV Minor Character, genderswap, unfortunate nicknames, bad jokes, dodgy references to people's sex lives, Defenestration, Women Being Awesome
Wordcount: 14,993 words
Summary: It wasn't every day you found a corpse pickling in a wine barrel.
NB: Originally started as a drabble[1] for Gileonnen, who had correctly guessed two of the fics I'd written for Yuletide 2009.[2]

Notes for this section begin on page 100.

To those of you still reading, thank you so much and I apologize for being a failbot. Thanks also to rosamund and angevin2 for beta-reading!

The characters of Stanley and his wife Margaret Beaufort (Lady Not Appearing In This Play) have been conflated for purposes of this story. Several other characters have been genderswapped, since that is one of the fun parts of a modern AU.

Edit (December 2018): I have been offered the opportunity to revise and extend this story for *Shakespeare and Creative Criticism*, and I'm pleased to announce that it is finished! Thanks also to Sara Stanley, Jess McCall, and Lea Frost for being wonderful and patient beta-readers.

Illustration 4.1: CSI: *Richard III*. Artwork by Rocco Russo ©.

Chapter 1

It wasn't every day you found a corpse pickling in a wine barrel.

'And thank God for that,' Detective Meg Stanley said, holding her nose as she peered into just such a barrel, even though the corpse in question was already with Forensics. 'Where the hell do you find wine barrels in Staten Island?'

'Fuck if I know.' Bill Hastings, Chief of Police, lit his eighth cigarette of the day and coughed heavily. 'Someone went to a lot of trouble. Of course,' he gestured in the vague direction of Forensics, 'not too many people will miss him.'

The corpse's name was George York. He'd spent the past two years in and out of the *Enquirer*'s back pages. Four trips in and out of rehab, arrested using any kind of drug imaginable, and weaseling out of jail because his family owned Broome Investments and had more money than God. Not to mention his younger brother Richard, possibly the best defense attorney in the state of New York.

It was impressive in its own way, especially in this image-conscious country. He'd been born with a twisted spine and, from what Hastings had told Meg, had spent most of his childhood shuttled between physical therapists. While he was able to walk, he needed a cane and rumor had it he popped pain pills like candy just to get through each day. The effect he had on juries was obvious, though, and Meg didn't trust him an inch.

Looking at the wine barrel, Meg sighed again. 'Have we got anything? Witnesses? An angry sommelier?' Hastings looked at her blankly. 'Wine expert. It was a joke.'

'Heh.' He grinned. 'You're a funny one, Meg. Why don't you let me take you to dinner sometime?'

'So not going there, Bill. Professional integrity.' Not to mention Hastings was a divorced man and a notorious lech to boot, and Meg wasn't remotely interested. A cry went up from the corner Forensics had claimed. Meg hurried over, Chief Hastings following close behind. 'What's up?'

'Multiple stab wounds.' Dr. Urswick, the pathologist, was prodding at the cold, discolored chest. 'Not to mention that I'm sure we'll find a full-on drug buffet in his system. I have no idea what killed George York. But I'm damn sure he didn't drown.'

'Well. That helps.' Chief Hastings looked green around the gills. 'Actually, it doesn't. But we work with what we have.' He raised his voice. 'Right, we've got a few leads. Where did this wine barrel come from? Trace it. Who last saw George York? Where? When? Do we have a cellphone? Move it, people!' Turning back to Meg, he dropped the finished cigarette and ground it beneath his heel. 'Anything else?'

'Does his family know?' Hastings made an eloquent gesture, prompting Meg to shake her head. 'I'm on it. Call me if you hear anything interesting.'

Edward York, George's older brother and CEO of Broome Investments, lived in a townhouse on East 68th Street that cost more than Meg would make in several lifetimes. It wasn't the first time Meg had been here; Edward was a well-known supporter of the Department, and if certain people were more inclined to look the other way whenever his brother was found in possession of something he wasn't legally permitted to have, so much the better. Although she didn't agree with this in principle, Meg allowed that George York hadn't actually *harmed* anybody other than himself – no drunk driving, no hookers in the closet, just lots and lots of drugs, usually indulged in the privacy of his multi-million-dollar apartment in the Village. She supposed he was keeping small micro-economies alive by way of take-out and delivery alone – if her informants were telling the truth, he might have been the best tipper in lower Manhattan. Not anymore, and for that if for nothing else, Meg was sorry.

The housekeeper who had let her in had disappeared, presumably to find whoever was home, and Meg took the opportunity to look around the marble-floored hall, badge in hand just in case. The last time she'd been here, the place had been full of politicians and Wall Street types. Not the best time to get a good look at anything, really. Above the massive ornamental fireplace was an old-fashioned portrait of a woman she recognized from the cover of a recent issue of *Vogue*. Edward York's wife, five years older than him but you'd never have guessed from seeing them together. Either the woman was hiding the Fountain of Youth in her bathroom or she had a great plastic surgeon.

The tinny sound of earbud headphones caught her attention and Meg glanced up to see a girl of maybe fifteen in the uniform of one of the fancy Upper East Side prep schools paused on the mezzanine level, hips gyrating madly.

'Pickin' it up, pickin' it up, I'm lovin', I'm livin', I'm pickin' it up–'

She had to work very hard not to laugh.

'Elizabeth Jacqueline York, do you think Roland is waiting for you because he thinks it's fun?' The strident tones boomed from several floors up, echoing impressively. 'You'll be late for school.'

'Yes, *Mom*.' Sullenly, the girl plucked the earbuds from her ears before she caught sight of Meg. Her eyes widened. 'Mom, why are there police here?'

'Police?' Meg could hear the click of stiletto heels on marble as Elizabeth Woodville descended the stairs. She looked every inch the Upper East Side queen, from the perfectly styled ice-blonde hair to the trademark red-soled pumps. 'Detective Stanley, this is a surprise. Is something wrong?'

'Well...' Meg paused. 'I guess you could say that, Ms. Woodville.' She'd kept her maiden name despite marrying one of Wall Street's youngest tycoons sixteen years earlier. 'Do you mind if we talk alone?'

'Of course.' A war of gazes ensued with her daughter that she, inevitably, won, although Meg smiled encouragingly at the girl. After the door had clanged shut behind her, Meg turned back to find Ms. Woodville regarding her curiously. 'Teenagers,' she said, with the smoothest helpless shrug Meg had seen. 'Do you have children?'

'One, but he's older than your daughter.' Henry had just started his first year at Langley, training for the FBI. 'I'm afraid I really need to speak to your husband, Ms. Woodville.'

'He's...' She fished her phone out of her pocket, '...in the air, I'm afraid. His flight left Dubai and is supposed to land at JFK in about three hours.' Pressing her fingers to her temples, she frowned. 'And there's a charity gala tonight at the Whitney. I'll pass on the news, whatever it is. I hope it's not something too bad.'

'I hope you'll excuse me, Ms. Woodville, but I need to talk to him directly.'

The frown lingered between her brows but she nodded. 'I understand. Perhaps if you came back around six this evening? We should have a little while before we're due to leave.'

Like clockwork, Meg knocked on the door again at 6:00pm sharp. Instead of the housekeeper she'd met earlier that day, she found herself facing Richard York, immaculate in black tie, who gestured with his cane for her to enter.

'Good evening, Detective Stanley, lovely to see you.'

'Counselor.' She nodded unsmilingly. 'Is your brother here?'

He waved the cane at the staircase. 'Upstairs. One doesn't like to intrude on alone time between husband and wife, know what I mean.' The smile he flashed at her was two shades short of a leer and she suppressed a shudder.

'I'm going to pretend you didn't say that. You're supposed to be a qualified legal practitioner.'

'Oh, Meggie, my colleagues get up to far worse.' She winced at the nickname but said nothing. 'And so do yours.' He leaned on the cane, eyes alight with laughter. 'You're just sore about that prostitution ring.'

'Chief Hastings had *nothing* to do with–'

'You and I both know that. But La Woodville,' he shook his head, teeth clicking, 'she sees only prostitutes, handcuffs, and her husband in a very compromising position.'

Meg crossed her arms and glared at him, but before she could say anything, footsteps sounded on the staircase, and the booming laughter associated with Edward York, darling of Wall Street and, according to some, a man who could read the global financial markets the way other guys read the morning paper.

'Detective Stanley, to what do I owe the pleasure?' He stepped forward and wrapped her in an unexpected bear hug. 'I'd grab you a ticket for the gala, but they're fresh out.'

'Not a problem, Mr. York. I just...' she glanced warily at Richard, 'I need to tell you something.'

'It's George, isn't it?' Richard interrupted. At Meg's horrified stare, he turned back to his brother and sighed. 'He was found dead this morning.'

'How do *you* know that?' demanded Meg.

'Hastings. He had some questions for me. Turns out I was the last person to see poor George alive, that we know of.' He shook his head. 'What a fucking mess. I guess we should've seen it coming.'

Edward's face had turned paler than the marble floor. 'What the hell are you talking about? George can't be dead. I left him in LA last week, at that new rehab facility. He was *fine*.'

'I'm afraid, sir,' Meg ventured, 'we found him this morning in a warehouse in Staten Island. Multiple stab wounds. Fair amount of heroin in his system, but not enough to kill him.'

'Fucking *hell*.' Edward turned away, one hand muffling his words. 'Richard, can you believe this?'

'Mr. York, I'm so sorry to have to ask, but can you think of anyone who might have had a grudge against your brother?'

'Every dealer from here to New Brunswick?' Richard let out a bark of bitter laughter. 'George wasn't a subtle guy.'

'He told me he was clean, Richard, he *promised* me he was clean!'

'Guess that's how much you could trust him.' Richard stared at the floor before looking back at Meg. 'Any chance you can keep this quiet, Detective? Wouldn't want to ruin the party.'

'Are you *sure*?' Meg ignored Richard, keeping her eyes fixed on his elder brother. 'I'm not saying a drug dealer is out of the question, but we could use a bit of help here.'

Edward swiped one hand across his eyes. 'Fuck, I don't know. George... well, Richard's right. He isn't – *wasn't* – a subtle guy. We tried to keep him out of trouble, but it just didn't work.'

'Hey, hey,' Richard reached out and clasped his brother's shoulder. 'It's not your fault. I loved George, don't get me wrong, but he was fucking unreliable on the best of days.' The past tense slipped so easily from his mouth that Meg narrowed her eyes. Just because she didn't like the guy didn't mean she should automatically consider him a suspect, but all the same...

Something just didn't sit right.

'You know what, there *is* someone who comes to mind.' Richard's voice dragged Meg out of her thoughts. He'd stepped away from his shocked brother, voice lowered conspiratorially. 'My lovely sister-in-law hated George. And she's got connections in all sorts of places if you know what I mean.'

Annoyingly, he was right. Elizabeth Woodville was a former model and continued to design for several couture houses, which did put her in contact with certain circles her brother-in-law had probably known well. She was clean, as far as anyone at the precinct knew, but they couldn't claim to have looked very hard. 'You don't honestly think she'd kill him?'

Richard shrugged expansively. 'Nothing about her would surprise me. She silently puts up with Edward's indiscretions when any other woman would have divorced him for half his millions and moved to the Caymans.'

'You don't seem to like her much.'

'I'm afraid she started that. Between you and me,' he glanced toward Edward, who had since been joined by his wife, 'I think she's uncomfortable around people who are...' he cleared his throat, '*different*. You might want to watch your back.'

Meg grimaced, as much at being grouped with him as by the implication about his sister-in-law. 'This is a serious accusation, Mr. York. Tell me you've got evidence to back this up.'

'Detective Stanley, as you yourself pointed out, I am a qualified legal practitioner. I know very well what it means to make an accusation of murder. Or at least manslaughter. I don't know if she's got what it takes to *kill* someone deliberately. She's more likely to rob them blind.'

Meg sighed. 'If you've got any *actual* evidence, tell me.' Though she might have said more, a great deal more, she was interrupted by a choked breath from the other side of the foyer.

'Oh, my God! Call 911!' Ms. Woodville had staggered back as her husband sank to the floor, his face growing bright red as he gasped for breath. Mechanically, Meg dialed the number and heard herself, as if from a distance, explaining that there was a man going into cardiac arrest and that he needed to get to a hospital as soon as possible.

As she lowered the phone from her ear, she caught sight of Richard watching her, his expression unreadable. It was only some hours later, after she'd made her report at the station and returned to her apartment, that Meg recalled why that had worried her – he hadn't even looked at his brother once. All his attention had been focused on *her* reaction. Almost as if he'd planned for it.

Almost as if...

But it didn't make any *sense*.

She typed Richard York's name into Google and clicked on his law firm's website. There wasn't anything she hadn't already known. Graduated from Harvard Law *summa cum laude* and started at Neville & Warwick, where, in just three years, he'd become the darling of their criminal defense group. And, considering the scum he'd defended, it was maybe not that surprising that he'd stoop to trying to kill his own brothers.

The question was *why*.

And that, Meg could not answer.

Chapter 2

'I ask you to report George York's death to his family, and *this* is what I get?' Chief Hastings' face was the color of a ripe tomato and

Meg couldn't help but worry that he was heading the same way as Edward. '*Two* bodies?'

'It was a heart attack,' Meg said softly. 'Nobody could have predicted that.'

'Edward York had a triple bypass last year.' It was then that she noticed that her boss's eyes were red-rimmed. 'I didn't think I needed to tell you to be careful.'

'It wasn't me!' protested Meg, heat rising in her cheeks. '*You're* the one who got Tricky Dick involved.'

Hastings blinked. 'Do people really call him that?'

'Everyone in the prosecutor's office. That shouldn't surprise you. But that's not the point, Bill. He's the one who told Edward, and I had no idea he even knew. Look,' she took a deep breath, steeling herself, 'I don't want to point fingers, but we've got him close to both men when things went haywire.'

'Are you accusing *Richard York* of killing his brothers?' All of the color drained from Hastings' face within seconds, an impressive display to say the least. 'You'd better have a damn good reason for this, Stanley.'

Meg sighed. 'Dammit, Bill, I don't know why. I just…I've got this feeling. I can't pin it down, but it's something about the way he looks at people. Like they're toys. Chess pieces. I bet he loves chess,' she added savagely.

'Regional champion in high school.. Edward said he'd teased Richard about it until Richard kicked his ass. First time he did it. Shocked the hell out of Edward, that's for sure.' Tears sprang to his eyes. 'Fuck, Stanley, why'd he have to go that way? He's younger than *me.*'

'Well, I'd bet you anything he didn't follow the doctor's orders after that bypass.' Even as Meg said it, she slung her arm around Hastings' shoulders, barely reaching his other side. 'I'm sorry. I know you were close to him.'

'He saved my life in Kuwait.' He rubbed at his eyes. 'I told you about that, right? Eighteen goddamn years old, joined up because he wanted to make his dad proud and pay for college. Well, he did.'

'You're saying something at the funeral, right?' Meg asked. 'He'd have wanted that.'

Hastings grimaced, wiping his nose. 'If I'm lucky and that wife of his lets me through the door. Widow, I guess. She'll have her brother make one of those speeches that nobody understands except the reporters from the *Times* and they'll write their fucking editorials about how it was such a moving occasion and all Edward would have wanted was for everyone to get drunk off their asses and have a great time on his dollar.'

'Oh, Bill. Let me buy you a drink. Or twelve.' Normally, Meg wouldn't have come within a mile of making this kind of offer, but she couldn't restrain herself. 'You said it's what he would have wanted.'

In retrospect, maybe it wasn't the greatest idea. She ended up buying at least a bottle's worth of Jameson's, to the point where the bartender had just handed the entire thing to her. It being the department's favored dive, she only had to pay wholesale, so that was something. And Hastings had at least stopped crying and had progressed to the maudlin nostalgia stage of drunkenness. She'd heard a fair amount about Edward York over the years, but Hastings seemed to be pulling out all the stories he'd kept to himself, and not without reason. Meg would never have pegged her boss for the experimental type, but apparently it was possible in the presence of a certain cocktail of substances and a woman referred to only as Jane.

Although Meg would have liked to run her theories about Richard York past him, Hastings was clearly in no state for rational analysis. He was slurring his way through a not altogether terrible rendition of 'Stairway to Heaven' as Meg practically dragged him out of the subway in Brooklyn.

Hastings saw the woman on his doorstep first. Meg might have, if all her attention hadn't been focused on keeping a man twice her size from falling over her.

'*Jane.*' At the word, Meg nearly stumbled, so shocked was she by the naked longing in Hastings' voice. 'Is that really you?'

'Oh, Bill. Oh, God, Bill.' She had the voice of a jazz singer. Meg supposed she couldn't blame Hastings *that* much. In a whiff of expensive perfume, Jane flung her arms around Hastings. 'I can't believe he's dead, I just *can't!*'

'Oh, babe,' he whispered, clinging to her as Meg disentangled herself from what was one hidden phone away from Hastings' worst nightmare. Thankfully he lived on a residential street and, nobody was around at this time of night. Oblivious to her, Hastings was saying, 'Dammit, Jane, if I'd known where you were, I'd have told you myself.'

Meg took that opportunity to discreetly withdraw. 'I'll see you tomorrow, Bill. Take care, okay?'

Much to her surprise, Bill looked her straight in the eye in spite of Jane sobbing hysterically into his shoulder. 'Thanks, Meg. You're a great friend.'

When she got home, she fixed herself a cup of coffee and stared blankly at the television, where it seemed like every channel was running retrospectives on Edward York and speculating on what would happen to Broome now that its golden boy's heart had given out at forty-five years old. He had kids, but they were all far too young–

Meg's heart twisted, remembering the girl on the stairs. Ellie York, apple of her father's eye, according to Hastings. She'd stop by, she told herself, after the funeral. Bill had insisted on a police escort for the family; two deaths within twenty-four hours, even if one was natural, merited some security.

'...he'd even talked about going into politics and rumor had it there might have been a spot for him in the Treasury Department if Clinton had won in 2016. Edward York will be sorely missed.' On the screen, the newscaster sighed visibly. 'There will be a memorial service at Saint John the Divine on Thursday for people to pay their respects.'

Meg clicked off the television and reached for the steno pad lying on the side table beside the empty coffee cup. Two words were written at the top of an otherwise empty page: *Cui bono?*

Whose benefit? Who would want both Edward and George dead? *Follow the money, Meg. Ninety-nine per cent of the time, you'll find your answer there.* But she wasn't finding any answers, at least not yet. Hastings, being one of Edward's close friends and, apparently, a beneficiary, was supposed to attend the reading of the will after the funeral and Meg had already arranged to meet him afterward.

She nearly dropped the pad.

'Follow the money. *Shit.*' Grabbing the phone, she hit the speed-dial for Hastings. In response to the unintelligible groan, she burst out, 'What was Edward leaving you, Hastings?' Do you know?'

'Meg, what t'fuck?'

'Is he leaving you shares, Bill? Shares in the company? Do you know?'

'I don't know, Meg.' In the background, she could hear the murmur of a woman's voice. 'My retirement account is at Broome. I don't know what happens except that I put money into it every two weeks and someday I might be lucky enough to use it. Now, why the hell are you calling me at 4 a.m.?'

'I'm sorry, Bill. But...' she sighed. 'We have two bodies. Brothers, shareholders in one of the biggest investment firms in the city, dead within twenty-four hours. Doesn't that seem at least a bit weird to you?'

'What are you talking about?' Hastings finally said, after several seconds of rustling. 'George wasn't a shareholder. Not anymore. He sold all his shares a few months ago, split them between his brothers. Edward said George was hard up for cash but he was sick of just handing it to him, so they came up with a compromise.'

Meg swore under her breath. 'So it can't have been for the money, I guess.'

'Not George, no. Although Catesby was chasing up a few leads that sounded promising. He said he'd meet me at the station before the funeral and let me know what he'd found. You interested?'

'Of course I'm interested. Sorry for waking you up.'

'Wasn't actually asleep.'

'You're a filthy man, Bill Hastings.' Laughing, she hung up.

* * *

Lieutenant Walter Catesby was thirty-five years old, balding, and wore Coke-bottle glasses ironically. He was also Hastings' right-hand man and had been for more than ten years now, turning down at least three different job offers in New Jersey on the assumption that, when Hastings retired, he'd be next in line.

'Detective Stanley, good to see you as always.' He shook her hand. 'I assume Bill's brought you up to speed.'

'More or less,' Meg said. 'You found anything new?'

'Well, Edward York's two boys and their uncle should be on the first train in from Boston today.' With a small sigh, Catesby looked at the ground. 'Poor kids. Ms. Woodville was planning to hire her own security detail to make sure the press didn't come swooping in, but it sounds like her brother-in-law managed to convince her they should keep things quiet.'

'Are we sure that's a good idea?' Meg frowned. 'The media are all over this story. Two fatherless boys in uniforms may be more than they can resist.'

'If they have any common decency–'

'It's the *press*, Catesby. They wouldn't know decency if it kicked them in the face and stole their cameras.'

She heard Hastings' snort of laughter from the doorway. 'No love for the tabloids, Meg?'

'They're vultures, Bill, and you know it.' But the words emerged with little force, so distracted was Meg by the expression on the police chief's face. He looked better-rested than he had in weeks, a look of lazy contentment in his eyes and in spite of the stiff black suit and tie he wore. Whoever Jane was, she clearly knew what she was doing. 'We should get going if we want to get in before all the crowds.'

Meg couldn't help but glance at the newsstand as Hastings wedged the cruiser into a truly unlikely parking spot. One of three shots of Edward York – twenty years old, in the full dress uniform of the United States Air Force and looking uncannily like a young Robert Redford; beside the stunning Elizabeth at Milan Fashion Week ten years ago; caught getting off a plane in Grand Cayman with a redhead in oversized sunglasses who, after the other night, looked very familiar to Meg – spilled across the front pages of the *Times*, *The Wall Street Journal*, and the *Post*, each framed by more text than she had time to read. But all seemed to be asking the same thing: What of Broome Investments? All of Wall Street had come to a standstill, according to the *Journal*, waiting with bated breath for what Ted York, the world's youngest billionaire at fourteen years old, would do.

At the sound of Hastings' yell, Meg gave in to temptation and bought a copy of *The New York Times*. As she reached his side, however, she was frowning at a tiny story on page three. 'Hey, Bill, check this out.'

'Harvard professor arrested on charges of child molestation?' Hastings rolled his eyes. 'Meg, really–'

'Look at his *name*, Bill!' Meg jabbed her finger at the text. 'Anthony Woodville. That's Edward York's brother-in-law.'

She and Hastings stared at each other for several seconds. 'No way. I don't believe it. If Woodville's gotten any action that wasn't his own hand and a bottle of lotion in the past fifteen years, I'll eat that paper.'

Meg rolled her eyes. The fact that Hastings had been Edward York's partner in crime – and apparently other things – ever since their Air Force days was not something that sat well with York's wife's family, and Professor Woodville had been especially outspoken against Hastings. 'Something is really wrong here, Bill. This is beyond your pissing match with the Professor. It's like someone is systematically taking down everyone associated with Broome Investments.' She didn't know if the professor had shares in the company, but it wouldn't have surprised her.

'A rival company?' Catesby suggested from Meg's other side. When they both looked at him, he shrugged. 'People do crazy things for money. Especially this kind of money.'

'It's got to be someone with a *lot* of influence, though. Or this has been in the works for years...' Meg took the paper back. Nothing useful, all anonymous sources and conjectures, and Woodville didn't even get a statement. Clearly his attorney was sleeping on the job–

Meg flipped back to the front page, unsure of exactly what she was searching for until she found it. '"Edward York named his younger brother Richard, an attorney with a prominent Midtown law firm, primary legal executor of his will." That makes him acting president of Broome Investments, Bill.'

'Meg, I know you don't like the guy–'

'I don't *trust* him. Liking has nothing to do with it.' Meg sighed. 'He's got everything to gain.'

'He doesn't *need* anything, Meg. For fuck's sake, he's in line to get his name on that damn law firm's building before his fortieth birthday.' Hastings straightened his tie as they reached the massive doors of the cathedral. 'Righto. Let's get this dog and pony show over with.'

But before they could open the doors, a high-pitched shriek echoed from within. Meg's hand immediately went to her shoulder holster as the door clanged open and Elizabeth Woodville stumbled onto the steps, one hand pressed to her mouth. For what had to be the first time in the more than fifteen years Meg had known her, Edward York's wife looked like a mess, hair falling loose from a chignon and mascara streaked across her face.

'God help us all, Detective Stanley,' she whispered, blue-grey eyes alive with horror. 'I knew it was only a matter of time. I'm never going to see my boys again.'

Chapter 3

The story, from what Meg could gather, was this. Ted and Bobby York had been picked up from their respective schools the previous afternoon, and had arrived at their uncle's house in Cambridge where they were to spend the night before leaving for New York. At some point during the night, the police had barged in – the details of the case remained undisclosed, much to Meg and Hastings' frustration – snatched up the boys, and handed them over to their *other* uncle, Richard.

Ms. Woodville had taken her shell-shocked daughter by the arm and all but manhandled her into a limo. With a dead look at Meg, Edward York's widow had said, 'If you need me, you have my number. But he's not getting Ellie. Not in a thousand years.'

As she followed her daughter, Meg heard her barking orders to the chauffeur. She opened her mouth but Hastings laid one hand on her arm. 'No, Meg. So long as Richard has her boys, she won't go far.'

Behind them, Meg heard the sound of a throat clearing. Framed in the doorway now was the ramrod-straight figure of Cecilia York, matriarch of the family and herself a shareholder in Broome Investments, in black from head to toe. She also had the dubious distinction of being one of the few people in Manhattan who could still frighten Bill Hastings and, by extension, Meg. 'Do you plan to stand out here all day, Chief Hastings?' she asked in a voice chillier than the Hudson in February. 'I seem to remember there was a funeral planned.'

There hadn't been a funeral for George – not a real one, at any rate. With his elder brother in the hospital, the only people who had been there were his mother and Robert Brackenbury, George's on-again-off-again AA sponsor.

'But what about–'

'Never you mind, Detective Stanley.' She closed her eyes briefly, an uncharacteristic hesitation. 'This day is for Edward. Anything else can wait until tomorrow.'

It didn't occur to anybody to question that. Even when Richard arrived some twenty minutes later, nobody said anything about the events of the previous night, although Meg could see Ted, painfully young in a blazer and school tie, constantly glancing back toward the door as if looking for someone.

The funeral was short and to the point. Hastings ended up speaking impromptu since Professor Woodville was absent, and everyone did their best not to look at the empty spots in the pew between Cecilia York and her silent grandsons.

The eulogy concluded simply. 'It was an honor and a privilege to call Edward my best friend. More than that, he was my brother. We–' He stopped, too choked to finish, and stepped down from the podium.

Meg had teared up more than once during the speech and even though the jokes were ones she'd heard a dozen times before, she found herself chuckling nonetheless. When Hastings returned to his spot beside her, she squeezed his arm. 'He'd be proud of you, Bill.'

He sniffed. 'Thanks, Meg. I'm just glad it's over.'

She fell into step beside Ted York as they left the cathedral after the service. He looked very like his mother, she realized when he looked at her. 'You're Detective Stanley, right? Dad told me who you were once, but I'm sorry if I'm wrong.'

'You're right,' she smiled. 'Were you looking for someone in there?'

'My uncle – Uncle Anthony, that is.' He swallowed. 'I don't know where he went. The police came and then he was gone. Nobody's telling me anything.'

'I...' Meg trailed off, at a loss. 'I'm afraid I don't know the details, Ted, but I'll tell you once I hear anything.'

'Promise?' There was an odd note of desperation in the boy's voice. 'Please promise. I don't want anything bad to happen to him. He didn't do anything wrong!'

'I know he didn't, and I'm sure the police in Boston will figure that out.' As she said it, Meg hoped she wasn't lying to the kid. Whoever planned this had covered their tracks incredibly well and she had the horrible suspicion that Anthony Woodville wouldn't be getting out of custody anytime soon. 'How are you holding up?'

Ted shrugged. 'Bobby doesn't get it. It's like he forgot when Dad was in the hospital last year. But Mom told me that this might happen. She said Dad didn't take care of himself properly.' He blinked up at her. 'Where *is* she?'

'I don't know, Ted–'

'Hamptons would be my guess.' Meg found herself facing Harriet Buckingham, Broome's top corporate counsel. Her purse was clearly doubling as a briefcase, even at a funeral, and the black suit she wore had subtle pinstripes, suggesting she was making a stop on her way to the office. 'You didn't see the pre-nup. If it hadn't been for me, this young man wouldn't have a cent.'

'She seemed very worried,' Meg said warily. 'I don't think she trusts her brother-in-law.'

Harriet gave a dismissive wave. 'She'll get over it. Or not. Either way, she's irrelevant. *You*,' she said, looking down at Ted, 'are the way of the future.'

'I'd rather see my mom, if you don't mind,' Ted said. 'Can you call her?'

'Would you call her, Ms. Buckingham?' she corrected him with a disapproving shake of her head. 'Kids these days have no manners, do they?'

'I'll call her, Ted,' Meg interjected, catching the other woman's eye. 'The car's waiting for you now.' She could still see his pale face in the window of the limo as it pulled away from the church and it occurred to her with a shiver that he looked like a ghost. Harriet muttered something about the office and stepped into a nearby Town Car with Broome corporate plates.

'Something walk over your grave, Detective?'

Meg spun on her heel to find Richard York making his way toward her, leaning heavily on his trademark cane. The rumor was it had one of those knives hidden inside it, but nobody had thought to ask. She shrugged, pushing the idle question aside. 'Not so much my grave, Mr. York. Though I have to wonder why your sister-in-law is so frightened of you.'

'You and me both, Detective. We've never been on the *best* of terms, I'll grant, but...' he gave a half-shrug. 'Who knows?'

'And what about Professor Woodville?' Meg crossed her arms and studied him warily. 'You sure seemed to be in the right place at the right time to grab your nephews when that went down.'

'What can I say? Police contacts have their uses.' He shook his head. 'Awful about poor Anthony, though. I wouldn't have thought it of him. But it just goes to show, you think you know a person.'

She briefly entertained the thought that he might be sincere. But you didn't become the youngest attorney in line for partner at Neville & Warwick – or any law firm – by being sincere. She would have questioned Richard further, but he excused himself to greet a young woman who had just arrived, wearing a veiled hat just this side of tasteful enough for a funeral. Meg supposed you needed something eccentric if you were out with Richard York and wanted to make an impression.

'I'm sorry, darling, the 1 was horrendously slow. I didn't miss everything, did I?'

Meg recognized her as soon as she pulled off her sunglasses. Anne Warwick's taste in boyfriends was as doubtful as her editorials in the *Atlantic* were sacrosanct, and she had a biting disregard for police officers and paparazzi alike. Meg read them – she'd been told that anyone with two X chromosomes should, though she had her own reservations about the very white quality of Anne's feminism – and she tried to give Anne the benefit of the doubt. Anyone who had come as close as she had to having Margot Lancaster as a mother-in-law deserved a medal for getting out alive, let alone making such a smooth transition to the winning side of this past decade's bloodiest corporate merger – in more ways than one. Nobody had ever figured out what caused Eddie Lancaster's little Cessna to plunge into the Atlantic, but his death had ensured Broome's undisputed place at the top of the NYSE's docket, and Anne had made tabloid history by appearing at his memorial service on the arm of Richard York. She might even have been wearing the same hat.

'You missed the service, I'm afraid, but we're on our way to the burial now. You know Anne, don't you, Detective?' Richard said, holding out his hand to catch his girlfriend's arm. 'Anne Warwick, this is police detective Margaret Stanley.'

Anne held out one hand with a cool smile, and Meg immediately noticed the ring. 'Detective Stanley. It's a pleasure to meet you. I just wish it were under better circumstances.'

'Likewise, Ms. Warwick. And if I may offer my congratulations.' Turning to Richard, she smiled. 'To you too, Mr. York. I wasn't aware that you were engaged.'

'Owing to the circumstances, we decided to keep things quiet.' So it had been recent. Meg couldn't help but wonder how recent. Not for the first time, she recalled the rumor so quickly silenced that Eddie Lancaster's death might not have been an accident. But now wasn't the time to look into old deaths; there were plenty of recent ones to go around. Straightening the uncomfortable suit that only came out of her closet for funerals, Meg joined Hastings and Catesby in the cruiser so they could drive to the cemetery.

* * *

Edward York's will was being read in the executive conference room at Broome Investments, on the seventy-fifth floor of one of the newest high-rises in Midtown. Meg found a spot on a bench in Bryant Park and called Henry, expecting to leave a message, but to her surprise, he picked up.

'Mom! I thought you had to go to Edward York's funeral today.' She could hear a roaring noise behind him. 'Sorry about that. The wind's crazy down here.'

'No problem. The funeral's over. I just wanted to hear your voice.' Meg winced at the quaver in her tone. 'That's all.'

'Mom, really.' She could hear the eye-roll in his voice. 'This isn't like you. What's wrong?'

'Nothing, Henry. You're right. I'm being silly.'

'Mom. Snap out of it and tell me what's up. You're weirding me out.' After a second, he added, 'I'm training for the FBI. You don't need to hide things from me.'

'I do if it's an ongoing case. You should know that.' Meg laughed in spite of herself. 'It's just getting to me. This case. I don't like it. Something about it smells wrong, y'know?'

'I thought Edward York died of a heart attack. That's what all the news channels are saying.' She heard a door close and his voice became clearer. 'Are they covering something up?'

'I'm not saying that, Henry, and you're not allowed to repeat a word of this, do you understand?' Without waiting for an answer, Meg continued, 'Yes, Edward died of a heart attack. I was an eyewitness. It's just...'

'Too convenient?'

Meg sighed. 'I know. You think I'm crazy?'

'You're never crazy when it comes to work, Mom.'

'I heard the caveat in that, young man. Are you sure you're going into the police and not the law?' Inevitably, that made her think of Richard York again and she had to suppress a shudder. 'Anyway, I'll let you go. I'm probably interrupting something important.'

'Just my lunch break. Love you, Mom.'

She said her farewells and hung up. The breeze had picked up by the time she reached Park Avenue and she was holding her suit jacket in a less than dignified manner when she stepped into the glass-and-wrought-iron lobby. Flashing her ID at the security guard even though she'd met him a handful of times before, she headed to the elevator that would take her all the way to Broome's corporate headquarters on the penthouse floor. The elevator ride was eerily smooth and so fast that Meg's ears had popped by the time the recorded voice announced that she had arrived at her destination.

She heard the crash and the scream within seconds of the doors opening. Meg snatched her gun out of her holster as she dashed forward and threw open the pair of double doors behind the startled receptionist's desk. The first thing she saw was Catesby, out cold on the floor. Then, the prone figure of Richard York, bent double over one of the expensive leather office chairs. And, behind him, one of the plate-glass windows, shattered.

Meg hadn't realized just how loud the wind could be on the seventy-fifth floor.

'Hastings.' She could barely make out the sound of her voice, and found herself shouting, 'Hastings, goddammit! Where the hell is Chief Hastings?'

Richard York held out one hand silently in the direction of the window. Swallowing the upsurge of bile in her throat, Meg crossed the room and peered out. At the end of the vertiginous drop to Park Avenue, she could see a growing crowd clustered around the smashed pulp that had once been Police Chief Bill Hastings.

'Oh, Jesus fucking Christ.' Meg resisted the urge to curb her own profanity and swung round to face the one witness she had. 'You tell me what happened. You tell me *right now*, or I am cuffing you this goddamn instant and you'll sing like a fucking songbird at headquarters.'

'Detective Stanley, please.' How could he look so damned *calm*? Fucking lawyers. 'There's a security camera near the window. It'll tell you everything you need to know.'

She took grim satisfaction in cuffing him all the same. He didn't protest, even when reporters swarmed round the patrol car as the officers shoved him into the back. He had something up his sleeve. Meg could *smell* it. But she had more important things to worry about. Like her dead boss.

Catesby had come to by the time Meg arrived at the station and he was seated outside the holding cell, a bandage around his head and an ice pack in one hand.

'What the hell happened in there?' Meg hissed. 'Tell me *someone* saw something!'

'It all seemed fine at first. It was just me, the chief, York, Buckingham, and the old family lawyer Morton, who was reading out the will. But we never even got there. York had to take a phone call as soon as the chief and I showed up and when he came back...' He stared down at the melting ice pack. 'Christ, Stanley, I can't even begin to explain it.'

'*Try*, Catesby. Pull it together.' Grasping his hands, she stared into his eyes. 'Our boss just fell from the seventy-fifth floor of a Midtown high-rise and it is our duty, our *first* duty, to find out how and why that happened. You got me?'

'It all happened so fast. York was saying how Ms. Woodville had connections to drug dealers and mentioned some floozy named Jane and suddenly Hastings goes at him like a bulldozer and York's elbow knocks me out cold.' He recited the words mechanically, as though repeating a story he'd already told several times, and it occurred to Meg that he must have been cross-examined all the way from the crime scene.

'Christ, Catesby, I'm sorry. I just got so wrapped up, I...' She stopped, took a breath, and let go of his hands. 'How are you holding up?'

He attempted an ambivalent shrug and winced, before raising the ice pack to his head. 'I'm acting chief of this precinct now, Stanley, and I can't even begin to...' He swallowed. 'I need your support. Do I have it?'

'Of course you do, Cate– sir.' She corrected herself, suddenly aware as never before of the difference between them in rank. He had always been so unassuming, Hastings' quiet and obedient shadow. Meg stood and straightened her jacket. 'What would you like me to do, sir?'

'Are there any more leads on George York?'

Meg had to think for a moment. Poor George. Forgotten in death as he had been in life. 'I have a lot of theories, but not so much in the way of leads. I guess I should talk to Forensics and see if they found any traceable drugs.'

'That sounds like a good start.' Catesby closed his eyes and Meg suspected he was probably steadying himself somehow. 'Leave Chief Hastings to me, Stanley. I'm afraid there's more to all of this than meets the eye.'

'You're telling me!' Meg wasn't certain whether to feel relieved that he shared her fears or terrified that they were being confirmed. 'Poor Bill. It's just too awful.'

Catesby looked at the ground. 'I'm afraid it's only going to get worse. Let's just say the chief showed you a very different side of who he was.'

Meg stared at him in growing horror. 'I don't understand.'

'Do you know what Hastings and Edward York got up to? The things Hastings covered up?' Catesby was shaking his head slowly. 'I do. I helped him, every step of the way, and I followed his orders and I kept it all quiet. It's not pretty, Stanley.'

'You're not going to posthumously charge him?' she whispered. 'Catesby, no. You were his friend. You know his *kids*, for God's sake.' Hastings and his wife had divorced soon after his return from the Middle East and Meg had only met her once or twice, but they all knew the chief's two daughters, who had visited him every other weekend like clockwork until they'd gone away to college.

'I'll do what I can to avoid that, but we have to say *something*. This is why I need you to find out who killed George York. That's what all of this is about. Richard York is convinced that his sister-in-law was behind it and that Hastings was protecting her.'

'But that's ridiculous. She and Hastings hated each other. I may not know all of the chief's dirty secrets, but I know enough to understand why. Catesby,' Meg waited until he looked up at her again, 'if Hastings was helping Edward's wife, don't you think we should ask *her*?'

'We will,' Catesby said, 'once we've got her in custody.' Into Meg's appalled silence, he added weakly, 'So, you see. It's doubly important that you get moving with Forensics.'

When Meg left the station, she made a beeline for the Zipcar lot, cellphone in hand. As she was crossing the Brooklyn Bridge, Ms. Woodville finally picked up her phone. 'Detective Stanley. I hope you're planning to explain what the hell is going on.'

She sounded like a woman hanging by a thread. They would make a fantastic pair. 'I'm afraid there isn't time, Ms. Woodville. They're about to put out a warrant for your arrest in connection with George York's murder. Now, listen to me. Don't panic. You *can't* panic.' She could hear the other woman's breathing, harsh and quick. 'I've just heard from Forensics and they've traced one of the drugs in George's system to a dealer in New Jersey. A dealer who sold once or twice to people in... circles you formerly frequented. Of course,' Meg added, '*his* boss was recently acquitted thanks to the legal pyrotechnics of your *other* brother-in-law, but I don't doubt Tricky Dick will see to it that the connection stays under wraps.'

There was a moment or two of silence. Then, in a voice like dragging chains, Elizabeth Woodville said, 'He has my boys.'

Meg had forgotten that. A yawning pit opened in her stomach. 'He can't do anything to them, Elizabeth. There are eyes on them all the time. Security details, reporters even. God, I never thought I'd be thankful for *them*.' She laughed uneasily. 'We'll get your boys away from him. For now, you need to get yourself a lawyer and set aside some money for bail. I'm on my way to East Hampton now. I'll take Ellie back to the city and make sure she's got a place to stay.'

Silence again. Meg suddenly realized that Elizabeth was crying. She remembered what the widow had said just earlier that day, what seemed like ages ago. *I'm never going to see my boys again.*

Three people were already dead. Meg had the feeling she was right.

Chapter 4

Meg woke up on her ancient blue couch, Ellie York draped half over her and sound asleep. As her vision came into focus, she discovered the source of the music that had awakened her – the DVD menu for *Veronica Mars*, Season One, playing on a loop. It had belonged to one of Henry's ex-girlfriends from college (who Meg had secretly hoped would stick around, to no avail) and she thought it might distract Ellie a bit before bed. Instead, the girl had sat for hours, glued to the screen, while Meg dozed off beside her. With a grim smile, she retrieved the remote and switched it off.

Ellie murmured something under her breath and clung tighter to Meg's waist. She'd talked a blue streak all the way across Long Island, and Meg's few puzzle pieces had transformed into a blurry but fairly complete picture. Richard York wanted Broome Investments for himself. That much was obvious.

The sharp knock at the door made her jump. Ellie's eyes snapped open and she crouched into the sofa like a hunted animal. Meg put one finger on her lips and crept toward the door.

'Detective Stanley, please let me in. I've got nowhere else to go.' It was a woman's voice – throaty, unmistakable, and clearly crying. Meg glanced back at Ellie before opening the door with a sigh. Jane stumbled through in a haze of perfume and threw her arms around Meg's neck. 'I'm so sorry for showing up like this, but Bill said to come to you if I needed help and it's all gone totally wrong...' She trailed off, distracted, and let Meg go. '*Ellie?* What are you doing here, honey? Where's your mother?'

The girl was leaning over the back of the couch, looking sheepish. 'Hi, Jane.'

Meg blinked. 'You...know each other?'

'Um.' Jane looked embarrassed. 'It's kind of complicated.'

'No, it's not,' Ellie said. Her lips were twitching as she tried to keep a straight face. 'Jane knows all the best thrift shops and she's way more fun than my mom.'

'That doesn't sound too complicated,' Meg conceded. 'Why don't you freshen up, Ellie, and let's get some breakfast?'

Jane's face fell into her hands as soon as Ellie closed the bathroom door. 'They're after me, Detective Stanley, and Catesby isn't returning my calls. I think he might be trying to save his own skin.'

'Oh, I'm sure of that,' Meg said. 'He's got everything to gain by helping Richard and throwing Bill under the bus.' As soon as she said it, she regretted it. 'I'm so sorry, Jane,' she said, as much to distract herself from that image as anything else. 'He was a good man.'

'He was,' said Jane with a wavering smile. 'Not a very good cop, though.'

Meg laughed. 'No, not very. How did you two meet?' Bill had told her the story, but it had been late enough in the evening that he'd been slurring his words.

Five years ago Jane had been brought into the precinct for having broken a bottle of Glenlivet 12 over someone's head. The full story came out at the station that she had left her much older husband in Indiana and run away to New York to pursue her dream of being on Broadway. At her very first job, a drunk guy got handsy and she grabbed the nearest thing she could find and whacked him over the head with it. Bill, unsurprisingly, had let her off with a warning.

'He also offered to get me into a few auditions,' Jane was saying. They'd never made it out for breakfast; instead Meg found some cereal and brewed a pot of coffee. 'I didn't question him; why would I? I needed the break. I'd just been fired from the nightclub gig, obviously, and I sure as hell wasn't going back to Matt. And then,' she said, after a sip of coffee, 'the doors just started opening. Casting directors started asking for me personally, that sort of thing. I hadn't believed Bill at first when he said he had connections.'

'That was his favorite part of the job – networking and fundraising. Though it helped that he and Edward had been friends all those years.'

Jane sniffed. 'Yeah, that's the thing, isn't it? Bill even offered to marry me once the divorce came through, but...' Her eyes strayed to Ellie. 'The heart's a stupid thing.'

Ellie hugged her. 'I miss him too.'

Meg studied them as she took a sip of coffee and it occurred to her just how much Ellie York resembled her dad. She filed the information away; they had more immediate concerns. 'We need a battle plan,' she said. 'These guys are moving quickly. I just wish I knew what the endgame was and *why*.'

'Richard wants all of Broome for himself,' said Jane flatly. 'That's what Bill thought. It was weird, though. That same morning you called Bill, Catesby stopped by. I was in the shower so I didn't hear anything, but Bill was pretty keyed up afterward.'

'You think Catesby was in on this earlier? You think he set Bill up?' Meg's mind was reeling. 'He's been Bill's second-in-command for years and he never said anything.'

'You know him better than I do.'

It was plausible. Catesby was a hard man to read on the best of days, and Bill was not easy to work for... but surely he wouldn't go so far as murder. 'Let's go at it the old-fashioned way.' Setting down her coffee cup, she retrieved an easel and a large pad of paper from the coat closet. On one side, she wrote her name, Ellie's, and Jane's. On the other, *Richard York*. Beneath it, *Catesby*.

Twenty minutes with Broome's corporate website unearthed mostly names for Richard's side. They added Ellie's mother and grandmother to their side, and her uncle Anthony, with a question mark beside his name. There hadn't been any further news about the Woodville case yet.

Meg leaned against the couch cushions with a grimace. 'We may need help.'

Jane frowned. 'What kind of help?'

'The Feds.' Even as she said it, she deflated. 'But we have no proof. Everything is circumstantial. Even that damn security video just shows Bill running at Richard and crashing through the window...'

'But aren't those supposed to be super glass or something?' Ellie asked. When both Jane and Meg looked at her, she shrugged. 'I remember my dad complaining about how much they cost. This was the conference room, right?'

'Do you think they may have replaced the window?' Jane's eyes widened. 'You think Richard set Bill up to fall from a high-rise?'

'It's a crazy idea, but...' Meg glanced at her phone. It would just be a quick conversation with the security guard at the building to ask if any window repairmen had come in before the 'accident'.

Jane and Ellie cleaned up the remains of breakfast while Meg got ready. 'I want you both to stay here. Don't leave the apartment unless I tell you. It sounds like you've got a lot of people looking for you. If you want takeout, it'll have to be the Indian place down the street. Menu and number are on the fridge. I've known the owner for years; she won't say a word to anyone. And Shivani makes the best paneer makhani I've ever had.'

Ellie was eyeing the DVD set on the table. 'I think we'll be fine. Jane, you *have* to see this show.'

Jane had assured her that she wasn't followed, but Meg doubled back and forth through the hallways of her building and took the fire escape into an alley. Just to make triple sure, even though she knew Henry would have laughed at her, she headed for a different subway station than usual, and by the time she was on the train, she was comfortable again.

There were four regular security guards who manned the front desk at Broome. Hastings had been on a first-name basis with all of them, but the man Meg found was a stranger with a distinctly brute-squad look. His eyes narrowed, one hand twitching toward the holster at his belt. 'May I help you?'

So that was how he was going to play it. Meg whipped out her badge. 'Detective Margaret Stanley, NYPD. I'm looking for Mr. Gregson.'

'Don't know anyone by that name. We all started this morning.'

Meg tried not to curse aloud. Of course Richard would have fired all the security guards. *Always one step ahead, the crafty bastard.* 'Thanks for your time,' she said, and started back toward the door.

'Detective Stanley.'

Fucking hell. Forcing a polite smile, she turned to find Richard stepping out of the elevator. 'Counselor. I see you're cleaning up the place.' She did her best not to glance at the orange cones and yellow tape blocking off most of the sidewalk outside the building. Catesby at least had the decency to leave the crime scene mostly undisturbed.

'The world still turns, Detective. It doesn't stop even for Bill Hastings. Or my brothers.'

'Yeah, about that,' Meg said, eyeing him warily. 'How are your nephews doing, Counselor?'

'They're in the corporate apartment probably glued to the X-Box playing something you cop types hate,' replied Richard with what Meg was deadly certain was an insincere sigh. 'Kids these days, right? One of my associates is babysitting. I told him he could bill the hours to Broome.'

'You mind if I pay them a visit? I promised Ted I'd look in on them, let them know anything I'd heard about their uncle.'

'*Do* you know anything about their uncle?' Richard was no taller than Meg, although he likely would have been without the bad back. He might have been a lot of things without that. 'Assuming, of course, that you mean Professor Woodville. I hate to be the bearer of bad news, but I had a call from Boston this morning. Poor Anthony was found dead in his cell. I could give you the details, but I assume you want to keep your breakfast.' He lowered his voice and leaned closer. 'Turns out they don't approve of messing with kids in prison.'

Meg's mouth worked for a moment before she could find her voice. 'Please tell me you're joking.' She couldn't let him know how much of a blow this was. 'Richard, this is not funny.'

His smile disappeared. 'Do I look like I'm joking, Meggie? Woodville's dead. You can stop barking up that tree. In fact, I'm going to offer you some free legal advice.'

'Oh, goody.'

'Don't piss me off, Meggie. You're smarter than that.' He was smiling again, Edward York's cajoling younger brother. *How the hell did he hide the psycho for so long?* 'Catesby's a great micro-manager, but you see the big picture the way neither he nor Hastings ever could. Come on, Meggie.' He stepped back and held out his hands. 'It's a new day, isn't it? The whole world's up for grabs and you could be right here in line.'

Devil's gonna tempt you one way or the other. She had no house, no car, no real assets, and she was a long way from a pension – if pensions even existed by the time she retired. Henry, thank goodness, had managed to land an athletic scholarship to Georgetown, and he'd taken full advantage of it even as his teammates coasted through on their parents' money. Still, he'd had to take out loans for housing and of course Meg had cosigned them. *Do I really care who's running Broome Investments?* She didn't. But she *did* care that Richard York thought he could play God with people's lives and get away with it.

So she smiled at him. 'I'll consider it. In the meantime, the associate who's taking care of your nephews. Care to give me his name?'

Richard didn't miss a beat. 'His name's Jim Tyrell. He's a second year summer associate from Yale. Nice kid.'

'I bet he is.' Probably still starry-eyed, willing to do anything if a partner gave him orders. *Even murder?* She knew in her gut that Richard was responsible for Hastings, Woodville, and his brother George, but what if Edward was also his fault? Surely that had to mean the nephews were next. 'Have a good day, Counselor.'

'You too, Meggie. I hope you'll take my advice.'

'I always listen to advice, Counselor, even if I don't take it in the end. For what that's worth.'

'Oh, Meggie, I do have one last question for you.' He'd waited until she was inches from the revolving door before speaking. 'I don't suppose you have any idea where I might find my niece?'

Meg grimaced. 'Have you asked her mother?'

'Her mother posted bail and is hiding behind her lawyer. Almost like she was warned this might happen,' Richard said. After a moment, he added, 'And one of the security guards at my brother's house in East Hampton tells me he saw you there last night.'

Fuck. She'd thought Elizabeth would have paid her security detail enough not to give her up at the first sign of trouble. *Of course, as deep as this goes, they may have been Richard's all along.* 'What do you want me to say, Counselor?'

'Is my niece with you or not? With her mother under investigation, I'm her next of kin.'

'One of her parents is dead and the other is insisting that his death wasn't an accident,' Meg finally said after some consideration. 'It seemed prudent to take her into custody.'

'I don't see anything on the books.'

'Don't push me, Counselor. Bill Hastings had a lot of friends and you're the last person who saw him alive. Whatever Catesby may tell you, you're still a suspect in this case.'

* * *

Meg stepped out of the subway station on the corner of Lexington and 68th Street and started toward Fifth Avenue.

A quick call to Elizabeth had confirmed that Broome had several corporate apartments across Manhattan, but the likeliest candidate was in a building overlooking Central Park, a few blocks north of the Plaza.

She was so deep in thought that she walked past the trio of women without seeing them until the eldest of the three spoke up.

'Detective Stanley, a word, if you don't mind.' The words could have been cut from crystal, so sharp were the woman's consonants. Meg spun on her heel, startled.

Cecilia York carried a cane that she clearly did not need in order to walk; she instead used it to clear a path through the clusters of tourists and shoppers on the sidewalk. Behind her, in too-large sunglasses and a high-collared trench coat, was Elizabeth, and Meg was shocked to recognize Anne Warwick, Richard's fiancée, as the third of their party.

'Detective Stanley,' said Cecilia York, wrapping both of her hands around the cane's curved handle, 'are you here to see my nephews?'

'I hoped to see them,' Meg replied. 'We can go in together if you want.'

'We were just thrown out. Rudely, I might add. I've taken the young man's name, but I have no doubt Richard will support him, so it's probably not worth filing the complaint.' She sighed and gestured toward the side street with her cane, nearly taking out a passing Chihuahua. 'There's a café a few blocks this way. I'd like a moment of your time, if you can spare it.'

'Of course, Mrs. York.'

The coffee shop was a tiny Italian place, cramped but empty at this time of morning. No doubt within an hour or two it would be swamped with tourists. After a few words with one of the baristas, they had the place to themselves and a 'Back in an hour' sign on the door.

Cecilia took a seat at one of the newly vacated tables. 'Let's get down to it. You think he's guilty, don't you?'

Meg gave her the capsule version. 'But I've got to hand it to him – I don't have any proof. Just my gut.'

'I wondered.' The rawness in the older woman's voice was as sudden as it was startling, and Meg realized there were tears in Cecilia's blue-grey eyes. 'You probably think I'm a monster, that he got it from me somehow. Maybe he did. He was just so clever, he and Edward both, but I couldn't help but love Edward more. Who could blame me? And Richard... it was just too hard. He was such a *difficult* child.'

'Tell it like it is, Cecilia,' said Anne, finally pulling off her sunglasses, though they'd been indoors for nearly ten minutes. Even beneath a layer of concealer, she had shadows under her eyes. 'He was a little shit, Detective, and he still is, only now the consequences are bigger.'

'Not a nice thing to say about your husband-to-be.'

'Not the first time it's happened. Eddie was a little shit too, but everyone said it was because his mama loved him too much, not too little. Just goes to show,' she added dryly, with a glance at Cecilia, 'you can't win with men.'

'Detective, do you think you can see them?' Elizabeth spoke so quietly that Meg barely heard her at first. She was fiddling with the sunglasses in her lap and when she looked up, her eyes were as shadowed as Anne's. 'My boys. Do you think you'll be able to see them?'

'I'll try my best.'

'If you do,' she said, reaching into her purse, 'will you give this to Ted?' It was a white paper bag with a pharmacy label. 'Better if nobody sees you.'

Meg read the label. 'What's he allergic to?'

'Walnuts. He had to go to the ER once in third grade because he was sneaking brownies at a class birthday party and didn't know they had nuts.' She gave a brief laugh. 'I just wish I could see them, even for a minute.'

'I know.' Meg said. 'But I need you to stay off Richard's radar for now. Where are you staying?'

'With me,' said Cecilia. The tears were gone, leaving not even a trace of smeared mascara in their wake. Meg couldn't help but notice the resemblance. 'Richard doesn't like it,' she pronounced, placing her hand firmly on Elizabeth's arm, 'but he can't find an objection that sticks.'

'Let's keep it that way. Care to join me, Anne?'

'Oh, I lack the clearance, apparently. Even this,' she waved her left hand and the light caught the diamond just so, 'didn't get me past the doorman. I must admit my engagement is not as advertised.'

'To be fair,' observed Elizabeth, 'you could have seen it coming. Richard doesn't play his cards *that* close to the chest.'

'Nobody mentioned the chronic insomnia.'

'Insomnia?' Meg asked, trying not to sound too interested.

'He never sleeps. At least that's what it looks like to me. Maybe he takes power naps at work, but he sure as hell doesn't when I'm around. Pain in the ass is what it is. Even if we do get married, I'm insisting on separate rooms. I can't work in these conditions.'

'Considering the kind of clients your father defended, it's a wonder *you* can sleep at night,' Elizabeth remarked. Meg tried to remember why there was bad blood between her family and the Warwicks, but was sure she didn't care.

Neither did Anne, who studied her prospective sister-in-law for a moment before shrugging. 'It's a life skill like any other. But Richard is about five levels above what I can handle. The one time I've seen him sleep, it took at least half a bottle of pills. And even then he woke up maybe an hour later, thrashing around like a fucking dolphin in a net. At which point he got up and went back to work and I finally got some goddamn sleep. Never again.'

'Huh.' Meg filed that away for later. 'You be careful around him.'

Anne gave her a brief, bitter smile. 'I'm always careful.'

Meg handed her a card. 'If anything happens, if you ever feel threatened, or you just want to get the hell away from him, you call me.'

'Or if I find anything incriminating?' She slipped the card into the black purse on the table in front of her. 'I know Catesby's in Richard's pocket, so you must be going rogue if you're trying to actually *solve* this case.'

'I'm old-fashioned. I don't approve of murder, least of all when it's murder for money.'

'It's not about money,' said Anne. 'Not really. Richard doesn't care about being rich. Money is a tool as far as he's concerned. What he wants are people. I think he read *Atlas Shrugged* too early and never recovered.'

'I don't know it, but I'll take your word for it. He wants followers? Like a cultist?'

'Not exactly, but close. It's just never occurred to him that what he's doing could be wrong.' Anne stood up. 'Seems a shame to hang around in here without having an espresso. Anyone?'

'I'll take one,' said Meg.

'Double,' said Elizabeth with the suggestion of a smile.

'Not for me, dear. It's bad for my digestion,' was Cecilia's contribution before turning back to Meg. 'Do you have a plan, Detective?'

'I need proof to go over Catesby's head on this. Solid, unmistakable proof. All I have right now is circumstantial, and I can't get to the case files without alerting him.' On her last visit to the precinct, she'd called in a few favors to sneak out a recorder, just in case. There would be hell to pay if she got caught and it might derail her career altogether. 'I don't suppose he's told you anything, Mrs. York?'

'Not by choice. He tells me what he needs to, or so he claims. I still hold twenty percent of Broome; he can't keep me completely in the dark.'

Hastings would have known that, but Meg hadn't been Edward York's best friend. For a moment, she had to bite her tongue to keep from bursting into tears then and there. She felt a pair of hands close over hers and realized they belonged to Cecilia York. 'I am so sorry about Bill Hastings. The only reason I wasn't at that meeting was because I was changing my will.'

Dry-eyed as suddenly as the tears had come on, Meg looked up at Cecilia. 'What did you change, if you don't mind telling me?'

'It doesn't leave this room.'

Meg nodded, as did Elizabeth. Anne, busy with the espresso machine, was too far away to hear.

'Everything goes to Ellie. The penthouse, the money, the shares. All of it.'

'Not to her brothers?'

'Not once I found out Richard had them.'

After a moment, Meg excused herself and stepped into the café's tiny kitchen. 'Henry,' she said when her son answered his phone, 'I'm going to need to talk to whoever you know that's high up in the hierarchy. I've got a situation here.'

* * *

By the time the barista returned and the café reopened, Elizabeth had received a text from her daughter that she was on her way to an FBI safe house. Jane was with her, according to the message Meg had received at the same time. Anne ducked out soon afterward, muttering something about a deadline.

When Meg, Elizabeth, and Cecilia stepped out of the café, Richard was waiting for them, flanked by two uniformed officers Meg recognized as pals of Catesby's.

'You disappoint me, Meggie.'

'Detective Stanley,' she corrected him coldly.

'And as for you, *dear* Elizabeth,' Richard turned to his sister-in-law with a look that chilled Meg to the core, 'you think you're so clever, don't you?'

'Richard, that's enough!' snapped his mother. Richard glanced at her as though he hadn't realized she was there.

'Mother.'

Cecilia shook her head, lips pursed and eyes blazing. 'Don't you *dare*. Not after what you did to your brothers.'

'Are you really going to believe *her*,' he threw a contemptuous look at Meg, 'over your own son?'

Meg and Elizabeth exchanged a quick glance, Elizabeth's eyebrows raised over her sunglasses. Meg supposed that if anyone had a prayer of rattling Richard York, it would have to be his mother. But Richard was glaring at her again now. 'You have no shame, do you? Turning my own family against me. That's some fucking nerve.'

'You did that on your own, Mr. York,' retorted Meg. 'Now, I'd like to see your nephews, please.'

'Catesby already saw them. If you're so goddamn keen, get a warrant.'

'And what about me, Richard?' asked Elizabeth. She spoke softly, but Meg could see her fists clenched at her sides. 'They're my children. You can't keep me from them.'

Richard leant close, pitching his words into Elizabeth's ear, just loud enough for Meg to hear. 'I think you'll find I can.'

One of the officers stepped forward with a pair of handcuffs. 'We'll need you to come with us, ma'am.'

Alarmed, Elizabeth turned to Meg, who shook her head. 'You don't need to cuff her. She'll cooperate.'

'Richard, you need to stop this.' Cecilia grabbed her son by the arm. 'What do you *want*, for God's sake?'

Richard fixed his mother with a look that almost made Meg pity him for half a second. 'Do you really need to ask?'

Taking advantage of his distraction, Meg shoved the voice recorder into Elizabeth's coat pocket. 'Whatever you need to get him to talk, just say it,' she whispered. 'I'll make sure it gets to the right people.'

Elizabeth squeezed her hand in assent and stepped forward, flanked by the two officers. 'Lay on, Macduff,' she said with a withering smile. Though Meg watched until she disappeared into the cruiser, Elizabeth did not look back.

Cecilia's shoulders slumped and, for the first time, she looked her age. 'Are you a religious woman, Detective Stanley?'

Startled, Meg shook her head. 'I'm a weddings and funerals only type of person,' she admitted. Her mother had gone every Sunday her whole life and it hadn't helped one bit when the cancer came.

'I sometimes wonder,' murmured Cecilia, 'that if I'd known my son was the devil, I might have stopped him sooner.'

'Mrs. York,' said Meg, 'the devil's a fairy tale. Richard's as human as they get.'

And Meg was going to bring him down if it was the last thing she did.

Chapter 5

Meg's apartment felt empty without Ellie and Jane, though she found a note from Ellie on the table asking if it was okay that she'd borrowed the DVD set. *The agent who picked us up told me they don't even have wifi at the safe house, but they did have a DVD player.* Meg cracked up at that. 'Kids these days,' she murmured, switching on the TV.

She would have expected Elizabeth's arrest to be on the evening news, but instead they were still airing the retrospectives on Edward. Clearly Richard was invested in keeping things quiet for now. She was about to switch it back off when her phone rang.

'Detective Stanley?' The woman's voice sounded familiar but Meg couldn't place her. 'Look, I don't have much time and, I'll be honest, I'm putting myself at risk by calling you.'

'Who is this?' Meg asked.

After a pause, the speaker hissed, 'Buckingham.'

Meg nearly dropped the phone in surprise. 'What's going on?'

'He's going to kill them. The boys.' Harriet Buckingham paused again, and Meg wondered if she was checking to make sure she wasn't overheard. 'I know you think I'm a stooge, but I didn't sign up for this. Not killing kids.'

Meg almost asked her if it was okay to send a cop falling to his death from a skyscraper, but reminded herself that Buckingham was a valuable source. 'How? When is he planning to do it?'

'Soon. I don't know exactly when; he won't tell me. I think he knows I don't like the idea.' She sighed. 'I thought he just wanted me to change Edward's will. I'm not the biggest fan of legal fraud either, but who the hell wants a fourteen-year-old running a multi-million-dollar company? I told myself it was for the best to have Richard in charge. But this?' Meg could hear the click of a cigarette lighter. 'This is fucked up.'

'How, Buckingham?' demanded Meg. 'How is he going to kill them? You have to give me something concrete.'

'He said Ted was allergic to peanuts or something. Like, really allergic. You know how easy it is to slip nuts into things. I don't know about his brother.' Buckingham gave an unmistakable cough and Meg rolled her eyes. 'I didn't know who else to call. Catesby's been paid off, he'd make sure everyone thought it was an accident.'

'Gotta give Richard credit. It's believable.' But for Elizabeth, Meg wouldn't have been able to guess either. 'Thanks, Harriet. You may not have much of a moral compass, but it's better than nothing.'

A few more seconds passed in a burst of coughing. 'Fuck,' muttered Harriet. 'I'm sorry about Hastings. I had no idea he was going to pull that shit with the window.'

'So that *was* how he did it,' murmured Meg. 'Bastard.'

'Take him down, Detective Stanley. I don't care if I go down with him. I'll testify in court and everything.'

There were so many things Meg wanted to say, but she restricted herself to relevant questions. 'First things first. I need you to tell me everything you know about the apartment where the boys are staying.'

After Harriet hung up a few minutes later, Meg sat in the dark, wondering if she'd just been played. But there was only one way to find out.

* * *

If there was one thing Meg knew about Richard York, it was that he refused to acknowledge anyone he deemed to be below his notice. Meg had spent many years in that category, only catching Richard's attention when it became clear that Hastings liked and trusted her, but still very much relegated there were the household staff at Broome's corporate apartments.

Using the intel Buckingham had given her, Meg managed to catch Loretta, the housekeeper, on her smoke break. She already knew the woman was from Queens, but by happy coincidence, it turned out she had a granddaughter at Henry's old high school. That – and the fact that Jim Tyrell was an asshole as only a legacy Yale law student could be – made it all the easier for Meg to convince her to sneak Ted his epi-pen while Tyrell was distracted. Meg also left her card and told Loretta to call her if anything unusual happened, no matter how small.

A quick stop at Cecilia York's apartment further up Fifth Avenue revealed that Elizabeth was still in police custody, but Cecilia handed Meg the voice recorder with a grim smile. 'I haven't listened to it, but Elizabeth called it a silver bullet.'

'Make it two. Buckingham's defected. I'll tell you the full story later, but if she gets in touch with you, see if you can help her get out of town, somewhere Richard can't find her. Just don't let her stay with you. She'll have the place stinking of weed before you know it.'

Cecilia wrinkled her nose. 'Thank you for the warning. I'm no stranger to the substance, as you well know.' For a moment, grief flashed across her face, and Meg felt a surge of overwhelming pity. Bad enough that two of her children had died in the space of a week, but knowing that the third was responsible for at least one of his brothers? She couldn't even imagine it. But just as Meg opened her mouth, Cecilia shook her head sharply and the mask was back in place.

On her way home, Meg left the voice recorder in the FBI drop spot that Henry had told her about the previous day. It was a relief to no longer have it; she'd been stupidly paranoid that Richard might find some way to pick her pocket, but she also knew he'd sink to just about anything.

What she did not expect was to find the Town Car waiting outside her building and Richard leaning against the passenger door. When she drew close enough to hear him, he looked the building up and down disdainfully. 'How many years have you been a cop, Meggie?'

'Long enough,' she retorted.

'And you live *here*?' He shook his head.

Meg rolled her eyes. 'Whatever you're selling, I'm not interested.'

'Your son's a different story, though, isn't he?' Meg froze. 'He's done well for himself. From this place to Georgetown and now the FBI...' She could hear the smile in Richard's voice. 'That's one hell of an accomplishment.'

'You don't know a damn thing about me, or my family.'

'I know several of your son's classmates from high school are doing hard time for drugs.'

For a few seconds, Meg could only see red. Her hands were clenched so hard she could feel her nails digging into her palms. 'Don't you fucking dare, Richard. Henry never touched that stuff. And I'm willing to bet those kids you're talking about shouldn't be in jail either.'

'That's not what the jury said.'

'I'm sure every one of them was white,' Meg spat, finally turning to face him. 'You're a piece of work, Richard York.'

'I'm good at my job. And I suggest you listen to what I have to say unless you want your precious Henry to have a very awkward conversation with the guys down in Langley.'

Meg wondered what his face might look like if she decked him. It was a satisfying image, but somehow didn't help. Tightly, she nodded.

'Buckingham gets chatty when she's had a joint too many.'

'It's a free country. She can talk to whoever she wants and so can I.'

'*Whomever*,' he corrected. 'What she told you was a violation of attorney-client privilege.'

'What she *told* me was that you were planning to murder two innocent boys. Not that that should surprise me one bit, given what I know about you.'

Richard was clearly about to say something when the phone in his pocket began to buzz. Glaring at Meg, he fished it out and held it to his ear. 'What? *What*? Goddammit, *how*? I told you to wait at least twenty minutes before calling, you moron–'

Meg could hear a man's voice, high and panicked, on the other end, but couldn't make out the words.

'You're kidding. How did he get–' That was when Richard looked at Meg and cold fury swept across his face. 'Never mind. Get our security guys to the hospital. Nobody gets in or out, *especially* not his mother. And this time, follow my fucking instructions.' He hung up.

Meg didn't say anything and tried not to smile.

'You think you're so smart, don't you? I'll have that fucking housekeeper deported.'

'You can't deport someone for talking to the cops, Richard. Not when she's just prevented a murder.' Meg was already composing a warning text to Loretta in her head. She'd get Cecilia to offer the poor woman a better job than the thankless one she had now, and protection from Richard. 'What were you saying about a hospital?'

'I think you've done enough. Keep the hell out of my way, Meggie, or I will destroy your son. Do you hear me?'

Without waiting for a reply, he climbed back into the Town Car and slammed the door. Meg's heart was beating a mile a minute. Once she was back in her apartment, she was halfway through dialing Henry's number when it occurred to her that she didn't know how long Richard had been waiting for her. *He might have bugged the place.* She texted Henry instead.

The reply came instantly. *Calm down, Mom. Good job getting us that recording. Boss says we may have enough to arrest York.*

Meg did a quadrant-by-quadrant search of her apartment and didn't find any bugs. Even still, she went into the bathroom and turned the shower on full blast before calling Henry.

'Henry, I just want you to be careful–' she said as soon as he picked up.

'Mom, chill out. Richard York has screwed up more than a few of our cases. They have his number and they won't believe anything he says about me. I promise.'

'Anything from Buckingham?'

'No.' She heard a door close on Henry's end. 'We tried the number you gave us but nobody's picking up. We're going to send someone over to her apartment when we're able.'

Meg's heart sank. 'You don't think Richard–'

'We don't know anything yet, Mom. But let's be real – she knew who she was working for. She gets credit for trying to do the right thing, but she had to have known Richard wasn't going to take it well if she gave away his plans.'

He wasn't wrong. Not that it made Meg feel any better about the prospect of losing one of her best witnesses against Richard. So she changed the subject. 'How's Ellie?'

'She's fine.' Henry laughed. 'I got her Season Two of *Veronica Mars* after she watched the first one twice.'

'That's very nice of you, Henry.' Thinking about Ellie had made Meg wonder. 'You know Richard's just going to hide behind a lawyer if you try to arrest him.'

'I have a plan, but you're not going to like it.'

Meg took a breath and listened. He was right; she did not like it one bit. But that didn't make a difference.

* * *

The following afternoon was one of the hardest of Meg's life, mostly because she couldn't do a damn thing. Henry had told her to stay in her apartment and wait until he called. *Nothing's going to happen to me, Mom. I'm a trainee for the FBI and there will be thirty agents within a hundred feet of me at all times. If this works, I'm basically guaranteed a job for the rest of my life.* Meg didn't say what she was thinking, though they both knew it: What if it didn't work?

Instead, Richard did exactly what they'd hoped he would do. When Ellie called him from just outside Central Park to say she'd run away from FBI custody and needed his help, he showed up on the spot. Within ten minutes, he was cuffed and in the back of an FBI car. To the glee of the watching crowd, Ellie leaned over the open window and hissed, 'That's for my family, you asshole!' before raising both of her middle fingers to him as the car drove away. The best photographs, to Meg's mind, were the ones that also caught her mother in the background, giving a radiant smile of approval.

It was almost anticlimactic. But Meg was at least able to call both of Chief Hastings' daughters to tell them the man who murdered their dad was going to jail for the rest of his life.

'It's weird,' said Katie Hastings, sniffling. 'Dad barely ever talked about him. It was always his brother Edward, you know? Did he really hate Dad so much?'

'Honestly, I don't think he hated him at all,' Meg replied. 'Richard doesn't see people as people; he only sees who helps him and who's in his way. And your dad, unfortunately, was in the second group.'

Catesby was also arrested for obstruction of justice. And when Meg went into work the following day, she found Harriet Buckingham in one of the holding cells. The lawyer shrugged when she saw Meg. 'Turns out that just because it's technically legal, you probably shouldn't smoke up on Park Avenue in front of a bunch of cops. Catesby just needed an excuse and I handed him one on a silver platter.'

Meg let her go home with a solemn promise that she not leave town until she'd finished testifying in Richard's trial. 'I can't promise you won't get punished. At the very least, you're probably getting some sort of slap on the wrist from the bar association.'

'I think they've got bigger fish to fry these days than little old me,' Harriet replied, 'but I'll take it under advisement.'

After Harriet left, Meg settled at her desk to sift through the enormous pile of papers that had accumulated in her absence. On the top of the pile was the final autopsy report for poor, forgotten George York, with a flash drive on top. The flash drive contained a single video file – grainy security camera footage of George leaving what appeared to be a fancy rehab facility, visibly shaking with withdrawal symptoms, pale and ghostlike. Beside him was Richard.

'I guess that solves the case of the guy in the wine barrel,' Meg said grimly. She closed the file, stacked it with the others from the case, and loaded them into a box to be delivered to the FBI. Whatever else happened to Richard York was out of her hands.

And she had plenty of other work to do.

Kavita Mudan Finn is an independent scholar who has published widely on medieval and early modern literature, Shakespeare, and fan studies. She has taught literature, history, and gender studies at Georgetown University, George Washington University, the University of Maryland at College Park, and most recently at Simmons College. In her (sadly minimal) spare time, she writes fanfiction. She credits this hobby for the successful completion of her D.Phil. thesis and many of her subsequent academic works.

Notes

1. **Drabble:** Short work of fanfiction, usually 500 words maximum and written in response to a prompt.
2. Yuletide is an annual fanfiction exchange where participants submit prompts in a variety of small fandoms (including Shakespeare's plays) and, in exchange, write a story of their own in response to someone else's prompt. The archive containing all the stories goes live at midnight on Christmas Eve, and the authors' names are all revealed on New Year's Eve.

Chapter 5
Enter Nurse, or Love's Labour's Won

Scott Maisano

LIST OF ROLES
DUKE *of Ravenna*
CAPULET, *an old gentleman*
BEROWNE, *a gentleman in disguise as* RAHERE
SPEDALINGO, *the hospital governor*
GARZONI DENTITRISTI, *the doctor*
SCRUPLE, *his apprentice*
HICKET, *a braggart knight sans arms*
SQUINT [or SQUIRT], *his squire*
ANTONIO AFRICANUS, *the confessor and chaplain*
PILLICOCK, *a fantastical sick-nurse of the men's ward*
SLAPBAG, *a lascivious gipsy*
TURTLE, *his ape*
ENDYMION, *a sleeping shepherd*
MOON, *the chorus*
LADY CAPULET, *a young gentlewoman*
LADY ROSALINE, *a gentlewoman in disguise as* NARCISSO FIRABELA
ANGELA, *a nun and sick-nurse of the women's ward*
CHIARA, *a miraculously preserved abbess*
LOCHIA, *a widow and midwife*
SUMMER
AUTUMN
SATYRS
WOODNYMPHS

LIST OF ROLES not in Q1 (1597) or Q2 (1598), the two quartos discovered in 2016. We have added this list for the convenience of readers and followed editorial precedent in ordering characters according to rank and gender. Shakespeare's decision to set this sequel to *Love's Labour's Lost* (*LLL*) in a hospital fulfills the promise made at the 'conclusion' of that comedy, when Berowne promises Rosaline that 'befall what will befall / I'll just a twelvemonth in an hospital' (5.2.847–8). In *Henry V*, Pistol refers twice to 'the spital' (2.1.67, 5.1.73), which a footnote in the *Norton Shakespeare* glosses as 'Hospital; in Elizabethan times, a filthy, disease-ridden place occupied by indigents near death' (2nd edition, 2008: 1493). This image of the Elizabethan hospital makes the task that Rosaline imposes on Berowne sound more like a death sentence than a romantic quest: 'to win me, if you please, / Without the which I am not to be won, / You shall this twelvemonth term from day to day / Visit the speechless sick and still converse / With groaning wretches; and your task shall be / With all the fierce endeavour of your wit / To enforce the pained impotent to smile' (Arden, ed. H.R. Woudhuysen: 5.2.836–42). The specification and repetition of 'a twelvemonth' as the allotted period for Berowne to reform his bitter ('wormwood') wit in the context of a hospital probably informs the one-year time scheme of the present play. This time scheme is inconsistent, however, and many events that presume the passage of months occur in a matter of days. In *Shakespeare's Medical Language: A Dictionary* (Continuum Press, 2011), published prior to the discovery of *Enter Nurse, or Love's Labour's Won* (*LLW*), Sujata Iyengar explains how 'Hospitals or 'spitals originated in priories or monasteries, as part of religious orders' duty to tend the sick, succor the poor and aid travelers' and notes how Shakespeare 'associates the hospital with festering or incurable disease' (166). Fortunately, there were Renaissance hospitals where even a lord like Berowne might feel comfortable, if not exactly at home. According to John Henderson's *The Renaissance Hospital: Healing the Body and Healing the Soul* (Yale UP, 2006): 'In the sixteenth century and beyond, information and favorable comments about Italian hospitals were carried north of the Alps by travelers from Martin Luther and Michel de Montaigne to Thomas Hoby and Fynes Morrison. Many of these gentlemen on their tours through Italy praised the magnificent appearance and services of these large civic institutions, which they viewed as important both as monuments and as examples of relief to the poor' (xxvi). Henderson's survey of sixteenth-century praise for Italian hospitals by Northern Europeans and Englishmen omits what is perhaps the most glowing account, which is provided by the fictional Jack Wilton in Thomas Nashe's *The Unfortunate Traveller*: 'O Rome ... there you shall have the bravest ladies, in gowns of beaten gold, washing pilgrims' and poor soldiers' feet, and doing nothing, they and their waiting-maids, all the year long, but making shirts and bands for them against they come by in distress. Their hospitals are more like noblemen's houses than otherwise; so richly furnished, clean kept, and hot perfumed, that a soldier would think it sufficient recompense for all his travel and his wounds, to have such a heavenly retiring place' (Penguin, ed. J.B. Steane, 1971: 330). These lines from Nashe are echoed in *LLW* when Berowne recalls the moment he first heard about Italian hospitals: 'So richly furnished, bellified, perfumed, / And cleanly kept by ladies gowned in gold, / Tis wonder any man would ever leave' (2.2.141–3). That *The Unfortunate Traveller* serves as one of several 'sources' for *LLW* should not come as a surprise given that Berowne's disparaging of lifelong scholars as 'continual plodders' in *LLL* (1.1.86) echoes the sentiments of Nashe's eponymous rogue, who denounces Wittenberg academics as 'Gross plodders ... that had some learning but no wit to make use of it' (296).

1. **DUKE** While dukes are most commonly found in Shakespeare's history plays, the comedies have their fair share too: a Venetian duke in *Merchant of Venice*, a Milanese duke in *Two Gentleman of Verona* (*TGV*) and rival dukes in *As You Like It*. Theseus is Duke of Athens in *A Midsummer Night's Dream*. Another Venetian duke appears in *Othello*, where his role is limited to Act One. The present Duke of Ravenna, by contrast, appears only in Act Five. In another late Elizabethan comedy, *Blurt, Master Constable*, Thomas Dekker and/or Thomas Middleton introduce(s) a Venetian duke in the final act. While Shakespeare never chose Ravenna as a setting for – or even mentioned the city in – another play, Thomas Middleton later made use of it in his tragicomedy *The Witch*. On this basis Professor Taylor credits Middleton as Shakespeare's coauthor and collaborator for *Enter Nurse*.

2. **CAPULET** A Shakespearean variation on the *senex amans* of classical comedy and medieval fabliaux. It is possible for an actor playing this part to double in the role of Lochia (see Appendix 1). The irony in that case is that the same actor would be both deceiver (midwife) and deceived (father) when in the play's final act Angela's baby is substituted for Lady Capulet's stillbirth ('What makes a child? Tis nothing but the name').

3. **BEROWNE / RAHERE** The 'class clown' of *LLL* has gained admission at the hospital by pretending to be a lunatic named Rahere, an allusion to the twelfth-century jester to King Henry I who (following a vision during his pilgrimage to Rome) founded St Bartholomew's Hospital in London.

4. **SPEDALINGO** A source has yet to be identified for this character, known only by his title, Italian for hospital director. The word *Spedalingo* appears in Tomaso Garzoni's *L'Hospedale de' pazzi incurabili* (1586), an Italian literary text which titillates its readers by taking them on a virtual tour of both the men's and women's wards at a hospital for the incurably insane. If, as Ken Jackson argues in *Separate Theaters: Bethlem Hospital and the Shakespearean Stage*, 'the hospital

was some sort of theater, a place of perverse and sometimes fashionable entertainment for Londoners' (U Delaware Press, 2005: 11), then Garzoni might have attempted to capitalize on a similar phenomenon in Italy. Garzoni's fiction, perhaps popularized by Shakespeare's *Enter Nurse*, was translated into English in 1600. Shakespeare's depiction of a sixteenth-century Italian hospital in this comedy seems remarkably modern at first glance and yet it conforms in many respects to the following description from Henderson's *Renaissance Hospital*: 'They [the hospital doctors] came to the hospital each morning at a set time and were greeted with a flurry of activity. When the head nurse on duty espied one of the consultants he rang a bell, which was a sign to the apothecary's assistant, who "runs to meet the doctor, bringing a white linen garment with which to cover his clothes".' (231). The white linen garment donned by the senior doctor before his daily rounds becomes a vehicle for mistaken identity and harrowing comedy in this play's fourth act. Despite some comic moments evocative of Grand Guignol, however, *LLW* generally affirms what Henderson calls Italian hospitals' 'reputation for excellent care' (*The Renaissance Hospital*, xxviii).

5. **GARZONI DENTITRISTI** The surname, unusual for such a minor character, means 'sad teeth'. The first name appears to derive from the author of *L'Hospedale de' pazzi incurabili* (see note for Spedalingo).

6. **SCRUPLE** 'Scruple' in sixteenth-century medical parlance, including *The Birth of Mankind: Otherwise Named, The Woman's Book* by Thomas Reynalde (1560), was an apothecary's measure equivalent to 1/24th of an ounce. Why Shakespeare assigned the name to Dentitristi's assistant also remains something of a mystery. Professor Smith points to a specific action in the play as justification for the name. Professor Jones, in a somewhat tortured argument, suggests that although 'scalpel', the word for a surgeon's tool, had not entered the English language at the time of the play's performance, the Latin *scalprum* may be 'faintly heard' behind the name, a garbling consistent with the fact that Scruple is 'deaf / As gravel' (1.3.80). In any case, Shakespeare's Scruple seems to have been inspired by the figure of Dr Zachary in Thomas Nashe's *The Unfortunate Traveller*. Shakespeare's anatomist's apprentice, however, is neither mercenary nor Jewish and so the anti-Semitism of the source is not an issue here. The parts of Scruple and Hicket were most likely written for William Kemp to double as both bear some relation to Dogberry, Bottom, and Sir John Falstaff.

7. **HICKET** 'The Hicket' meant hiccups. Perhaps the only armless character to appear on the early modern stage. Presumably, the actor tucked his arms into his doublet.

8. **SQUINT** In Q1 (1597), the character is always referred to as 'Squint' but in Q2 (1598) the name is consistently amended to 'Squirt', except for one speech prefix that reads 'Sin-

cklo'. The Q1 name, a better fit for a character with poor eyesight and supposedly prone to hallucinations, has been chosen for this edition (but see Appendix 2). The singular substitution of 'Sincklo' indicates that the part was written for John Sinklo, a member of the Lord Chamberlain's Men best known for his lanky physique. Both Squint and Rosaline (in her disguise as Doctor Narcisso Firabela) are described as especially thin characters. See, for example, the Duke's query: 'Which is the doctor here? And which the bones?' (5.2.25). More than likely, Sinklo doubled these roles. Indeed, if Sinklo doubled the roles of Rosaline (Narcisso) and Squint, and William Kemp, his plump comic counterpart in Shakespeare's company, doubled the roles of Scruple and Hicket, then the two actors would have taken turns playing servant and master vis-à-vis one another.

9. **ANTONIO AFRICANUS** If Shakespeare modelled Antonio on St Benedict the Black or 'il Moro' (1526–1589), born to African slaves but later leader of and confessor to a Sicilian hermitage, it is not clear how he came to learn of him. If Benedict the Moor did not spur Shakespeare's imagination to create Antonio Africanus then the parallels between the two are nonetheless remarkable. The name Antonio probably draws on Saint Anthony of Egypt, 'desert church father and founder of monasticism', in the words of Cynthia Lewis, who argues persuasively for the saint as prototype for a multiplicity of 'stage Antonios' in works of Shakespeare and his contemporaries. The 'very name Antonio', writes Lewis, 'suggested to audiences of high English Renaissance drama a willingness to compromise one's own well-being for a person or principle seen as more important – or higher – than the self'. See 'Wise Men, Folly-Fall'n: Characters Named Antonio in English Renaissance Drama', in *Renaissance Drama* 20 (1989), pp. 197–236.

10. **PILLICOCK** Vulgar slang for 'penis'. Shakespeare would later use the word in *King Lear* when Edgar, in the guise of Poor Tom o' Bedlam, sings 'Pillicock sat on Pillicock's hill. / 'Allow, 'Allow, loo, loo!' (3.4.73–4). The name also appears to play on the fact that Pillicock uses his ostentatious heirloom codpiece as a container for peppercorns and other medicines which he dispenses to the patients. Pillicock's codpiece, equivalent to Othello's handkerchief, is practically a character itself.

11. **SLAPBAG** Shakespeare only uses the word 'gipsy' to refer to Egyptians such as Cleopatra (see both *Antony and Cleopatra* and *Romeo and Juliet*). The fact that Slapbag possesses a crystal ball, however, and tells the fortunes of other characters suggests that Shakespeare might have intended for him to be of Romanian or Eastern European descent. The name also recalls Shakebag, the ruffian whose foibles in tandem with Black Will supply some of the funniest moments of *Arden of Faversham* (circa 1592), a domestic tragedy to which Shakespeare probably contributed Scene 8. Described by Angela as 'swart' (3.1.34), the actor playing the role of Slapbag most likely doubled as

Antonio Africanus (the two never appear onstage at the same time). Such doubling, however, invariably results in both confusion and surprise for audiences when Slapbag's true identity is revealed at the end of the play.

12. **TURTLE** Slapbag's 'ape', presumably a monkey, appears in 3.4 (Q2), an additional scene that does not appear in Q1.

13. **LADY ROSALINE** Having worried over Berowne's fate and learned of his whereabouts, Rosaline arrives at the hospital disguised as **NARCISSO FIRABELA**, an overreaching (mock-Marlovian?) physician and curioso. Professor Lee suggests that the name is an anagram of François Rabelais, whose *Pantragruel* was 'first ascribed to a [different] anagram, "Alcofribas Nasier"' (see Anne Lake Prescott, *Imagining Rabelais in Renaissance England*, 2). Although Shakespeare seems to have taken inspiration from *Pantagruel* when naming the pedant in *Love's Labour's Lost* Holofernes, Lee's conjecture strikes the present editors as an example of making rather than finding contextual evidence. The influence of Rabelais's earthy and sexual humour, no doubt honed during his own training as a medical doctor, is more obviously felt in Pillicock's paean to his codpiece. But Shakespeare did not bestow an ingenious anagram on Pillicock.

14. **ANGELA** According to the *OED*, the modern meaning of the word 'nurse' – that is, 'a person (historically usually a woman) who cares for the sick or infirm' – enters the English language in Shakespeare's *Comedy of Errors*, when Adriana says: 'I will attend my husband, be his nurse, / Diet his sicknesse, for it is my Office' (Folger Shakespeare Library, ed. Barbara A. Mowat and Paul Werstine, 5.1.102–3). Although the *OED* dates this usage to the publication of the First Folio in 1623, *The Comedy of Errors* was written in the 1590s. Moreover, the *OED* is probably mistaken in its assumption that Adriana, a housewife insisting on her duty to care for and look after her husband, is the kind of 'nurse' who has made caring for the sick or infirm among the general populace – not just members of her immediate family – her profession or vocation. And yet on further examination *The Comedy of Errors* contains a nurse of this professional sort: Aemilia, the Abbess, who does not yet know that the man taking refuge in the abbey is her son, explains why she is better suited to caring for the ailing Antiopholus in lines immediately following those cited by the *OED*: 'I will not let him stir / Till I have used the approved means I have, / With wholesome syrups, drugs, and holy prayers, / To make of him a formal man again. / It is a branch and parcel of mine oath, / A charitable duty of my order. / Therefore depart and leave him here with me' (5.1.106–12). Aemilia's regimen of 'wholesome syrups [and] drugs' in addition to 'holy prayers' reflects what John Henderson describes as 'the hospital's two main functions, the cure of the soul and the cure of the body' (*The Renaissance Hospital*, 113). By referring to her care for the sick as 'a branch and parcel of mine oath, / A charitable duty of my

order', Aemilia, a widow at this point in the play, makes clear that she has taken vows to serve as the convent infirmarer. Perhaps prompted by Adriana's use of the word 'nurse', Aemilia defends her occupational space and its accoutrements – 'the approved means' of 'syrups', 'drugs', 'oaths', and 'orders' – against what she perceives as the inadequacies of home healthcare. Shakespeare's most well-known 'nurse', of course, is Juliet's raucous and pragmatic wet nurse, whose name is Angelica (*Romeo and Juliet*, 4.4.5). Angelica's backstory can be glimpsed when she speaks of her dead daughter, Susan (1.3.19), who would have been Juliet's age had she lived, and her late husband, who made bawdy jokes when as a toddler Juliet was concussed during an earthquake (1.3.36–58). Angela in *LLW* is a somewhat younger Angelica, most obviously when she gives birth to her daughter, whom she intends to name Susan. This mid-1590s work from Shakespeare's lyrical period therefore constitutes at once the long-lost sequel to *Love's Labour's Lost* and a porny but poignant prequel to *Romeo and Juliet*. Despite its relatively late date of publication, Professor Conkie speculates that Shakespeare might have written this play, the only one of its time to depict signs of the plague on stage (when in 1.2 Angela consults Pillicock about the black spots – 'ungodly tokens' – on her groin, neck, underarms, and fingertips), as early as 1593, in which case its sequel would be *Romeo and Juliet* and its prequel *LLL*.

15. SUMMER The seasonal complements to Winter (Hiems) and Spring (Ver) in *LLL* appear at the end of *Enter Nurse*. Their appearance is further warranted by the fact that the play begins on 31 July, the eve of Lammas Day, which is the first harvest, and ends a year and a day later, following Juliet's (and Susan's) birthdate. Pillicock's 'Latter Lammas' ballad (1.2.80–95) alludes to a proverbial 'day that will never come' (*OED*) because Lammas comes but once a year. *Enter Nurse* might be said to defy the proverb by setting its final act at a second (or latter) Lammas. Surely, Shakespeare must have considered using *Latter Lammas* as a title (cf. the seasonal comedies *A Midsummer Night's Dream* and *Twelfth Night*), thus alliterating till the last word: *Latter Lammas, or Love's Labour's Won*. But for reasons of his own or the stationer's, what we have instead goes by the less satisfying name of *Enter Nurse*.

16. AUTUMN Perhaps inspired by Nashe's *Summer's Last Will and Testament*, Shakespeare presents Autumn as the heir to Summer, who enters in the epilogue on a sickbed.

ENTER NURSE, OR LOVE'S LABOUR'S WON

1.1 *The grounds of the Hospital. Enter SLAPBAG and ANGELA. A banquet laid out.*

SLAPBAG [*removing ANGELA'S shoes and holding her feet*]
Two feet alike in dignity, new-sprung
Before mine eye, perfected, plump and pink;
Each flower's nectar beckoning my tongue,
Ten toothsome toes make eight health-giving chinks!
Instead of Montague versus Capulet   5
This feud is one of laterality –
Tis Dexter versus Sinister; Right, Left –
O Blessèd Cursèd Bipedality!
Somewhither would one have me, somewhither
Else the other; such sport mars my labour;   10
Impeded hither, and likewise thither,
Wherefore choose one and neglect its neighbour?
Ecce panis angelorum! Tis most sweet

1.1 Location: Ravenna. 'A banquet laid out' is an error here. These stage properties do not appear until the next scene.

SD: Neither quarto contains stage directions for this dialogue and some may object to our inserting them here as overstepping editorial licence. Our commentary, however, attends to matters of the stage as well as the page and in theatrical performance it seems necessary for Angela to lie on her back, with her head toward the audience, and for Slapbag, facing the audience, to hold her feet in his hands and to talk to them, turning from one to the other. The scene might recall Lance's speaking to his shoes while holding them aloft ('this left shoe is my father') in *TGV* 2.3.1–27.

1 Slapbag's speech echoes even as it alludes to the choric Prologue to *Romeo and Juliet*. The sexual innuendo here seems to surpass anything else Shakespeare had written for the stage but for a comparable passage see the 'deer park' episode in his epyllion *Venus and Adonis* (229–40).

See Rogero's 'Like to the Capulets and Montagues' from John Marston's *The Insatiate Countess* (1.1.186) in *Four Jacobean Sex Tragedies*, ed. Martin Wiggins (OUP, 1998).

8 **Bipedality** For a discussion of this Shakespearean inkhorn term and its Darwinian afterlife, see pp. 66–9.

13 *Ecce panis angelorum* Latin. Literally, 'Behold the bread of angels'. Inscribed near the altar in Catholic churches, it refers to the Eucharistic host. Q1 reads '*Ecce penis angelorum*', a printer's error. But Jones argues for 'a deliberate pun which calls attention to the boy actor even as its muddled Latin insinuates "Behold Angela's penis"'.

By yon mound where these same two jarring foes
    (as friends) do meet.

ANGELA
  Dolce morte! Though my perpetual 15
  Reward were lost, no angel will e'er know
  Delights incarnate as these his kisses.
  Even Venus in arms of Adonis clad
  Would trade her bliss for mine.

SLAPBAG
  Tomorrow harvest is; Slapbag feasts tonight: 20
  And where I feed, I whet her appetite.

              Enter MOON in a cloud aloft.

MOON
  This little globe's a stage I look upon
  From greatest seat where graceful watch I keep
  Divining deaths as though I were a swan
  Not my own death but rather those that sleep, 25
  Or wake, or do such collied deeds by night
  As they surmise no other will suspect
  The sequent day when with sated appetite,
  They visors put on, glib discourse affect.
  This counterfeit Egyptian I've seen before, 30
  Though many nights since Moon saw him last,
  His painted face resembling much a Moor.
  Its borrowed hue of umber shall soon be cast

---

14 In a forthcoming essay, 'Two Feet ... do meet', Jones notes that the final line of Slapbag's sonnet is a 'fourteener', containing two metrical feet in excess of the standard pentameter. However, Maisano's comment that the final line of Angela's reply is 'missing' two metrical feet, 'as if she had donated them to Slapbag', is not persuasive.

15 **Dolce morte** Italian. Literally 'Sweet death'.

21 **whet** Possibly a pun. **appetite** *OED* 'spec. Craving for food, hunger'. But also, as in Crystal and Crystal's *Shakespeare's Words*, 'sexual desire, passion' (19).

22 This line appears to combine Jacques's *theatrum mundi* topos from 'All the world's a stage' in *As You Like It* with Prospero's metatheatrical allusion to 'the great globe itself' in *The Tempest*. But in this case appearances are deceiving: *Enter Nurse* was written (and published twice) prior to the opening of the Globe Theatre in 1599.

> Upon such privy places as ne'er see the sun,
> The humblest, hidden holes of this most holy nun. 35
> An earthly month, for me, is but a day;
> One year is twelve nights; two years, twenty-four;
> In only hours your weeks I do survey
> And blanch as blackest tidings come ashore –
> Calamities far off do touch me near, 40
> Tiny tragedies I sensibly peruse,
> Remotest sobs resound against my ear –
> Such distant heartache I cannot refuse.
> As in a tiring house these actors unlace
> In the dark, disporting naked, or almost, 45
> Conceiving themselves unseen in secret place.
> But think me not a moralizing host:
> *Though Moon is fabled a virgin queen,*
> *She too has a side that cannot be seen.* Exeunt

1.2 [Withheld from the present excerpt]

1.3 *Enter SPEDALINGO somewhat fast.*

SPEDALINGO
> He will come straight. I'll hide me even here.
> [SPEDALINGO *hides behind the curtain.*]

> *Enter BEROWNE disguised as RAHERE*
> *in the motley of a court jester.*

BEROWNE
> Disconsolate am I, and shall I be,
> Friends, viands and music boot me not,

36–37 The action of the play spans one year in mundane, terrestrial time, which amounts to twelve lunar days. From Moon's perspective, the calendar year depicted on stage, from one Lammastide to the next, might appear as a Twelfth Night festival or feast of the Epiphany.

48–49 **Though ... seen** If, as the Q1 title page indicates, this comedy was first 'PLAIED BEFORE THE QVEENE'S MAIESTIE ON TWELFE DAY AT NIGHT', one can only guess at the reaction of Elizabeth I, idolized as Cynthia (goddess of the moon), to this scene's concluding couplet.

Till she, if she, unless my hoped-for she
Should show her face among the faces here.
My eyes oft make my heart a fool and start
The tender sleeper with visions, dreams,
Phantasms conjured forth from sighs
Commix'd with desperate search for her I lost:
Any human figure gives me shape enough
To paint her face upon before it turns,
Or nears, revealing eyes, a smile, not hers,
Whereupon my breathless heart, having waked
And dressed fantastically with colours wild
To greet the moment garishly displayed,
Discovers only ghostly memories arrayed
In borrowed strangers' faces, brows and frowns.
Betrayed again my heart can take no more:
Were her shadow here I'd with it converse
All day, or longer, till wearied with talk
About her nose, about her chin, arms, hands,
Together lying side by side, we'd die,
Disanimated by that we once possessed.
The fair, the fine, the foolish Rosaline!
Though she's the fool, 'tis I the motley wear
In quest of laughs from feeble lungs and dead
Applause from wrinkled hands, palsied sore,
'I'll jest a twelvemonth in an hospital',
To her I swore, 'or else be there forsworn'.
Perchance she knew or perhaps foresaw
How kept from her decrepit I'd become
And ache the air I part with every step.
I, that have late dissected others' love,
Anatomized and lectured o'er its corpse
Untouched by Cupid's affliction and scourge,
Now find my brain dull as his bird-bolt,
My heart's bowstring broke by his ambitious pull.
No longer Berowne, I play a clown's part –
A red-flannel coxcomb covers my wit
(For Rosaline would have me chastise it) –
A jester errant, travelling actor strayed
From a band of entertainers, Rahere my name.
But none suspect I feign the hectic part,

For who can *tremor cordis* or fever feign?
The ablest player proves unable to play 45
Unable. How should I, less able than he,
Perform my illness well?
And though I know the cause of this my cause
It shall remain obscure, a mystery hid,
A matter within to madden those without. 50
Berowne, be gone! My spectators are about.

SPEDALINGO [*aside*]
Aye but, young cozener, I have eyed you ere this play began.

Enter ROSALINE in disguise as FIRABELA
with his assistant SCRUPLE.

FIRABELA
This man's in love – I see it in his eyes.

SCRUPLE
His size would dwarf a Cyclops. This man is monstrous huge.

FIRABELA
Not his size, Scruple, but his eyes. Look here. 55

SCRUPLE [*turning away*]
Has he more than one eye? Then the monster is many times
a Cyclops. I'll not look on such a giant again.

FIRABELA [*to RAHERE*]
Art thou sick with love, poor fool?

BEROWNE [*as RAHERE*]
Contagion! O contagion! Running boils
And botches, welts and bruises bluish black! 60
In sooth my ling'ring sickness knows no cause
Nor knows itself for't changes ev'ry day:
Headache today, tomorrow liver pain;
One hour my lip has lumps, next limps my leg.
In me thou dost behold death's ensign pale, 65
A wasted cheek; inhale superfluous fumes,
The spleen's surplus; collect eye-blinding rheum,
A watry gulf (enough to glut the ground,

Or drown a salt fish); and hear the heart's drum,
Whose wild, irregular sound does marching lead 70
Disease down worn-out sinews, stretch'd, aflame,
Its powerless powers advancing bellyward,
To disrupt digestion and food send back
As surfeit, though the while I shrink and starve.

SCRUPLE

Carve? Would the monster be carved? Have its wings
and horn extract? Why, then, it shall be well served here 75
in hospital. We have fine utensils for carving. And though
I am old I am but newly called to the surgeon's trade and
haply learning even now the carver's art. But I shall do it
without mine eyes for I dare not look into its.

FIRABELA

I beg your pardon, mimic to foreign kings, 80
Some handsome prince's fool. This aged man,
My assistant here, is sand-blind and deaf
As gravel. Very little he sees and hears
Even less. To him all the world's a dumbshow,
A pantomime: 'tis better, then, to gesture broad, 85
Speak scarce, and never bare your neck, or arms,
Or legs, lest seizing a vein he lets your blood.

BEROWNE

I am not in the giving vein today.
[*Aside*] I feel a kind of inward and subject joy
That fain would character itself, 90
Unfold and yield its marks to extern sight,
Yet fears that e'en now, over-eyed and read,
The signs, though changing not, would meaning change:
Betrayed by mean imprint, surveyed and prone,
No joy in joy, and I no longer I. 95

89–95 Berowne's aside hints at his attraction to the young male doctor. He might simultaneously worry about his same-sex attraction and what it portends for his relationship with Rosaline, for whose love he has come on a quest to this hospital.

FIRABELA
May I peruse the plumpy lumps upon your lips?

BEROWNE
Who sees me, sees a cipher; who ciphers me sees what
   I cannot.

FIRABELA
This moan is full of matter.

SPEDALINGO [*still behind the curtain*]
[*Aside*] Aye, and this matter full of bombast. 'Tis all
   padded out and put on for show.

[The remainder of 1.3 and all the rest of the play, with the exception of 3.3, have been redacted.]

3.3

ANGELA
Procreant lust, my lord, comes not always
Attended by affection. His hard hands
By force did take my never-given gift,
The tender treasure kept lockt, sealed fast,
Until such day as I, a virgin bride,   5
Might change it for a moiety most like,
Having died, my Jesu's gift of true love:
Abiding, endless, noble (and salt) love.

---

96 The repetition of bilabial consonants (m, p) in this question suggest that the actor playing Rosaline (as Firabela) should exaggeratedly pucker his or her lips at once mimicking a kiss and demonstrating for Berowne the expression he should make in order for Firabela to conduct his clinical examination.

1 **Procreant** *OED* 'that procreates, that begets offspring, generative'. Cf. *Macbeth* where Inverness is described ironically as a 'procreant cradle: / Where [birds] most breed' (1.6.8–9). See also the noun form in Othello's command to Emilia to 'Leave procreants alone and shut the door' (4.2.28). See Kelsey Norwood's unpublished Honours Thesis, 'Leave Procreants Alone: Lesbianism, Loss, and Shakespeare's *Othello*' (UMass, Boston, 2013).

8 **salt** Lustful and lascivious. Angela imagines even sacred love as carnally rewarding.

SPEDALINGO
> Three month since, Angela, three month since
> The secret gipsy stole upon the path   10
> You trod and said: 'She shall my strumpet be'.
> Yet in all that time none save you and Squint,
> A madman sent to us for cure, have seen
> This Slapbag, who o'ertook you in your walks
> Against your will, and made his will 'gainst thine. 15
> Suppose 'tis true, suppose fond fumbling could
> Bring forth issue without begetting heirs.
> What scape might a goodly maid contrive
> To rid herself of children not desired?

ANGELA
> I'd sooner expire for my child than she   20
> Expire for me –

SPEDALINGO
> What 'she'? Why should not groatsworth of mankind
> To manhood grow, to brave the bastardy
> Upon him thrust by's ill-breeding mother?
> To pine to know what fop, what patch, what rot   25
> His father might be? Wherefore not despair
> When he be shent 'mongst men, envenomed
> Against them, haunted by his lack of name?
> His matron having been leman to no
> Gentleman but Sir Stranger, Sir Shadow,   30
> Who over-canopying the path she trod
> One night, he's told, did quicken life in her
> As sunbeams stirred Chrysogone to twins.

ANGELA
> Slapbag, the gipsy singular and swart,
> Exists. Not I nor Squint could him have dreamt.   35

Enter PILLICOCK at one door and SCRUPLE at the other.

---

15 **will** The word is used here first as 'desire' and then as 'sexual organs' (male and female). Cf. Sonnet 135.
27 **shent** Blamed or shamed. Q2 reads 'sent'.

PILLICOCK
There is at the postern, Spedalingo, a widow wanting work.
  Will you see her?

SCRUPLE
A widow wanting work? *Hysterica passio*, let no man doubt.
Bring spatulas and other engines searching yet delicate!

PILLICOCK [*to* SCRUPLE]
Employment, sir. The woman wants to be of service.

SCRUPLE
Cervix, say you? The pain is in her neck? I'll see to her
  haste-post-haste.   40

SPEDALINGO
I'll see to him that he do her no harm.

Exeunt SPEDALINGO and SCRUPLE.

PILLICOCK
Behold how Nature doth protect the seeds
Of beans and peas with firm-set husks and pods,
Safeguarding the jewels of generation –
Fair posterity! – O joys of life to come!   45
What needs the stone a shell? Armour, armour?
Yet walnuts no less than tender snails do hide
Encased in gauntlets of their own design:
Hardness more harder than that that's hard at hand.
E'en diamonds are crowned with cushion of earth   50
As these my diamonds are in codpiece housed.
This fragrant, ornamented upholstery large,
With pockets and dials good for telling time,
Did late my father, but newly deceased,
Bequeath unto me. Stuffed with peppercorns   55
And syrups wholesome for lunatics, I keep it.

---

49 **hard at hand** Close or nearby.
50 This line is anapestic rather than iambic. The irregular meter here and elsewhere throughout this scene are taken by Professors Taylor and Smith as signs of textual corruption and/or collaboration with a lesser playwright.

Keep it, said I? – It keeps me, in good sooth.

ANGELA
Privy matters are best kept to yourself.

PILLICOCK [*moving towards her*]
Tell me you want to smell me. [*Scream heard from within.*]
I go, madam, but will return for thee. To thy unborn bairn,
   'Father' shall I be. 60

Exit PILLICOCK.

ANGELA
God-a-mercy! Where aches my poor heart now?
It stands somewhere wet in yon woods, I wot,
Pale-dead in the dark, burthening some bough,
Sad-faced among limbs, an owl that hoots for naught.
Yellow eyes gilding a lifeless gloom, 65
Feathers failing or fallen, damp with chill –
Yet full of life beneath its tufted tomb! –
Mantled in melancholy, tail to bill.
Yesternight it flew from me, this fool fowl,
Left flutt'ring silent to its Valentine, 70
Impatient with Nature, my little owl
Pursueth its humour, undoeth mine!
Slapbag, my heart is taken to the wood,
Envying the good hap of my maidenhood.

---

57 Compare Aaron's 'To wait upon this new-made empress. / To wait, said I? – to wanton with this queen' (*Titus Andronicus* 1.1.519–20).

61–74 Angela's sonnet here echoes Slapbag's in 1.1. Maisano's additional observation – that the sonnet's first thirteen lines form the acrostic 'GIPSYFY MY LIPS' – is unwarranted and gratuitous.

Scott Maisano is Associate Professor of English Literature at the University of Massachusetts Boston. His work on Shakespeare has been featured in *Lapham's Quarterly, Smithsonian Magazine, Scientific American, The Telegraph, Ideas with Paul Kennedy* (CBC Radio), and *The Science Show* (Australian Broadcasting Company). His publications include "Shakespeare's Revolution: The Tempest as Scientific Romance," about Prospero and particle physics in *The Tempest: A Critical Guide* (Bloomsbury Arden Shakespeare); "Now," about Einsteinian spacetime in *The Winter's Tale*, for *Early Modern Theatricality* (Oxford University Press); and "Rise of the Poet of the Apes," about intelligent apes and monkeys in plays from the beginning to the end of Shakespeare's career, for *Shakespeare Studies*. He is coeditor of *Renaissance Posthumanism* (Fordham University Press) and is currently completing a new Shakespearean comedy entitled *Enter Nurse, or Love's Labour's Won*.

Chapter 6
Echo and Narcissus, or Man O Man!
A Very Tragical Comedy in One Act, possibly Two.

Mary Baine Campbell

Echo and Narcissus, or Man O Man! is the only surviving fragment of an early dramatic work of Shakespeare's, perhaps his first – some critics argue it was composed before he left home and saw his first play performed. It shows signs of immaturity in its stagecraft. (Though a well-funded contemporary production could work technological magic with the pool in which Narcissus sees his mirror image and, perhaps, hears his mirror voice. Or sees his mirror-voice.) Shakespeare would return to Ovid for material more than once in his career (Carroll, 1985), and his wry, choric clowns are often taken, as here, from folk culture, but the sense of imminent catastrophe evident in even the casual opening lines of his tragedies is missing in this early effort, as is the barely suppressed power struggle of the initial exchange in his first completed Ovidian comedy *Midsummer Night's Dream*. Greenblatt has suggested that this fragment, apparently abandoned, was sketched by the young playwright during detention, as a display of nonchalance intended to frustrate an embittered Latin teacher (*Shakespearian Negotiations*, 1989).

Dramatis Personae

Echo, a strapping lass, muscled, highly verbal, multi-talented, who has been felled by Love

Narcissus, a lad named after a flower, oddly seductive to some tastes, who can't get over himself, also can't swim

Little Red Riding Hood, a clown

A wolf

Act II, Scene I. *Echo is discovered crouching in the ferns near a forest pool.*

Echo: The thing that drives me crazy is the fact
That I can't say it if he doesn't say
It first.
   That isn't all, of course:
I could complain all night, and will, until
He comes and shuts me in the chamber of
His sighs. For instance: who do these sighs pursue?
Whose name do our two meters with one breath
Harry and hunt down, whom do we call up
With our name magic, fashion with magic
Of the eyes from the heart's exhalations,
From whose eyes seize, both of us, heart's ease or
Heart's Hell? His – whose pupils harbour his own,
Whose love is a standing wave between his
Eyes and eyes that are his and his alone.

She rises from the ferns, moved.

I am invisible, and I'm annoyed.
But 'who shall give a lover any law?' –
As Chaucer said, in good pentameter.
Ay, there's the rub: no one could sympathize
With lawless Nárcissus better than I
Who share each suffocated breath, each bruise
Of spirit, ev'ry blinded gaze, whimper
And shudder of joy in the deep drowning
Of the double vortex of his liquid
Eyes. I am invisible, I, and I
Cannot be heard when he comes on the scene –

*Enter **Narcissus**, his left hand fanned across his neck in an erotic clutch. **Echo** drops suddenly back into her crouch.*

Narcissus: Alack!

Echo: Alack!

Narcissus: Alack!

Echo: ...'lack ...'lack

Narcissus: Alas!

Echo: A lass! A lass!

Narcissus: A lad, alas, a lad
In love, or do I mean a god ...

Echo: Aladd-
In. (*whispering*) Quick, come rub your lamp, love's Genie longs
To ease you if that way she steal a touch –

Narcissus: SILENCE, all gnats and midges! Silence, leaves
That slide and whisper one against another!
Silence you moles and voles, owls, everything
So I can hear the throb of diastole
And systole in the breast below the pool's
Soft skin, wet skin, to touch which is to drown.

***Echo** keeps her hand clasped tightly over her mouth till she bursts out –*

Echo: –Ow–, –ow–!

Narcissus: Is that my soul, my howl, I hear?

***Little Red Riding Hood** passes across the stage apron swinging her basket, wearing a starched pink A-line dress, very short, and white anklets. **Echo** and **Narcissus** freeze in place.*

Little Red: Is that a 'bow-wow' ringing in my ears?

(*Sings*) Mama said there'd be sounds like this,
There'll be growls and woofs, Mama said.
Mama said there'd be sounds like this,
There'll be growls and woofs, Mama said.
My eyes are wide open, but all I can see
Is dogs and wolves are callin' for everyone but me.

Yes, that's right – the original lyrics say 'all I can see / Is chapel bells callin'', which suggests that the Shirelles were on drugs. Mama said everyone was taking drugs in the sixties. She said synaesthesia was a common feature of psychotropic drug experience. I have had this experience myself at the Museum of Science where I went on a field trip with my third grade class. It wasn't a historical exhibit about the sixties, it was about cognition. Cognition is something that can go seriously haywire under the influence of drugs, or love. My cognition is in tip-top shape if I do say so myself. (*Little Red turns to address the audience directly.*) Hey, do I remind you of Sylvester the Cat's son Felix who clearly attends the Bronx High School of Science and Art? I would very much like to attend that school but unfortunately I live in the woods in a pre-modern hamlet and am not destined for great things.

Narcissus (*unfreezing*): Silence, all gnats and midges, mites and snails!
Silence, you very molecules and sub-
Atomic particles: be still, spin not:
I heard the flutter of my lash upon
His cheek, or is that mine? I heard his tongue
Gliding along his lip to catch that droplet –
Yearning's accident, mistaking hot
Muscle and skin for long-desired food –
Leaked hungry from beneath the tongue and saw
Shine on the lip's brim – there! – or was that dew,
Seeking a petal warmer than my name-
Sake nárcissus, that springs up gold and cold
From snow's white sheets, can offer in his season?

Little Red: There's a word for that, when somebody overdoes the sentence they're in to the point that you can't parse it: it's what Mama calls *asyndeton*. He was doing OK till he got to 'shine on the lip's brim' – but 'shine' has no object to complete it, grammatically.

I'd say judging from context that *this* cognitive disruption is *love*, not drugs, Echo and Narcissus being mythical figures located *in illo tempore*, outside of historical time, and therefore of the drug trade – which is interesting – I mean, that there's love (invented in twelfth-century Provence) *in illo tempore*, but not *drugs*. Because Mama told me fly agaric formed the basis of a *very ancient* Greek mystery cult, pre-Homeric in origin –

Narcissus: SILENCE –

Echo: SILENCE –

Narcissus: – gnats and midges!

Echo: – midgets!

Little Red: I'm one of those kids in *The Drama of the Gifted Child*. We're often told to go up to our rooms, if we have them. I live in a one-room cottage so it's moot. Still, I think I'll skedaddle now. Hey, nonny nonny ….

> *Little Red scurries away, singing*
> *'hey nonny nonny' under her breath.*

Narcissus: What was I saying? Hard to keep in mind
The matter of poetry when its own
Self and model, that which exceeds it, tongue
And trope and all, lies wet, lies longing
Under the lucent skin of this woodland pool ….

Echo: Under the lanolin of this woolly mole?

> *Narcissus rearranges himself so he's lying on his side along the pool's bank, his back to Echo, gazing down fixedly at his double. He makes a 'come hither' gesture with his hand. Echo imitates it, sticking her hand up out of the ferns, a micro-second later.*

Narcissus (*addressing the surface of the water*): Speak to me,
do I look like a Greek god
To you? You do to me: are you a god?

Echo: Are you a cod?

Narcissus: Your black eyes are a god's.

Echo: A cod's.

Narcissus: Whip me with lashes of long gold
And cure me with medicines the gods know –

Echo: God knows, I would –

Narcissus: Would that I knew the gods'
High craft, to lounge thus under the water
Without breath – we'd be together, breathless
Now and ever, mouth to mouth and heart –

Echo: – and fart?

Narcissus looks back over his shoulder.

Narcissus: I've had enough, Miss Smarty-pants!

Echo: 'Miss Smarty-pants'!

She crosses her hands over her heart and looks moonily at him.

Narcissus: Don't be abject! Just scat!
Begone! Vamoose! If there's one thing I hate
It's abject wenches lurking in the ferns.

Echo (*rising, indignant*): 'Lurking in the ferns'?

Narcissus: Oh, get thee to a –

Echo: Doo-wah –

Narcissus: – nunnery, you eco-fairy!

Echo: *Echo*-fairy.

Narcissus: Let's pretend she isn't there.

Echo (*sadly*): She isn't there.

Narcissus: She isn't there.

*Enter **Little Red**, dashing across the apron, arms extended stiffly in front of her, pursued by an offstage wolf. **Echo** and **Narcissus** freeze.*

Little Red (*stops to listen, panting*): A wolf! (*Batting her lashes*) I think he likes me! But I have to act a little coy, n'est-ce pas? Wolves don't like it when you're easy to catch. That's what Mama told me anyway. I wonder what'll happen when he catches me? Probably something called 'sex', about which I am rather confused, since when I asked Mama about it she just gave me a book with pictures of chickens in it called *Growing Up*. Wolves are famous for eating chickens but there were no wolves at all in this book. It's difficult being a child 'on the brink of adulthood'. For instance, what is a 'wolf whistle', and why am I not allowed to answer it? I was actually very disposed to answer when I heard it, but I did what Mama said.

*She stares, distracted for a moment, at **Echo**, as she eases back into her crouch among the ferns, and **Narcissus**, stroking the tops of the ripples by the pond's edge, then turns to the audience.*

Speaking of 'on the brink', will you get a load of these two?! I'm not old enough to work out the details here, but even I can see something is *way* off. For one thing, they're shedding avoirdupois at lightning speed – I was just here a couple minutes ago, now they're practically skelingtons!

***Narcissus** and **Echo** unfreeze.*

Narcissus (*moaning*): Nárcissus!

Echo: Nárcissus!

Narcissus: I faint, I die!

Echo: I die?! – of what?

Narcissus: I die of lust, you goose!

Echo: *You* goose!

Narcissus: No you!

Echo: No, *you*!

Narcissus: No YOU!

Narcissus and Echo freeze again.

Little Red (*sings*):
In the greenwoods
Canopy
Birds are laughing
At these three:
Her and him and who
He loves –
I guess that's just two
Turtle doves.
The other one's
A fantasy –
Wait, no it's not –
So are there three?
I am getting
All confused:
Her and him and who
Is who?
Will one boldly
Make a move?
Will they puzzling
Pleasures prove?

High above this
Two or three,
Birds are laughing
In the trees.
Down below
A panic brews:
He and he and
She is two,

Or he and him and she
Are three
Or fading, drowning,
Nobody ....

*A **wolf** enters stage right at a rapid clip,
chasing **Little Red** across the apron and offstage left.*

Mary Baine Campbell is Professor Emerita of English, Comparative Literature and Women's and Gender Studies at Brandeis University and the 2019–20 Kennedy Professor of Renaissance Studies at Smith College. She is the author of two scholarly books, *The Witness and the Other World* and *Wonder and Science*, and is currently writing a history of early modern dreams, "Dreaming, Motion, Meaning: Oenirics in the Early Modern Atlantic." Founder of the Creative Writing program at Brandeis, she has published two collections of poems and a chapbook and composed the libretto of Martin Brody's chamber opera *Feral* from her translation of Marie de France's Breton lai, *Bisclavret*.

Chapter 7
The Fair Maid of Alexandria, or The Glass Tower

Dan Moss

From Spenser's *Faerie Queene* (1590)

> Who wonders not, that reades so wonderous worke?
> But who does wonder, that has red the Towre,
> Wherein th'Ægyptian *Phæo* long did lurke
> From all mens vew, that none might her discoure,
> Yet she might all men vew out of her bowre?
> Great *Ptolomæe* it for his lemans sake
> Ybuilded all of glasse, by Magicke powre,
> And also it impregnable did make;
> Yet when his loue was false, he with a peaze it brake. (3.2.20)

The Fair Maid of Alexandria, or *The Glass Tower*

The Persons of the Play

PTOLEMY, Pharaoh of Ægypt
HERODOTUS, a young adventurer from Helicarnassus
SOLON, his elderly tutor and travelling companion
GLOBOSUS, a sycophantic courtier
PERDITUS, a malcontented courtier
DEMETRIUS, a lord
AMON, chief of the palace guard
HERMES TRISMEGISTUS, chief magician to Pharaoh's court
ARGUS, an eunuch, warden of Phao's prison
MORION, a fool in Pharaoh's court
APICIUS, chief baker to Pharaoh
BIBULUS, chief butler to Pharaoh
MANETHO, an ancient soothsayer
TOBY, his English servant, a clown
CALLIMACHUS, a librarian in the Library of Alexandria
SPORADICUS, keeper of the Pharos Lighthouse
HALIEUTICUS, a fisherman of Nile

NEFERTITI, Queen of Ægypt
BAST, her lady-in-waiting, formerly a witch
PHAO, a noble Ægyptian maiden
NUT, her servant
A blind BEGGAR-WOMAN

Courtiers, Soldiers, Librarians, Magicians, Assassins, Beggars

1.1 *Enter Herodotus and Solon, dripping wet.*

HERODOTUS Wondrous, is't not?

SOLON Phew! Wondrous.

HERODOTUS Art thou not enchanted by this River Nile?

SOLON Aye, the nymph thereof hath chained my nostrils to her.

HERODOTUS Canst imagine, even now, we voyaged here from the coast in boats of paper!

SOLON And as staunch and steady as boats of æther. My shoes and backside – both annihilated – speak to the wonder. And canst imagine, the journey down four miles of river devoured as much time as the journey over four hundred miles of ocean!

HERODOTUS Hush, querulous fellow! Let me perform all filial rites.

He kneels.

> O father worthy of a worthier son,
> And wise withal, to waft me to this Ægypt
> With your utmost breath, for what in the wide world,
> Or anywhere in Asia, wields such wonders!

SOLON Welladay, and what whale wetter than we? For without question, thou hast found out the very hieroglyph for 'w'. But find we some hearth to warm us once again into mankind, for verily I wobble on fins until these weeds be dry.

Enter a rabble of beggars.

HERODOTUS O Solon, not since Io first stampeded hither have these shores heard such complaints as thou makest. Yet thou stumblest on some reason. Let us remove from these docks and look for lodging. Mayhap one among this crowd of welcomers will help us to a house.

SOLON They will welcome our purses from us if we be not wary. That one riverbank should hold so many beggars is this day's greatest wonder.

FIRST BEGGAR Welcome, worthy wayfarers!

SECOND BEGGAR Wouldst witness wonders? Wend with me!

THIRD BEGGAR Whither from this wharf, your worships?

SOLON Nay, is't in the water?

HERODOTUS Good sir, here's for thee, know'st of any lodging hereabout? Or thee, take these denarii, wilt guide us to some honest house? And for thee, fine fellow, we seek but a bed.

SECOND BEGGAR Why, blessed patron, which of us do you prefer?

FIRST BEGGAR For another denarius, I will show your worships to three beds!

SOLON Master, thy charity will be our undoing. I beg thee, let me bestow my hands on them as freely as thou dost thy coins, before we beggar ourselves.

HERODOTUS Away, thou churl! Hast thou no compassion?

SOLON Milord, passing is all I would have us do. But what is this shape lurches toward us, and so appals our new friends?

Enter the Blind Beggar-Woman of Alexandria.

FIRST BEGGAR Ware! 'Tis the witch!

THIRD BEGGAR We must hence, or she'll worry us!
Exeunt Beggars.

HERODOTUS Alas, our guides have deserted.

SOLON By Jupiter, we're better to be strangers.

BEGGAR-WOMAN Strangers to our shores! Would you know the secrets of this land?

HERODOTUS Ay, damsel, dearly would I know them. Here's gold for thee.

SOLON 'Damsel'? She's a dynasty or more hobbling hither. Good master, let us hail the next paper waterman, and take her back to Greece, to sell piecemeal as mummy.

BEGGAR-WOMAN I need no eyes to find a fool. We've store in Ægypt.

HERODOTUS Nay, good madam, I prithee disregard my menial! Yea, I beseech thee, accept of this further humble offering. Know'st thou, among thy treasured secrets, of a lodging beside these docks?

BEGGAR-WOMAN Thou wilt never rest thy head in Ægypt.

HERODOTUS (*to Solon*)   O slave, thus to bring curses down upon us!

SOLON (*to the Beggar-Woman*)   I prithee disregard my master. In the storehouse of thy second sight, dost perceive whither I will rest my head in Ægypt?

BEGGAR-WOMAN   Ægypt holds no cushions for thy pate neither.

SOLON (*to Herodotus*)   Then truly, milord, I am sorry so to have offended the gods.

BEGGAR-WOMAN   Thou offendest them by naming them with thy stinking breath, but even for thy generous lord's sake will I admit thy place within my friendly prophecy.

HERODOTUS   Good lady, still thy words are dark as any pitch. If anything I can provide will help thee into plainer speech, demand it.

BEGGAR-WOMAN   Look to thine ears,
Hark not to thine eyes.
Trust not to seers,
They've naught but lies.
But I do see
What comes to pass:
Thy dearest lady
In her prison of glass.

SOLON   My lord, this speech is no plainer.

HERODOTUS   Alexandrian Sybil, even on my knee I beseech thee, help me to interpret this impenetrable charm, for I do feel it draw me into Ægypt, as a shiver of iron to some massy lodestone.

BEGGAR-WOMAN   Well, you Greeks have many oracles, but no sense of them. For another piece or two I'll tell you all.

SOLON   Nay, trusting master! How long must we take this python for Pythia? Please thee, let me charm her hence with this rope's end, or she will swallow thy tribute whole.

HERODOTUS Without thou mend thy lines, varlet, she's like to fore-ordain your neck to a rope's end.

BEGGAR-WOMAN You do me kindness, sir, to silence him, yet the world I foresee is never so just. He will live to old age and gain a far repute for wisdom.

HERODOTUS Wisdom?!

SOLON Sure, master, here's proof she has no eagle's vision. I protest I've never been mistaken for a wisdom-monger.

BEGGAR-WOMAN Yet countless learned fools will deem thee wise, and all for some dotages thou'lt mumble, of a drunken afternoon, to a barbarian king called Croesus, a fellow yet more fool than thou art. (*To Herodotus*) But you, most magnanimous of men, shall leave such record of truth behind you as generation's moiety will ever hail you history's prime mover.

HERODOTUS Nay, good madam, in this thou flatter'st me, and now I do begin to doubt thy motive be metallic, as my servant said 'twas. We'll trouble thee no more. (*Turns away.*)

BEGGAR-WOMAN O linger, gracious sir, for your impatience at my overmuch praise, though born of right humility, may yet deprive an innocent maid – for virtue and beauty the nonpareil of the world – of her very life, and you of her love.

HERODOTUS (*turning back*) Love?

SOLON Good my lord, of all such anglers' baits, this same worm of love betrays the most and greatest fishes. Let us swim from this Charybdis, and betimes.

HERODOTUS I bear my wits about me, Solon, and though my experience of love as yet be little (or rather, none), I do suspect the poets something overvalue Cupid's charms, as thou exaggerate'st his terrors. Be it so, yet to try of love is parcel of the education my good father bid me seek in Ægypt. For if love be the angel some have portraited, I shall embrace him, or if he be the monster thou defamest him as, I'll sweep him from my lifelong path. For all that, I predict the pursy blindfold boy will show himself but slow and short-sighted.

BEGGAR-WOMAN   Now sir is your man the wiser, for you nothing reck the power of that oldest and mightiest god. Hark to my lore, and soon enough you will worship at his alter, none more ardently.

SOLON   The prophecy fulfilled, I am lauded for my wisdom!

HERODOTUS   Proceed, good lady, pardoning my earlier chastisement. Tell me, where shall I find love in Ægypt?

BEGGAR-WOMAN   Then prepare your fancy, venturous Greek, for what I tell you now is no mere tale, but quite as true as 'tis beyond all credit. Mistake me not, for there be tales enow in Ægypt; yea, many roaming this dockside will tell you of wars between the cranes and pygmies, of the immortal phoenix, of great horned serpents, of a tribe of ants that mine the desert sands for gold and guard their treasure jealously, and much nonsense else.

SOLON   Our boatman swore he'd seen these ants at their labour. Doubtless an effect of the river's fumes.

HERODOTUS   Silence, Solon. Interrupt her not.

BEGGAR-WOMAN   A fisherman's tale, no more. But this I presently shall speak is history, no tale: six-and-twenty moons ago this night, our Pharaoh Ptolemy, whilst he consulted with his Master of the Quarries, beheld amongst the Hebrew slaves (that wretched tribe we ever keep in servitude) a maiden beautiful past measure, and far beyond the fading beauty of his lawful wife and sister Nefertiti.

SOLON   Sister?!

HERODOTUS   Nay, sirrah ...

BEGGAR-WOMAN   So our kings have used to marry, time out of mind. Yet this same queen, whose nature tends toward jealousy (not without cause), soon suspected her injury, from her lord's altered manner and some words let fall in sleepy negligence. Advising with her creature Bast – a pygmy witch who claims to equal Hecate in craft, yet cousins her in malice only – she had the quarry-master sealed live within his obelisk, and plotted the general massacre of the inoffensive Israelites, had not her husband overruled her edict (their labours being needful) ...

SOLON   Mwah? Nm. Pippins.

BEGGAR-WOMAN   What imports your man?

HERODOTUS   Nay, good lady, he never doth import. Thy tale too intricate for him, he nods. Prithee continue.

BEGGAR-WOMAN   Then will I be brief. Our Ptolemy, in hopes to quiet his unruly lady, gave her apparent proofs of the Hebrew maid's demise, as manufactured by his own arch-mage – a conjuror of great proficience, known through the world as Hermes Trismegistus – who then, at Pharaoh's bidding, built a prison for that dear unfortunate. Indeed, her only fault is faultless beauty; her only crime an innocence our nation, in its present stage of decadence, not knows!

HERODOTUS   Thou hast rehearsed enough, and more than so!
For though your Ægypt sink beneath its vice
Deeper than this fabled stream at's crest,
Yet in Hellas still we cherish honour,
Beauty, innocence! What life I have henceforth
'Longs to ... Pray, the fair maid's name?

BEGGAR-WOMAN   Phao of the Hebrews.

HERODOTUS   'Longs to Phao!

BEGGAR-WOMAN   Yet hear me, good sir ...

HERODOTUS   Solon! Wake! There's work to do!

SOLON   Wha? Wake? Work?!

BEGGAR-WOMAN   Yet one word more, bold Grecian ...

SOLON Oh, somewhere Aeolus grieves his winds have 'scaped
their cave and blown themselves into this leaky bag. I will
re-dispose myself to slumber.

HERODOTUS Fool! Wake, I say! What wouldst thou, dame? Thou
holdst me back 'gainst my most active will. Here's drachmas!
Which way lies this prison? The walls thereof I'll atomize!

SOLON Adam's Eyes! Which prison?!
Whichever, lord, this crone hath witched us both,
Let's slip before we're bound. Ho, ferryman!

[Remainder of Act I not extant.]

3.2 [*Scene: The Library of Alexandria.*] *Callimachus discovered; enter Herodotus and Solon unobserved.*

CALLIMACHUS Herondas ... *Mimes* ... Hesiod ... *Theogony* ... *Works and Days* ... *On the Shield of Herakles* (note: doubtful attribution) ... Hipparchus ... *Lives of the Sophists* ...

SOLON (*to Herodotus*) What madness possesses this fellow?

HERODOTUS (*to Solon*) Hush! Let's not disturb him.

CALLIMACHUS Hippias Major ... *Minor Works* ... Hippias Minor ... *Major Works* ... Hippocrates ... *On Medicine* ... Hippolytus ... *Hippolytus* ...

SOLON (*to Herodotus*) Eureka! he is a scholar, doomed to *melancholia*.

CALLIMACHUS Homer ... *Batrachomyomachia* (note: a paltry effort at humour for so great an one) ... *Hymns* ... *Iliad* ... *Odyssey* ... *The Returns* (note: checked out; overdue) ... Horticus ... *On Gardening* ... Hyginus ... *On the Constellations* (note: scroll corrupt with worms; transfer to papyrus) ...

SOLON (*to Herodotus*) Papyrus? Be there no poets 'twixt the H's and the P's?

HERODOTUS (*to Solon*)   Peace, or we'll be found.

CALLIMACHUS   Hypsipocles ... *On Geese* ...

SOLON (*to Herodotus*)   Geese?

CALLIMACHUS (*overhearing*)   'Tis a book of cookery. Silence in the Library! Iambicus ... *Iambics* ... Ibis ...

SOLON (*to Herodotus*)   Do th'Ægyptians cook such fowl?

CALLIMACHUS (*overhearing*)   Fool! Quiet, I say.

HERODOTUS (*stepping forward*)   Most learned sir, we mean no disrespect,
Nor would we add our tedium to your task –
For camels want no superflux of sand –
We mean to ask direction, nothing more;
For you, of all in Ægypt, sure must know
The way to Pharos isle?

CALLIMACHUS   Why, what art thou that I should tell thee? The mysteries of Ægypt are not to be divulged to vagabonds from barbarous lands. Is there not light enough in Helicarnassus – is't too far north? – but thou must thieve it from our storied lamp? Or dost thou hope its flame will singe whichever one of Juno's gadflies drove thee hither across our ocean?

SOLON   Master, he is some wizard. How else should he know a Helicarnassian from a Hyperborean? Let us leave him to his incunabuluses, lest he change us into frogs.

HERODOTUS   Indeed, sir, how have you divined our nativity?

CALLIMACHUS   Thy voice betrays thee; of all the Minor Asians, ye Helicarnassians are the least happy linguists, incapable of the smallest *sigma*. (*Mimicking him*) 'Kind thir, cantht tell uth the way to Phththaroth? Ith it not thouthpheatht of Phthia?' Yet thy companion – or perhaps only his tongue – suffers from hyphaeresis; evidently he hails from the ignorant peninsula of Attica.

SOLON   I must protest, my tongue is innocent, (*sticks out his tongue*) ath you perthieve.

CALLIMACHUS   Well.

HERODOTUS   Forgive my man's impudence; your question was not undue.
Then know, most learned sir, my worthy sire,
Lyxes of Helicarnassus, e'er praised
This Ægypt for the first home, chiefest shrine,
And only school of wisdom. Yea, he spent
His latest breath in bidding me sail hither,
Take science as 'twere meat from Thoth's own beak,
And nourished thus, return surpassing wise
To Hellas, to live by this instruction,
And someday write the story of my travels.
This loyal servant, my tutor from a boy,
He sent to guard my youth.

SOLON (*aside*)   A long breath 'twas!

CALLIMACHUS   Why, this excuses altogether thine intrusion. O worthy embassy! Hadst thou not told me your father's name, I would deem so wise a Greek Odysseus himself, and thou Telemachus, and I shall be a Mentor to thee.

SOLON (*aside*)   Then am I out of my part, or am I to play Penelope?

HERODOTUS   We thank thee for thy kindness, yet only wish to know the way to Pharos. We would not hinder thee thine awesome task.

CALLIMACHUS   Ah, my *Pinakes*, or catalogue of the Library? Nay, by Ammon's horns, let that rest awhile, for to speak truth, of all Pharaoh's edicts 'tis the most tyrannical, that I must waste mine eyes to tadpoles in such a stream of names and titles. Sisyphus' stone excepted, there is no more endless nor more thankless labour than an index. But come, let me tell thee of Ægypt, for 'tis a land of wonders.

HERODOTUS Aye, we have heard tell of them, yet must we postpone the pleasure of hearing them again recounted, for in our haste ...

CALLIMACHUS Pray, what hast thou heard, and from what source?

SOLON A blind beggar-woman on the Bankside, most aged in her wisdom. You must add her name to your *Pinochles*.

CALLIMACHUS Pshaw! These crones swarm the banks as thick as do the crabs, yet are they worse for pestering travellers with gossip. I hope ye gave her no money and paid her no heed?

HERODOTUS Why, we offered some small charity, and were richly repaid with tales of Ægypt.

CALLIMACHUS Tales indeed! I beseech thee, worthy Hellene, let not such dockside ignorance, like a contrary wind, hinder thy voyage for wisdom! Rather, I pray thee use me – the foremost scholar of the world – to fulfil thy father's dying wish. Ah, the wonders I will tell thee! For even the smallest creatures in this land perform miracles. Nay, look not incredulous, for far within the western desert, a singular tribe of ants extracts gold ore from deep within the earth! How do they this, thou wilt now ask? First, they form a column thousands-strong ...

HERODOTUS Nay, we've heard tell of the ants.

SOLON Aye, these ants file thorough Ægypt millions-strong, as we'd left a rind of cheese a week on a window-sill, or Hector's redolent corpse on the ground fore Achilles' Myrmidons. Prithee, no more gilded ants.

CALLIMACHUS Then let me tell thee of a most remarkable animal that lives upon the Nile – a monster not to be believed ere seen – called the crocodile ...

SOLON Oh sir, we spied many of these cockadoodles under the bridge on our way here. Perchance thou dost not leave the Library so oft?

HERODOTUS Indeed, most learned sir, our pressing haste ...

CALLIMACHUS   Why then ... know'st thou then of great *cerastes*, the horned serpent?

HERODOTUS   A snake with horns say'st thou? Well. Monstrous to our Greek imaginations, and most interesting withal. Horns, Solon! What more is there to tell? And now, about that Tower ...

CALLIMACHUS   And on this very topic of herpetology, we possess here in the Library the definitive papyrus on *ophies pteretoi*, a serpent fledged as the hawk!

HERODOTUS   Aye, of these monsters likewise we've been told.

SOLON   Flying, if't be creditable, through the atmosphere.

CALLIMACHUS   A heaven swarming, I assure thee, with greater wonders than such winged serpents! For here in miraculous Ægypt, or rather southerly toward mystic Thebes, there is millennially birthed, and millennially immolated, the sole and supermortal Phoenix!

SOLON   Yea, th'Æthiopian Memnon?

CALLIMACHUS   Ha! Osiris almighty! Æthiopia?! The pea-brained Pygmies hold that parched waste to be the source of Nile, whenever the Cranes disgorge them long enough to testify. Nay, the Phoenix is absolutely and uniquely Ægyptian.

HERODOTUS   Grant this fowl solely Memphian, not one jot Memnonian, yet I prithee remember our first inquiry into the Tower of Pharos ...

SOLON   News of this Tower, indeed, were to us all the ant-gold and phoenix-feather of Africa.

CALLIMACHUS   The Lighthouse of Pharos? Why, 'tis the highest structure this side Asia (or, to tell scholarly true, the highest visible structure)! Have ye Grecians eyes? Canst not perceive that Tower from anywhere in the city – nay, through this very casement?

SOLON   Truly, there rises a most visible Tower of lofty proportion!

CALLIMACHUS   For a swallow of beer, or anything like a coin, one of the fishermen will ferry ye to the island.

HERODOTUS   And from this Tower's height, that of Glass shall be perceptible?

CALLIMACHUS   Nay, I promise ye not that. The Glass Tower may never be perceived by mortal eye; it is as lost to the lynx or the eagle as to us. Yet if any Alexandrian know its secrets, it is Manetho.

HERODOTUS   What's he?

CALLIMACHUS   A seer of hundredfold foresight, though after his hundredfold years on earth, he's as blind as the eldest mole-rat in Sinai. He dwelleth two streets over.

HERODOTUS   Sweet librarian!

SOLON   May thy researches ever yield thee esoteria of thy farthest fantasies!

CALLIMACHUS   The *roc*, thou mean'st? With quills like spear-shafts and feathers like main-sails, seizing in its elephantine talons the wild beasts of the earth?! 'Tis rumoured, lost in this Library, we possess a map leading to its nest in Madagascar, laden with adamantine eggs!

HERODOTUS   And truly, good Callimachus, I wish thee fortune in all thy researches, whether into papyrus or rocks, but for this moment, know'st thou some egress from this wondrous building, nearest the Tower of Pharos? For we continue in haste.

CALLIMACHUS   Yea, knowledge-seeking sons of Greece, use the librarians' exit to the left, through the geography section.

SOLON   Ah, now there I might devote some hours. Indeed, Callimachus, hast thou heard of a land – or a land that was, ere sunk beneath the sea – called Atlantis, once a powerful Greek city-state?

CALLIMACHUS   An Ægyptian empire of old, I assure thee, though sunk indeed, and not to be recovered until the Pharaoh Akhnaton, a millennium hence, will raise it through hydraulic science beyond our ken.

HERODOTUS   And until that glorious day, worthy Callimachus, we wish thee well, and must now take our leave.

SOLON   About this Atlantis, I suspect more research might re-establish it a Greek isle after all ...

HERODOTUS   Solon, let us go, and leave Atlantis to her depths, for we are in present haste.

SOLON   Farewell then, worthy bibliographer. I shall scribble to thee.

CALLIMACHUS   And I shall keep thy writings safe, good Pelasgian.
Exeunt.

[Act 3, scene 3 not extant.]

3.4   [*Scene: Pharos; lower stage is the beach; upper stage is the Lighthouse*]; *enter Herodotus, Solon, and Halieuticus, the two latter drunken.*

HALIEUTICUS   And thish, my mashtersh, ish Phpharosh.

HERODOTUS   Make haste, Solon, for that babbling librarian and this bibbling ferryman have between them devoured much of our table of time.

SOLON   And much of my wineskin of wine.

HERODOTUS   O Poseidon, have we wronged you, that this fellow rowed us half to Ormus and back merely to prolong his tippling? An hour lost. Wise mentor, to thine eyes, seems the heaven darker than 'tis wont at this hour?

SOLON   Nay, mine eyes are bleared with age and with this selfsame wine wherewith we have bribed our ferryman.

HERODOTUS (*taking the wineskin*)   Hast drunk no more than so? Then this southerly sun hath warmed thy little spirit into fumes, which reeking thence into thy little brains, have wasted what little wisdom time had left thee. And still thou swim'st better than this great whale, for – I will write upon't – nothing sinks faster than a Nile fisherman. Bacchus, angry at the Ægyptians for his maltreatment as Horus, hath curs'd them with weak stomachs, and drowns them by the thimbleful. Yet we need his boat; delay him, good tutor, some half an hour, until I return from the Tower.

SOLON   Even now he is delayed full length on the strand, and snoring as to be heard above Thule. How now, Halieuticus?

HALIEUTICUS   GGGGGGWWWWWWAAAAAAAHHHHHHH!!!! SZSZSZSZSZSZSZSZ ...

SOLON   Homer had his Stentor, Herodotus his Halieuticus.

HERODOTUS   At all events, wake him not, but leave some of thy wine by his side, so he rises not but to renew oblivion.

SOLON   Good my lord, this unmixed Chian cost me many a drachma in our last Hellenic port; sure I have spent enough on him already?

HERODOTUS   Bad my man, thou know'st 'tis the foulest garbage any port swindler ever sold to an old sot. I here promise thee an hundred of true Chian when we return, and thou shalt toast my wedding with bright Phao. But let us not remain here below, observing this fellow snore, when th'ecstatic sight of her we seek floats a staircase above us!

SOLON   Fisherman, dream on bream and wake not, lest my life's-blood purple these barbaric shores.

HERODOTUS   Nay, linger not, for thou hast more in thy pocket, as sure as snakes do fly.

SOLON (*producing another wineskin from his pocket*)   Indeed, sir, Pythia never spoke truer. I have a dram yet. But this door is fast, and too thick for our shoulders. I'll knock.

He knocks lightly on the door.

HERODOTUS Knock louder, for 'twill grow dark while we stand here on the porch like tax-men. Keeper! At home, good keeper?!

SOLON (*pounding on the door*) Keeper! Ho! Keep'st thou at home?

SPORADICUS (*within*) Go away!

SOLON (*pounding louder*) Present thy colours, or 'twill be thy tower's ruin! Good captain, let us use these oars for rams!

HERODOTUS Nay, bombastic ensign, or we are stranded, for they must carry us again to Alexandria.

SOLON Thy wisdom shows thee still an Odysseus, nor would I wish more time with this ornery Calypso here. I'll knock yet louder.

He kicks the door. Enter Sporadicus above.

SPORADICUS By the last asp of Nile! What barbarous army, strayed from the field, so tattoos my misfortunate door?

HERODOTUS Good keeper! Greetings from faraway Greece! We crave but a few moments of your time. Pray you, open this door unto us, and let us view the city from your aerie. I shall load you with drachmas!

SPORADICUS Fool! Know'st not that door to be as far vertically from where I stand as thou art southerly from Greece? With thy breath and thy man's, I'd not attempt these stairs for all the ambrosia on Olympus. Beside, Pharaoh's man keeps me in beer. Away with you!

HERODOTUS (*to Solon*) 'Beer'? What is it? Is't currency?

SOLON (*to Herodotus*) I've never heard of it. (*To Sporadicus*) How many beers for one skin of undiluted wine of the first water?

SPORADICUS 'Wine'? Is't some Greek commodity?

SOLON 'Tis what th'ancients meant by 'ambrosia'. Descend, my chuck, and I'll instruct thee in the ways of Zeus, when he is most delightful.

HERODOTUS (*to Solon, indicating Halieuticus*)   Ay, rest him here by stormy Poseidon, so long as he opens this door.

SOLON (*to Herodotus*)   Like thunder or a crashing wave, I'll bring him down. (*To Sporadicus*) A merry challenge, lad! Let's change healths, myself with thy bear, thou with my *vinum*, and an angel to the first touches bottom.

SPORADICUS   I'll touch bottom to angle with thee, worthy Grecian! A moment, whilst I fetch my beer.

HERODOTUS   Ay, fetch thy bier indeed, so thou wilt open to me this door.

[Remainder of *The Fair Maid of Alexandria* not extant.]

Dan Moss is an associate professor in the English Department at Southern Methodist University in Dallas. He received his B.A. from Brandeis University and his Ph.D. from Princeton University, where he was a Mellon Fellow. Specializing in late 16th-century poetry and drama, Dan's book, *The Ovidian Vogue: Literary Fashion and Imitative Practice in Late Elizabethan Poetry* (Toronto, 2014), maps the wide-ranging effects of Ovid's pre-eminence as a source for imitation by the poets and playwrights of the 1590s. His work has also appeared in *Modern Philology, Critical Survey, Spenser Studies, The Spenser Review*, and in edited collections. Dan's book in progress, *The Play within the Plays: Shakespeare, the Chamberlain's Men, and the Continuity of Metatheater*, argues that Shakespeare's professional circumstances gave rise to a systematic and continuous metatheater, which transcended the individual play and provided regular playgoers with an evolving "shadow-play" starring fictional versions of company personalities.

Chapter 8
A Tragedy of the Plantation of Virginia

David Nicol

Readers of this volume will by now be familiar with the surprise discovery of six pages from a hitherto unknown quarto edition of the lost 1623 play *A Tragedy of the Plantation of Virginia*. The pages, found stuffed behind a wall in the Cock and Bull public house in the village of Blayton Tokes, must rank among the most remarkable finds of this century. We here present the first annotated, modern-spelling edition of the fragile but still readable fragment.

Previously, *The Plantation of Virginia* had been known only from an entry in the office-book of Sir Henry Herbert, Master of the Revels:

> August [1623]
> A Tragedy of the Plantation of Virginia, the <prophaness left out> contayninge 16 sheets and one <leaf> may be acted <els not for the> companye at the Curtune
> Founde fault with the length of this playe & <commanded a> reformation in all their other playes.[1]

Scholars had long been fascinated by this entry, as it records the earliest English play known to have been set in the North Ameri-

Notes for this section begin on page 160.

can colonies; the earliest *surviving* play had been Aphra Behn's *The Widow Ranter*, written some sixty years later.[2] The new discovery has exceeded expectations, as it reveals *The Plantation of Virginia* to have been the earliest known dramatization of the lives of Captain John Smith, the governor of Jamestown, and Pocahontas, the daughter of Chief Powhatan who married the plantation owner John Rolfe and became a celebrity in London before her untimely death in 1616. The revelation of this subject matter now gives added point to Smith's complaint in 1630 that 'they have acted my fatall Tragedies upon the Stage'.[3]

The author of the play is unknown. The surviving scene includes several words and phrases that David J. Lake considers to be strong indicators of the presence of Thomas Dekker and John Ford.[4] However, other characteristics argue against the author being a professional playwright, in particular the unusually close reliance on sources. The verse is often clumsy, and the most metrically awkward sections occur at those moments when the wording of the source material is followed most closely. In other places, the author steals passages outright: the lengthiest examples are John Rolfe's encomium to Virginia, which is a lightly adapted version of a passage about the Spice Islands in John Fletcher's *The Island Princess* (1621), and Pocahontas's panegyric to Britain, which is a patchwork of quotations from Michael Drayton's *Poly-Olbion* (1612–22). Such sequences go beyond the normal amount of borrowing in early modern drama, suggesting the work of an inexperienced playwright. One way of harmonizing the evidence is to propose that Dekker and Ford revised the work of an amateur playwright who was enthusiastic about the colony. This hypothesis is supported by the fact that several of the play's sources were unpublished at the time of writing and must have been read in manuscript, including John Smith's *General History of Virginia, New England, and the Summer Isles*, which was not published until the following year, and John Chamberlain's private letters to Sir Dudley Carleton. The unknown author may, therefore, have known Chamberlain or Carleton, and must have had a close relationship with individuals associated with the Virginia Company.

Readers expecting a play faithful to documented fact will, however, be disappointed, as *The Plantation of Virginia* includes the earliest known example of the fictional romance between Pocahontas and Smith that would be reworked endlessly in the centuries to follow.⁵ It is easy to understand why the author chose to do this, as the last events of Pocahontas's life – her marriage to Rolfe, their journey to London, and her death from unknown causes – are lacking in conventional drama. The surviving scene is located at the beginning of Act 5, and takes place in England. In the previous acts, we must presume, the English have arrived in Virginia and the legendary rescuing of Smith by Pocahontas has occurred, but before love could fully blossom, Smith has been injured in an accident and so has had to return home, with Pocahontas left believing him to be dead. Upon the arrival of more colonists, she has been abducted by the English and has married John Rolfe after being baptized. In the surviving scene, the author dramatizes an event from Smith's *General History* in which Smith re-encounters Pocahontas in Brentford and has an enigmatic conversation with her. The author adds a fictional rivalry between Rolfe and Smith that culminates in them exiting to a duelling field. It is uncertain what was to happen in the final scenes, although presumably Pocahontas died – perhaps by running between their swords as she promises at the end of the fragment.

The portrayal of Pocahontas is undeniably a product of the colonialist mindset of the time. Inspired perhaps by John Chamberlain's remark that Pocahontas was reluctant to return to Virginia, the author places into her mouth a panegyric to Britain, borrowing lines directly from Michael Drayton's *Poly-Olbion*; there could be no better illustration of the ways in which Pocahontas's image could be appropriated to advertise English colonial expansion. Yet despite its reiteration of romantic clichés and imperialist discourse, the play's version of Pocahontas has considerable defiance and poise. Although she wears English dress, in the manner of the Simon van der Passe engraving of 1617, and although she is referred to as Rebecca Rolfe (the author uses the speech prefix 'Rebecca' throughout this scene, although it might have been different earlier in the play), her bearing is reminiscent of Quisara, the Indonesian heroine of Fletcher's *The Island Princess*. Gordon McMullan has argued that Fletcher's play has thematic connections with the marriage of Pocahontas and Rolfe;⁶ conversely, Quisara's regal and only partially exoticized demeanour may have been the author's model for Pocahontas, who was promoted in 1616–17 as the daughter of a mighty emperor.⁷

Any originality lacking in the main characters is made up for by the minor characters, as the author's wide reading produced some remarkable characterizations. One surprise is the appearance of the letter writer John Chamberlain, portrayed as a waggish figure always ready with a jovial quip. Even more startling is the depiction of Tomocomo, a holy man who accompanied Pocahontas across the Atlantic and stubbornly rejected Christianity: the author has transformed him into a classic Jacobean malcontent.

However, the most extraordinary feature of *The Plantation of Virginia* is that the surviving text inadvertently preserves the marginal comments of Sir Henry Herbert, made during his censorship of the text; apparently the compositor did not understand that the offending passages were to be cut.[8] Herbert was clearly outraged by Tomocomo's favouring of his own god Okeus over the Christian god, and by his disappointment with King James. His comments are a rare glimpse into the workings of the Revels Office, and illustrate the political sensitivity of the ideas that the colonization of the Americas was raising.

Yet the greatest mystery of all concerning this text is the presence of ideas, images, and even lines of dialogue that echo Terrence Malick's 2006 film *The New World*. The similarities are undeniable, and yet the film was made several years before the discovery of the *Plantation at Virginia* fragments. This extraordinary coincidence has of course provoked scepticism about the authenticity of the fragments. Yet analysis of the paper and ink proves without doubt that they were printed in the late 1620s. Malick's legendary avoidance of interviews makes further questions fruitless, and even the most rational scholar is reduced merely to speculation on great minds and their likeness of thought.

A Tragedy of the Plantation of Virginia

ACTUS QUINTUS, Scæna Prima.

Enter as from dinner, CHAMBERLAIN[9] *and* WATFORD.

WATFORD   In truth, my friend, the princess is indeed
More fair than any English lady known.

CHAMBERLAIN   She is a princess and she must be fair:
That's the prerogative of being royal.[10]

WATFORD   Why, sure you jest! Were she but a serving
  Wench, she'd blast the charms of any she
  Who'd claim the royal'st lineage in the land.

CHAMBERLAIN   Pish, no fair lady is she – yet with her
  Tricking up with titles and high styles
  You'd think her and this Rolfe to be someone.
  Know you not that the Virginia Company,
  Merely to clothe her, gives 'em four pound a week?[11]

> *Enter* ROLFE, TOMOCOMO, *gentlemen;* REBECCA[12] *attended by ladies both English and Virginian. Tomocomo stands apart.*

ROLFE   Join us my friends, and let us celebrate
  Our dear Rebecca, whose presence here
  Hath charmed our nation and buoyed our spirits.

> *All cry, 'Rebecca, Rebecca'.*

REBECCA   My English hosts, you shame me with this warmth.
  'Tis more than I deserve; I blush to hear you.

TOMOCOMO [*aside*]   She shames herself to fawn thus on these English.

WATFORD [*aside to Chamberlain*]   She's formal and she's civil in her manner![13]
  Yet who's that man who with his savage air
  Doth cast upon us all so dark a pall?

CHAMBERLAIN   Tomocomo is his name and he's her
  Father's counsellor[14] – a melancholic
  And one who shows no love for being here.[15]
  Come, let's join 'em.

WATFORD   Master Rolfe, you bless us
  With the presence here of this your lovely wife.
  I have seen English ladies worse in looks,
  Proportions and behaviour.[16]

1 LADY   'Tis true sir,
   She's been esteemed by many noble sorts
   And by the King himself.[17]

REBECCA   You flatter me. And
   Let not rumour thus report my fame so falsely.

TOMOCOMO [*aside*]   She flatters them and masks herself with
   words.

ROLFE   And now, my friends and good companions,
   Gather, for I have news you all should know.
   Let all here be the first to hear: it pleaseth
   Me that instantly, my dearest wife and I
   Will swift return to fair Virginia's shore.
   Our crops of sweet tobacco wait us there.

TOMOCOMO [*aside*]   I like this well, 'tis music to me![18]

REBECCA   Say'st thou so, my lord? And not in jest?
   We've been in England but six month. Think'st thou
   To return so soon? I've yet seen little
   Of this land.[19]

ROLFE   My sweet Rebecca, speak'st thou
   Aright? Dost thou not long to see thy home?

REBECCA   It moves me not. 'Tis thy new world, not mine.

CHAMBERLAIN   She's too much an Englishwoman now, sir!

ROLFE   Sweet lady, canst thou spurn thine own Virginia?
   Thy home is blest among the Western lands!
   Its every wind that rises blows perfumes
   And every breath of air is like an incense.
   The treasure of the earth there dwells and
   Nothing we see but breeds an admiration.
   The very waters, as we float along,
   Present us oysters and the cod to court us.
   The soils of the land do swell and bloom
   With corn, tobacco and the noble squash;
   Nothing that bears a life but brings a treasure.

> The people they show brave, too: civil-mannered,
> Proportioned like the masters of great minds.
> The women, which I wonder at –

WATFORD   Ye speak well!

ROLFE   Of delicate aspects, fair, clearly beauteous,
> And to that admiration, sweet and courteous.[20]
> Rebecca, is this not your land? Why spurn't?
> Pray tell me, is it not a wond'rous place?

REBECCA   It is. But I have seen it.

ROLFE   What of our son? Must he not see his home?

REBECCA   He is not of Virginia nor
> Is he of England. He is a world himself.

CHAMBERLAIN   It seems she'll go back sore against her will, sir![21]

TOMOCOMO [*aside*]   She'll lose herself and all her father taught her.

REBECCA   Oh sweet my lord, I've been here but three month,
> And all I've known is London and Gravesend.
> Wilt thou remove me thus, before I've seen
> The wonders of your glorious Albion here?
> Carried you me across an ocean, yet
> Wilt thou permit a taste of England only?
> To me, this country is a brave new world[22]
> And seems to me a paradise on Earth.[23]
> The summer's not too short, the winter not
> Too long; the heat kills not the cold nor cold
> Expels the heat; no rain's too heavy nor
> No wind's too great;[24] this isle's the Golden Mean.
> And oft I hear of Britain's wonders too.
> Of Plymouth, where the navies lie, as do
> The thund'ring cannons that the world defy.[25]
> Of Wales, that ancient land, which still has been
> The craggy nurse of all the British race.[26]
> Of Durham's stately seated towers,[27] and
> Of the burning rock called coal from Newcastle,
> Famed no less than India for its mines.[28]

Of Evesham's Vale and Avon's winding stream,
Where thick and well-grown fog doth mat the green
Pastures where the dainty clover grows[29] and
Leads the way to Warwick's mighty fort.
Of that great edifice the Pictswall, built by
Romans full eighty miles in length twixt Tyne
And Eden,[30] standing still firm 'gainst ruin.
And of the mighty peaks of Cumbria,
Upon whose hoary heads cold winter long
Doth keep, yet pleasant springs and large-spread lakes
From them their clear beginnings make and flow.[31]
Oh Master Rolfe! How can we home so soon
When unseen wond'rous marvels still await
In this my new-found land of Britain? Pray
Pity me and let us stay a longer while!

ROLFE   It cannot be, my love. Our fields of fresh
Tobacco call, and thou, my wife,
Must keep still at my side.

CHAMBERLAIN   Come, gentle lady!
If you're to be an Englishwoman, you'll
Obey, for disobedience is foreign.

TOMOCOMO   Matoaka,[32] Powhatan awaits you,
And will not brook delay. Obey your man.

REBECCA   On every side I am beset.[33] [*To Rolfe*] My lord
I'll go, but with a disappointed heart.

ROLFE   My love, I swear to you I'll make a home
There for us where we'll live in bliss.

Knock within.

WATFORD   Who's that who knocks? 'Tis late, and woundy cold.

Enter SERVANT.

SERVANT   One Captain Smith desires entrance, sirs.

ROLFE   Captain Smith?

TOMOCOMO   Ha?

REBECCA   What means this?

CHAMBERLAIN   Captain
Smith!
I partly know the man. The fellow's brave,
And helped to found your colony.

ROLFE   Why yes,
But little do I know him. [*To servant*] Show him in.

                                         [*Exit servant.*]

REBECCA   It cannot be!

ROLFE.   Rebecca?

REBECCA   Say not so!
This must but be a dream, my honoured lord.

Enter SMITH *as from riding;*[34] REBECCA *falls in a swoon.*[35]

WATFORD   Look to the lady there!

ROLFE   Rebecca!
What means this?

1 LADY   Nay sir, give her some air there!

[*The women tend Rebecca aside.*]

ROLFE   Why Captain Smith, what means this sudden entrance?
You see the lady's startled.

SMITH.   Your pardon,
Master Rolfe, I had no ill intention –
'Twas meant to be a happy visit. When
Learned I of your presence here in Brentford,
I thought to make acquaintance, and to see
Once more the lady Pocahontas.[36] [*To Chamberlain and Watford*]
Sirs,
I'm glad to see that you are here as well.

CHAMBERLAIN   The delight is ours!

WATFORD   I joy to hear your talk.

TOMOCOMO [*coming forward*]   Chawnzmit.[37]

SMITH   Can it be? Do these mine eyes deceive me?

TOMOCOMO   They did tell us always you were dead, Chawnzmit.
   Our king did not believe them.[38] I see now
   That he judged aright, and understands you all.

ROLFE   Thus comes it, sir, that she is so perplexed.
   Thy presence is cause of great alarm
   As thou may'st see. Perhaps 'twere best you leave.

SMITH   My lord, I meant no harm in coming here.
   If't please you, I'll speak one word more here with
   This gentleman, whose news I long to hear.

ROLFE   As you wish.

        [ROLFE *attends* REBECCA *aside.*]

SMITH   What think you of England, my friend?

TOMOCOMO   My lord Powhatan bade me find you out,
   And see your God, your King, your Queen and Prince
   You told us so much of.[39]

SMITH   And saw you them?
   What think you of our God?

TOMOCOMO   I have not seen
   Your God. You Englishmen talk much of him
   And yet I see him not. With these mine eyes
   I've seen Okeus.[40] I'll serve no hidden God.   *I like not this*[41]

SMITH   Then Tomocomo wilt thou not repent
   And love our Lord? Wilt thou be damned to hell?

TOMOCOMO   If thou must preach, preach to the boys and girls
   Of my nation. I am too old to learn.
                              Profane and must be left out[42]

CHAMBERLAIN   I' faith, the fellow is very zealous
   In his blasphemous superstitions![43]

SMITH   What think you of our King?

TOMOCOMO   We saw not him.

CHAMBERLAIN   Why, sure, you did. D'ee[44] not recall the masque?
   I saw that you were placèd well. And there
   It was His Majesty did honour you.[45]

TOMOCOMO   We met no King that day.

WATFORD   You did, you did!
   King James himself did nod to you, and smiled.

TOMOCOMO   Was that man the King?
                              Full of faults and must be corrected.[46]

SMITH   'Tis sure, nothing more sure![47]
   [*Pause.*] Why art thou silent?

TOMOCOMO   You gave Powhatan
   A white dog, which Powhatan fed as himself.
   But to me your King gave nothing, and I am
   Better than your white dog.[48]
                              Leave this out wholly, at your own peril.[49]

                    REBECCA *stirs.*

1 LADY   She stirs! Good sir, step back a little.

ROLFE   Rebecca!

REBECCA   My lord! Forgive my folly.

1 LADY   Let her stand.

REBECCA   I am standing. Pray excuse
   My fond and foolish weakness, good my lord.

ROLFE 'Twas not thy fault; this brash intrusion did
   Thee startle so. I'll have the man removed.
   [*To Smith*] Pray leave us, having frighted so a lady
   With your uncouth and ill-judgèd entrance.

SMITH I'll take my leave and never see thee more.
   Rebecca, adieu.

REBECCA   Stay yet! [*To Rolfe*] Good my lord,
   Allow me still some discourse with the man.
   Though yet his ghostlike entrance startled me,
   Able am I now to keep composure.
   Pray let me speak some words with him.

ROLFE My lady, he's a vagabond, a dull
   Wretch turned from mercenary to author.
   Why wouldst thou give an ear to such a man?
   As thou art my wife, desist: let Smith begone.

REBECCA I speak not as thy wife but as ambassadress
   Of my dear father's empire. This man was
   Once Powhatan's bosom friend who bade me
   Seek him out. I say I'll speak with him and
   Not be silenced in this matter.

CHAMBERLAIN   'Tis true,
   The lady doth outrank you, sir! If she
   Hath diplomatic business, 'tis her due.

ROLFE One minute only may you speak with him,
   For we must preparation make for sea.

ROLFE, CHAMBERLAIN, WATFORD, TOMOCOMO, LADIES *withdraw; Rolfe looks angrily on* SMITH *and* REBECCA *who speak in private conference.*

REBECCA And did you find your Indies, Captain Smith?

SMITH I fear I sailed right past them, Mistress Rolfe.[50]

REBECCA They told us you were dead, father. 'Tis both
   A joy and grief that I was thus deceived.
   Would that time could turn backward. But 'tis done.

SMITH Rebecca, thou must not call me 'father'.

REBECCA Did you not promise Powhatan that what
 Was yours was his? And did not he the like
 To you? You called him 'father', being in
 His land a stranger, and 'tis reason I
 Must do the same for you.

SMITH   Nay, thou must not:
 I durst not let thee title me that way,
 For thou art daughter of a mighty king,
 And I am but a captain, rude and low.

REBECCA Yet wert thou not afraid to come into
 My father's kingdom, causing fear in him
 And all his people (save but me)? And fear
 You here that I should call you 'father'? No,
 I say to you I will, and you shall call
 Me 'child', and so I will be for ever
 And ever your countryman. They did tell
 Us always you were dead, and I knew no
 Other till I saw thee here; yet Powhatan
 Did command Tomocomo seek you and
 Know the truth, because your countrymen will
 Lie much. Enough. My embassy is done.
 Farewell.

 Exit, bearing a well-set countenance.[51] *Ladies exeunt after.*

ROLFE [*coming forward*] She is offended. See, she stalks away.[52]

TOMOCOMO [*aside*] 'Tis well, I see she's not all English yet!

ROLFE You have insulted my sweet lady, Smith.
 How answer you this? What saidst thou to her?

SMITH I'm all this while a-going, sir.[53]

ROLFE   Stay, sir.
 What didst thou say?

SMITH   'Twas nothing, good my lord;
   I'll leave you.

ROLFE   Villain! I have too long borne
   Your bitter scoffs in silence.[54] Thou, thou art
   A scoundrel and an overweening rogue.

SMITH   I mean no quarrel with you, sir, nor with
   Your virtuous wife. I'll trouble you no more,
   And will undertake a voluntary exile.[55]

ROLFE   False upstart! I have heard what's said of you.
   You would have made yourself a king, they say,[56]
   By marrying Rebecca in Virginia.[57]
   I fancy still thou harbour'st those desires.

CHAMBERLAIN   Nay, sir, you take too much of that for truth.
   'Tis true he ever much respected her,
   But marriage could no way have titled him
   A king, nor was he e'er suspected so,
   For in troth he no more regarded her
   Than in honest reason and discretion.[58]

TOMOCOMO   My lord, I'll speak now, with a plain man's words.

ROLFE   What's this? Virginian, tell us what thou know'st.

TOMOCOMO   I knew this man when lived he with my people.
   If he would, he might have married her; nay,
   Have done what him listed, for there was none
   That could have hinder'd his determination.[59]

ROLFE   This flame will fire me into present ashes![60]
   Captain Smith, you have insulted me, my
   Household and my wife. I'll meet thee on the field.

SMITH   Master Rolfe, I wish not this.

CHAMBERLAIN.   The gentleman
   Has dared you, sir, you're bound to quarrel.

SMITH. Then so be it. Lead on sir, I will follow.

> *Exeunt* [SMITH, ROLFE, CHAMBERLAIN *and* WATFORD] *as to the field. Manet* TOMOCOMO, *smiling at the event.*[61] *Then enter* REBECCA.

REBECCA Why sir, where goes my lord and Captain Smith?

TOMOCOMO The English dogs are gone to use their swords.
They love you both and both, I hope, will die.
I smile to see the discord thou hast sown.

REBECCA Oh cursèd fate! I'll stop them yet! I'll run
Between their swords and save them both!   *Exit.*

TOMOCOMO Go, Pocahontas, trait'ress to thy land!
Go Smith, go Rolfe, both English swine alike!
This new-found land's a dog-hole; I'll away.
I've hated England ever since I alighted,
And whosoever dies I'll be delighted.   *Exit.*

David Nicol is Associate Director of Theatre at the Fountain School of Performing Arts, Dalhousie University. His principal research area is Jacobean drama; he is the author of *Middleton and Rowley: Forms of Collaboration in the Jacobean Playhouse* (University of Toronto Press, 2012) and has published numerous articles on Rowley's plays in such journals as *Comparative Drama, Early Theatre, Medieval and Renaissance Drama in England, Shakespeare Bulletin* and *Studies in English Literature*, as well as in the *Encyclopedia of English Renaissance Literature* (Blackwell, 2012). His most recent work is the stage history section of the forthcoming New Variorum edition of *A Midsummer Night's Dream* for the Modern Language Association and he is currently working on an edition of Rowley's *All's Lost* by Lust for Digital Renaissance Editions, as well as his ongoing online project, *Henslowe's Diary ... as a Blog*. He has also published an article on Terrence Malick's *The New World* for the film journal *Screening the Past*.

Notes

1. N.W. Bawcutt, *The Control and Censorship of Caroline Drama: The Records of Sir Henry Herbert, Master of the Revels* (Oxford: Clarendon Press, 1996), 141–2. The angle brackets enclose words used by only one of the two transcribers of Herbert's office-book.

2. For a summary of scholarship on the play, see David McInnis, 'Plantation of Virginia, The', *Lost Plays Database*, 2014, http://www.lostplays.org/index.php/Plantation_of_Virginia,_The.

3. John Smith, 'The True Travels, Adventures, and Observations of Captaine John Smith' (1630), in *The Complete Works of Captain John Smith*, ed. Philip L. Barbour (Chapel Hill: University of North Carolina Press, 1986), vol. 3, 141.

4. David J. Lake, *The Canon of Thomas Middleton's Plays: Internal Evidence for the Major Problems of Authorship* (Cambridge: Cambridge University Press, 1975).

5. The love affair narrative was popularized by John Davis's *Travels in the United States of America* (1803); see Robert S. Tilton, *Pocahontas: The Evolution of an American Narrative* (Cambridge: Cambridge University Press, 1994), 35.

6. Gordon McMullan, *The Politics of Unease in the Plays of John Fletcher* (Amherst: University of Massachusetts Press, 1994), 222–35.

7. Karen Robertson, 'Pocahontas at the Masque', *Signs* 21 (1996), 553.

8. This accident is not without precedent. The printed text of Thomas Jordan's *The Walks of Islington and Hogsdon* faithfully reprints Sir Henry Herbert's licence at the end. See Gerald Eades Bentley, *The Profession of Dramatist in Shakespeare's Time, 1590–1642* (Princeton: Princeton University Press, 1971), 146.

9. **CHAMBERLAIN.** Apparently a caricature of the socialite John Chamberlain, whose letters to Dudley Carleton provide some of the few surviving references to Pocahontas's reception in London. There is clear evidence that the author(s) had read Chamberlain's letters, and the characterization of him reflects his generally condescending attitude toward Pocahontas.

10. **She is ... being royal.** A direct borrowing from Fletcher's *The Island Princess*, 1.1.45–6. Act, scene and line references to this play refer to *The Dramatic Works in the Beaumont and Fletcher Canon*, ed. Fredson Bowers, vol. 5 (Cambridge: Cambridge University Press, 1982).

11. **Pish ... a week?** *Cf.* John Chamberlain, *The Letters of John Chamberlain*, ed. Norman Egbert McClure, vol. 2 (Philadelphia: The American Philosophical Society, 1939), 56–7: 'Here is a fine picture of no fayre Lady and yet with her tricking up and high stile and titles you might thincke her and her worshipfull husband to be somebody, yf you do not know that the poore companie of Virginia out of theyre povertie are faine to allow her fowre pound a weeke for her maintenance'.

12. **REBECCA.** Pocahontas was christened 'Rebecca' before she married John Rolfe. The playwrights use her English name in the surviving fragment, although it is conceivable that they used 'Pocahontas' in earlier scenes.

13. **She's formal ... her manner!** *Cf.* John Smith, 'The Generall Historie of Virginia, New-England, and the Summer Isles' (1624), in his *Complete Works*, vol. 2, 258: '[Pocahontas] was become very formall and civill after our English manner'.

14. **Her father's counsellor.** *Cf.* Chamberlain, *Letters*, vol. 2, 50: 'The Virginian woman Poca-huntas, with her father counsaillor hath ben with the King'.

15. **Yet who's ... being here.** Although the representation of Tomocomo as a malcontent relies on Jacobean stage convention, it apparently has an element of truth; Samuel Argall, 'Samuel Argall to Council for Virginia[?], June 9, 1617', in *The Records of the Virginia Company of London*, ed. Susan Myra Kingsbury, vol. 3 (Washington, D.C., 1906), 73, describes Tomocomo returning to Virginia after Pocahontas's death, where he 'rails against England, English people'.

16. **I have ... behaviour.** Cf. Smith, 'Generall Historie', vol. 2, 261: 'divers Courtiers and others ... generally concluded ... they have seene many English Ladies worse favoured, proportioned and behavioured'.
17. **She's been ... King himself.** Cf. Smith, 'Generall Historie', vol. 2, 261–2: 'I have heard, it pleased both the King and Queenes Majestie honorably to esteeme her, accompanied with that honourable Lady the Lady De la Ware, and that honourable Lord her husband, and divers other persons of good qualities'.
18. **'Tis music to me!** A phrase characteristic of Dekker, paralleled in *Match Me in London* and *The Spanish Gypsy*; it may be evidence for his authorship of this section. See Lake, *Canon*, 224.
19. Pocahontas's reluctance to return to Virginia is mentioned in Chamberlain, *Letters*, vol. 2, 50: 'She is on her return (though sore against her will) yf the wind wold come about to send them away'.
20. **Thy home ... and courteous.** This long passage is taken almost in its entirety from Fletcher's *Island Princess*, 1.3.16–36, with some adjustments to make it refer to the characteristics of Virginia rather than the Spice Islands of Indonesia.
21. **Sore against her will.** See note 19 above.
22. **Brave new world.** An obvious borrowing from *The Tempest*, 5.1.183. Act, scene and line references to Shakespeare's plays refer to *The Riverside Shakespeare*, ed. G. Blakemore Evans (Boston: Houghton Mifflin, 1974).
23. The remainder of this long speech is a patchwork of quotations from Michael Drayton's *Poly-Olbion*. Chapter and line numbers refer to *The Works of Michael Drayton*, ed. J. William Hebel, 2nd edn (Oxford: Basil Blackwell, 1961), vol. 4.
24. **The summer's ... too great.** *Poly-Olbion* 1.6, 3–4.
25. **Of Plymouth ... world defy.** *Poly-Olbion* 1.229–30.
26. **Of Wales ... British race.** *Poly-Olbion* 4.107–8.
27. **Of Durham's ... seated towers.** *Poly-Olbion* 29.72.
28. **Of the ... its mines.** *Poly-Olbion* 29.123–5.
29. **Of Evesham's ... clover grows.** *Poly-Olbion* 13.353, 399, 401.
30. **Of that ... and Eden.** *Poly-Olbion* 29.325–6. The 'Pictswall' is Hadrian's Wall.
31. **And of ... and flow.** *Poly-Olbion* 30.126, 128–9.
32. **Matoaka.** Tomocomo uses Pocahontas's personal name, which was recorded on her 1617 portrait. See Robertson, 'Pocahontas', 558, 570.
33. **On every ... am beset.** Cf. Thomas Dekker, John Ford and William Rowley, *The Witch of Edmonton*, 'On every side I am distracted' (1.2.191), in a scene believed to have been written by Dekker. Act, scene and line references refer to *The Dramatic Works of Thomas Dekker*, ed. Fredson Bowers, 4 vols (Cambridge: Cambridge University Press, 1958).
34. The image of Smith riding in haste to Brentford is curiously paralleled in Terrence Malick's 2005 film, *The New World*.
35. ***Falls in a swoon.*** The author has exaggerated a moment in Smith, 'Generall Historie', vol. 2, 261: 'without any word, she turned about, obscured her face, as not seeming well contented; and in that humour, her husband, with divers others, we all left her two or three houres'.
36. **When learned I ... Lady Pocahontas.** Cf. Smith, 'Generall Historie', vol. 2, 260–1: 'hearing shee was at Branford with divers of my friends, I went to see her'.
37. **Chawnzmit.** Helen C. Rountree, *Pocahontas, Powhatan, Opechancanough: Three Indian Lives Changed by Jamestown* (Charlottesville: University of Virginia Press,

2005), 6, claims that the Powhatan people probably pronounced Smith's name 'Chawnsmit'; it is thus intriguing to see the same name appear in the play.

38. **They did ... believe them.** *Cf.* Smith, 'Generall Historie', vol. 2, 261: 'They did tell us alwaies you were dead, and I knew no other till I came to Plimoth; yet Powhatan did command Uttamatomakkin to seeke you, and know the truth, because your Countriemen will lie much'. The playwright intensifies the drama by having Pocahontas and Tomocomo unaware that Smith is alive until this moment.

39. **My lord ... much of.** *Cf.* Smith, 'Generall Historie', vol. 2, 261: 'hee told me Powhatan did bid him to finde me out, to shew him our God, the King, Queene, and Prince, I so much had told them of'.

40. **With these ... seen Okeus.** *Cf.* Samuel Purchas, *Purchas his Pilgrimage*, 3rd edn (London: Henry Fetherstone, 1617), 954: 'I learned [from Tomocomo], that their *Okeeus* doth often appeare to them in His House or Temple ... walking up and down with strange words and gestures'.

41. *I like not this.* One of the most remarkable features of Q is the inadvertent printing of marginal comments added by Sir Henry Herbert, Master of the Revels, next to lines that were presumably cut from the play before performance. The words 'I like not this' also appear in Sir George Buc's comments on Fletcher and Massinger's *Sir John van Olden Barnavelt* (1619); see Janet Clare, *'Art Made Tongue-Tied by Authority': Elizabethan and Jacobean Dramatic Censorship* (Manchester: Manchester University Press, 1990), 176.

42. *Profane and ... left out.* *Cf.* Herbert's entry in his office-book: 'A Tragedy of the Plantation of Virginia; the <prophaness left out>', quoted in Bawcutt, *Control and Censorship*, 141–2.

43. **If thou ... blasphemous superstitions!** See Purchas, *Purchas his Pilgrimage*, 955: Tomocomo 'is very zealous in his superstition, and will heare no perswasions to the truth; bidding us teach the boies and girles (which were brought over from thence) He being too old now to learne'.

44. **D'ee.** This idiosyncratic contraction of 'do ye' is characteristic of John Ford and is the best evidence for his part-authorship of the play. See Lake, *Canon*, 220.

45. **Why, sure, ... honour you.** *Cf.* Chamberlain, *Letters*, vol. 2, 50: 'The Virginian woman Poca-huntas, with her father counsaillor hath ben with the King and graciously used, and both she and her assistant well placed at the maske'.

46. *Full of ... be corrected.* *Cf.* Herbert's entry on William Rowley's lost *Fool without Book*: 'full of faults, and must be Corrected, if allowed'; see Bawcutt, *Control and Censorship*, 211.

47. **Sure, nothing more sure!** *Cf. The London Prodigal* 10.78; this anonymous play is sometimes attributed to Dekker. Scene and line references are to *William Shakespeare and Others: Collaborative Plays*, ed. Jonathan Bate and Eric Rasmussen (Basingstoke: Palgrave Macmillan, 2013).

48. **You gave ... your white dog.** *Cf.* Smith, 'Generall Historie', vol. 2, 261: Tomocomo 'denied ever to have seene the King, till by circumstances he was satisfied he had: Then he replyed very sadly, You gave Powhatan a white Dog, which Powhatan fed as himselfe, but your King gave me nothing, and I am better than your white Dog'.

49. *Leave this ... own peril.* *Cf.* Sir Edmund Tilney's comment on *The Book of Sir Thomas More*: 'Leave out the insurrection wholly ... at your own peril'. Quoted in Bate and Rasmussen, *William Shakespeare and Others*, 350.

50. **Did you ... Mistress Rolfe.** By an extraordinary coincidence, almost identical words appear in Terrence Malick's film *The New World*.
51. **Rebecca, thou ... well-set countenance.** *Cf.* Smith, 'Generall Historie', vol. 2, 261. 'She began to talke, and remembred mee well what courtesies shee had done: saying, You did promise Powhatan what was yours should bee his, and he the like to you; you called him father being in his land a stranger, and by the same reason so must I doe you: which, though I would have excused, I durst not allow of that title because she was a Kings daughter; with a well set countenance she said, Were you not afraid to come into my fathers Countrie, and caused feare in him and all his people (but me) and feare you here I should call you father; I tell you then I will, and you shall call mee childe, and so I will bee for ever and ever your Countrieman.'
52. **She is ... stalks away.** An unexpected place for an allusion to *Hamlet*, 1.1.50.
53. **I'm all ... a-going, sir.** A borrowing from *The Changeling*, 1.1.44. Act, scene and line references to plays by Thomas Middleton refer to *Thomas Middleton: The Collected Works*, ed. Gary Taylor and John Lavagnino (Oxford: Clarendon Press, 2007).
54. **I have ... in silence.** *Cf. Richard III*, 1.3.102–3, 'I have too long borne / Your blunt upbraidings and your bitter scoffs'.
55. **And will ... voluntary exile.** A phrase characteristic of John Ford; it can also be found in *The Lovers' Melancholy*, *The Broken Heart* and *The Spanish Gypsy*; see Lake, *Canon*, 223.
56. **You would ... they say.** *Cf.* John Smith and others, 'The Proceedings of the English Colonie in Virginia' (1612), in *Complete Works*, vol. 1, 274: 'Some propheticall spirit calculated hee [Smith] had the Salvages in such subjection, hee would have made himselfe a king, by marrying Pocahontas, Powhatans daughter'.
57. **By marrying ... in Virginia.** An unusual use of a hexameter line, but one that permits emphasis on the assonance of 'Rebecca' and 'Virginia'.
58. **'Tis true ... in discretion.** *Cf.* Smith and others, 'Proceedings', vol. 1, 274: 'Very oft shee came to our fort, with what shee could get for Captaine Smith, that ever loved and used all the Countrie well, but her especially he ever much respected ... [.] But her marriage could no way have intitled him by any right to the kingdome, nor was it ever suspected hee had ever such a thought, or more regarded her, or any of them, than in honest reason, and discretion he might'.
59. **If he ... his determination.** *Cf.* Smith and others, 'Proceedings', vol. 1, 274 (following immediately from the quotation in the previous note): 'If he would he might have married her, or have done what him listed. For there was none that could have hindred his determination'. The author of this passage of *The Proceedings* seems to be using these words to defend Smith from the accusation that he wanted to marry Pocahontas, but the playwright turns the words against him by giving them to the malevolent Tomocomo.
60. **This flame ... present ashes!** A borrowing from Thomas Middleton and William Rowley's *A Fair Quarrel*, 1.1.352–3, also about the build-up to a duel.
61. **Smiling at the event.** *Cf. The Changeling*, '*Enter Deflores after all, smiling at the accident*' (4.1.0.3).

Chapter 9
Othello, Original Practices
A Photographic Essay

Rob Conkie

In October 2013 I directed an 'original-ish practices' staged reading of *Othello*. What follows is a photographic documentation of that event with occasional annotations. What did 'original practices' mean in this context (La Trobe University, Melbourne, Australia)? Here is what I wrote for the programme notes:

> We are playing a game with 'Original Practices'.
> Here are the Rules of the Game:
> 1. all-male cast;
> 2. all actors are in make-up;
> 3. thrust stage with audience on three sides;
> 4. the audience is in the same light as the actors;
> 5. the actors directly address the audience;
> 6. the actors double parts;
> 7. the text is cut to 'two hours' traffic';
> 8. the production plays without an interval;
> 9. there are two entrance/exits;[1]

Notes for this section begin on page 179.

10. period costumes (recycled from company stock); and
11. minimal rehearsal (twenty-four hours).

I will (literally) illustrate one of these rules – that of doubling (#6) – via some of the production photographs (taken by, and reproduced with thanks to, Olivia-Kate Glynn).

Illustration 9.1: Doubling: Desdemona/Bianca (top) and Roderigo/Emilia (above). Photos © Olivia-Kate Glynn. All following images in this essay © Olivia-Kate Glynn.

There were other doubles but these are the most significant for the discussion/illustration that follows. Anyone who is quite familiar with this play might already be wondering how we solved the difficulties that these doubles bring into *play*. Part of the answer, drawing on Jeremy Lopez's *Theatrical Convention and Audience Response* (2003), is that these difficulties were and were not solved. Lopez writes that:

> the potential for failure of many of the theatrical devices indigenous to or inherent in early modern drama is an essential part of understanding their potential success ... [. T]he drama and its audience were very much aware of the limitations of the early modern stage, and that the potential for dramatic representation to be ridiculous or inefficient or incompetent was a constant and vital part of audiences' experience of the plays.[2]

At times, this, original-ish practices staged reading of *Othello* was at least ridiculous, perhaps inefficient, and in several ways incompetent, but it was also surprisingly quite magical and brilliant. I will be more forthright, and this is my central provocation: part of this production's magic and brilliance was indebted to its ridiculousness, inefficiency, and incompetence (which is no reflection on the cast, all of whom are trained, disciplined, and dedicated). To apply this provocation a little more broadly, I am suggesting that the kind of (potential for) failure described by Lopez and perhaps revived by an original practices production such as the one described here offers a challenge to orthodox practices of Shakespearean production which enshrine polish, precision, and psychological nuance.

One brief anecdote before I continue: I was hoping to observe some of the roughness I am describing here at a recent visit to the American Shakespeare Center but the three Actors' Renaissance Season productions that I witnessed were all the very final shows of their respective runs and they were smooth as silk. Even the one moment where an actor dried and requested a prompt was met by such a speedy and seamless reply from the book-holder that there was almost no rupture of which to speak.

The remainder of this photo-essay will feature examples from our production of things going wrong and describe how they added up to things overall going right.

General Cock-ups

The context for the big cock-up that is coming up is a series of smaller cock-ups from *the* beginning of Act 2. Damien Millar (Illustration 9.2) played the Herald (2.2.1–8).[3] This is text I would usually cut (and did so the first time I directed this play). I don't remember hearing it much in productions of the play that I have seen (probably 15–20). I certainly wouldn't have directed Damien to play the part the way he did (Damien is a multiple award-winning playwright and nationally reputed teacher of directing as well as one of Australia's most sought-after dramaturgs, but he's a bit camp as an actor), but with the rush of rehearsals I wasn't keen to intervene too much in the individual contributions of the actors, nor to smooth out inconsistencies of tone. Damien played the Herald pretty much as the Clown (who was cut), with celebratory party blower (lying around in the rehearsal room) and streamers. There were a lot of laughs and it struck me how beautifully this approach served the dramaturgy of the play, providing a caesura between the relentless pace – and the whole production was very fast – of the war council scene and the hyper-charged emotional scenes that were about to unfold.

Illustration 9.2: Damien Millar as the Herald.

In the notes I was writing as the production was playing I recorded Tom Davies's Cassio saying, 'Welcome, good Iago, and welcome to you ... (pause, he's gone off script, can't remember who he's looking at) ... too ...' (big laugh from the audience). What makes this cock-up even more of a cock-up is that I can't identify the moment in the text that this happened. If it was at the start of the watch scene (2.3), then someone must've been on stage who wasn't supposed to be (my money would be on Bob Pavlich's Roderigo). Below is Cassio's come-uppance for that blunder, but what's wrong with this picture? Cassio lies maimed (5.1), but the goblet is still sat on the edge of the stage (Illustration 9.3), the actors having failed to clear it after the drinking and fighting. The image nicely frames the potential consequences of intemperance but I spent most of the time hoping that it wouldn't be

Illustration 9.3: A goblet unmoved.

kicked at a crucial moment. It mocked both me and the seriousness of the last scene, during which it continued to proudly announce itself. The moment recalls an anecdote related by Russell Jackson. One night Ian McKellen drops his matches during his spellbinding turn as Iago in Trevor Nunn's much-praised 1989 RSC *Othello*. He then bends down and picks up every match, not just not breaking character for a moment, but perfectly within, even enhancing that character. That is a moment of failure, even in the most poised and accomplished of performances, which elevated that performance to a new, unplanned, and unplannable level.

Big Cock-ups

Here are the lovers of the production, Tom Considine's Othello (Illustration 9.4) and Andre Jewson's Desdemona (Illustration 9.5).

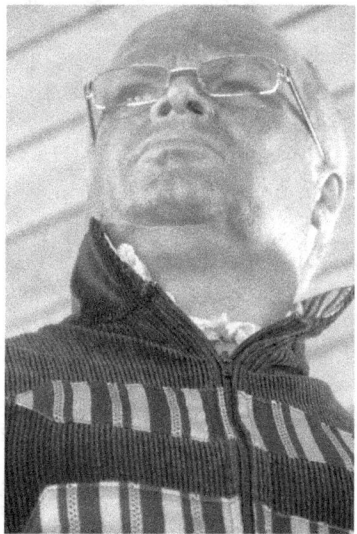

Illustration 9.4: Tom Considine as Othello.

Illustration 9.5: Andre Jewson as Desdemona.

And here are further photographs that help to fill in a bit more of what the overall production looked like (Illustrations 9.6–9.9).

Illustration 9.6: Roderigo (Bob Pavlich) and Iago (Trent Baker) sitting on a step in the stage.

Illustration 9.7: A long, narrow thrust with audience on three sides.

Illustration 9.8: The difficulties of fighting with scripts.

Illustration 9.9: An unholy alliance.

And Now, the Kiss ...

How we didn't quite anticipate this moment I can only put down to the rush of getting the whole production on in, by contemporary standards, a very short time, but after Othello was reunited with and kissed Desdemona, the actors left very visible make-up smudges, each upon the other. And not only this, but Othello, with one especially marked smudge right on his nose, looked like a clown (Illustration 9.10). The audience laughed a lot. Even though I wonder above about how I/we didn't anticipate this moment, the kiss and its after-effect was not done, as some might suppose, unthinkingly. I've written about Olivier's and Zadek's smudges[4] and the programme notes contained – as well as customary citations of Hugh Quarshie on black actors avoiding Othello and Margot Heinemann on, after

Brecht, playing these old works historically – the following, as it turned out, remarkably apposite quotation:

> A black Othello is an obscenity. The element of the grotesque is best achieved when a white man plays the role. As the play wears on, and under the heat of lights and action, the make-up begins to wear off, Othello becomes a monstrosity of colours: the wine-red lips and snow white eyes against a background of messy blackness.[5]

Was the production (or play) destroyed or marred by this moment of unintended hilarity? Not as far as I could tell. My feeling in the room at the time was that the audience was swept up in the joy of the Othello/Desdemona union and that their laughter became a celebratory confirmation of this. And soon after came one of the most powerful moments of the production: Desdemona smoothed the smudge on Othello's face. It was, at one and the same time, the actor Andre taking care of the actor Tom, but also, quite beautifully, a young bride taking care of her new husband.

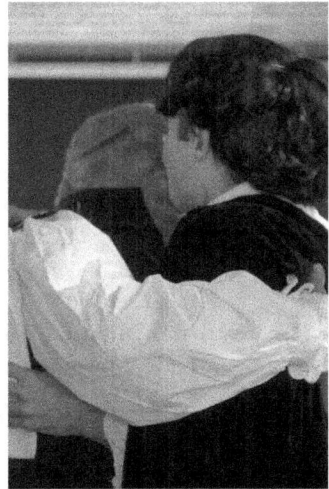

Illustration 9.10: The kiss, the clown.

The directorial intention (or one of them) behind the blacking up was to probe the 'traumatic residue' of blackface, to offer, after Ayanna Thompson, an appropriative critique through an 'activated and oppositional gaze' at the play. But given that Thompson also observes that 'Intention, practice, and reception cannot be disentangled',[6] my nervousness about the production meant that I wasn't sure I could do the same show in a public, rather than a university and research-driven context. The wonders of the kiss, though, the laughs, the smudge, the way it drew the audience into the production, and perhaps, set them up for the tragedy to come, could not have happened in a polished, tightly orchestrated, and psychologically driven production. Here's another such moment: Emilia's fabric management.

The production was staged in The Playroom at La Trobe University, one of the spaces managed by Student Theatre and Film at the university and presided over by the Artistic Director, Bob Pavlich. Bob played Emilia in the production. His wig was pretty ridiculous. Late in the production I had to fiddle the script slightly to make the Roderigo/Emilia double work, or at least potentially work. After Roderigo was slain by Iago (5.1) his killer dragged him off. Very soon after, Emilia had to appear, asking, 'Alas, what's the matter?' Bob had managed that switch in the full rehearsal in the morning, but for the afternoon's production he couldn't find the dress backstage. Out he came, wig askew, and carrying the dress in his hand, somehow trying to mask the black tights he was wearing. Again, cue big laughs. This was exacerbated by the fact that many of the students in the audience have worked a lot with Bob, but I like to think this represents a very faint analogue of the sort of laughs that the Polonius actor garnered with his line about being 'killed i'th' Capitol' (*Hamlet* 3.2.99).

It was just before this moment that another of the production's misfires provided an unplanned reward. In the unpinning scene (4.3), it took Bob a long time to unlace the corset (Illustration 9.11). It not only didn't matter, but enhanced the scene and production considerably. Desdemona was very definitely the centre of this all-male production and this wasn't just because of Andre's beautifully controlled (amongst the chaos, perhaps there's the rub) performance (two days later he was cast as the head hyena in the Sydney production of *The Lion King*). Maybe I was unconsciously placing her/him centre stage for many of his/her scenes, but there wasn't too much deliberate blocking going on. As Bob laboured with what Carol Chillington Rutter has labelled the 'technical nightmare' of unpinning and untying Desdemona, Andre just kept singing 'Willow, willow'. Still untying, still singing. It highlighted Desdemona's beauty and serenity (against all odds) and vulnerability. Like the Herald earlier, this moment demonstrated the dramaturgical ingenuity of this scene as everything slowed down and took a deep breath for what was about to unfold: the playing very much affirmed Rutter's argument that the 'unpinning is "big fuss," and its complicated physical business, written so that it must be conducted in front of spectators' eyes, constitutes both the significant labor and the theatrical meaning of the scene'.[7] When I first directed this play I largely cut the unpinning and singing, partly because I had a young, female student actor in the role that I didn't want to over-expose, partly to facilitate a lickety-split, ninety-minute, physical theatre adaptation, but mostly because I am an idiot. The scene, and its unintended lengthening, was crucial to the production's overall affective force.

There was another moment of the actors helping each other, and this one was only possible because it was a staged reading, rather than a full production. Whilst Bob untied, Andre held both of their scripts and held Bob's so that he could see it to speak Emilia's lines. Later Bob described the production as flying by the seat of its pants, a moment most summed up by him having to come on carrying, rather than wearing, his dress in 5.1. I like to think of Lopez's argument in terms of stumbles. If the actor does not stumble then there is no possibility to help him (or her in another production) up. Sometimes it is the fellow actor who helps, as in the case of fixing the smudge or holding the script, and sometimes it is the audience who lifts the actor (or

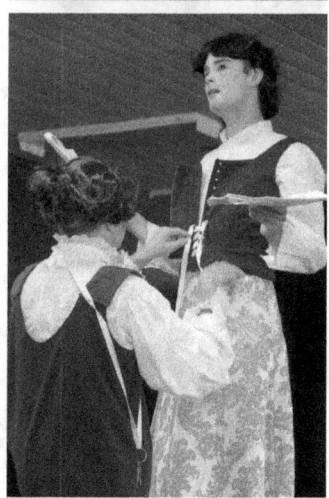

Illustration 9.11: Emilia's fabric management.

production) from a stumble, as in the generous response to a ridiculous or untidy moment, and they – I'm going to stick with collective here for all its complications – are further drawn into the production as assistants in its success (via failure). If an actor dries on stage and their fellow comes to the rescue, that helping up from a stumble is a demonstration of virtuosity (and fraternity/sorority) impossible without the stumble.

I think, like Grupo Galpão's *Romeu e Julieta*, that the tragedy of this original-ish practices production of *Othello* was enhanced by the

Illustration 9.12: Desdemona asleep.

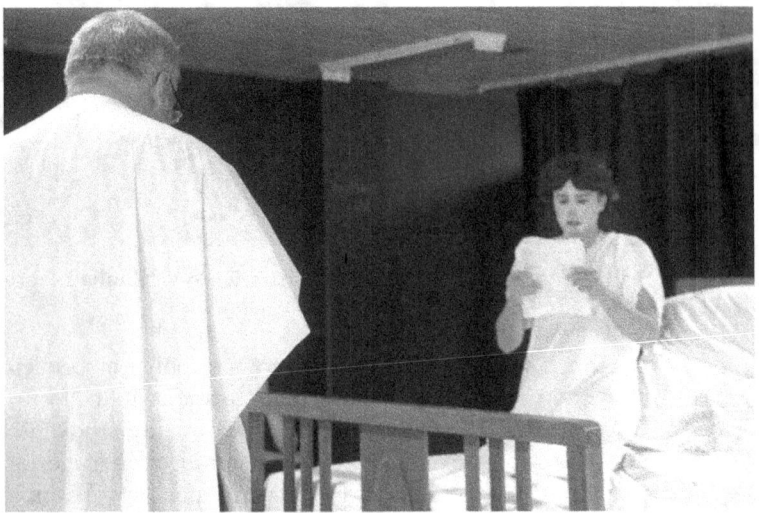

Illustration 9.13: 'Think on thy sins.'

Othello, *Original Practices* 175

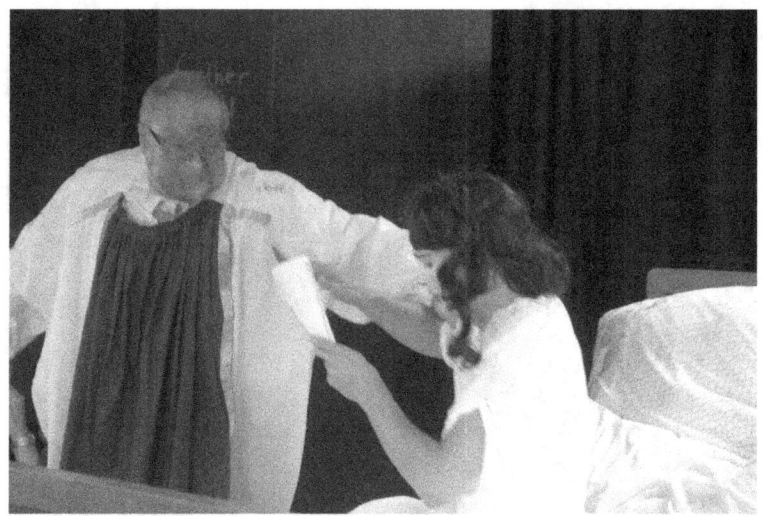

Illustration 9.14: 'Out strumpet! Weep'st thou for him to my face?'

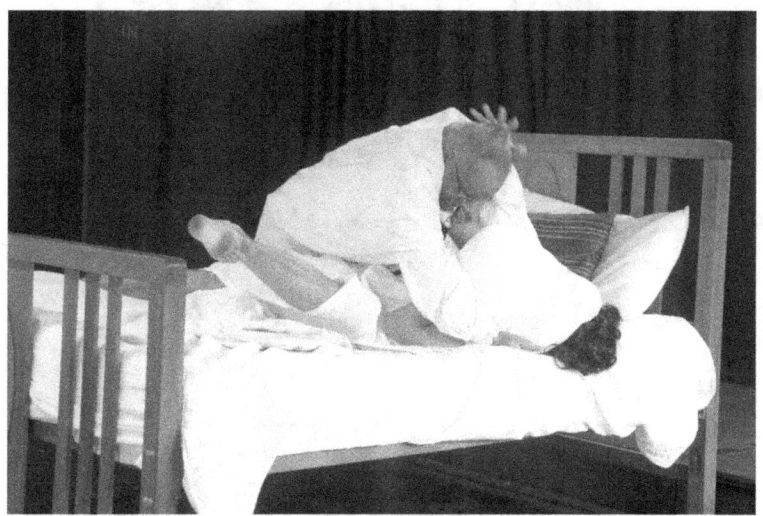

Illustration 9.15: 'Down, strumpet.'

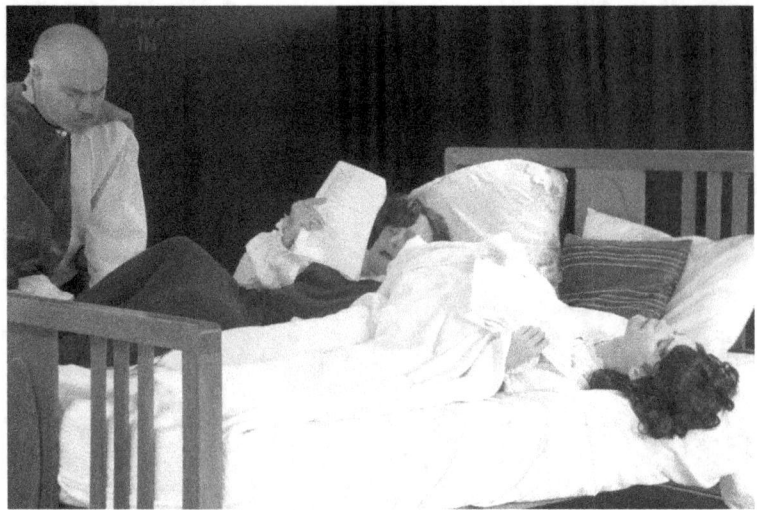

Illustration 9.16: 'What did thy song bode, lady?'

Illustration 9.17: I've not witnessed a more emotionally wrought Othello than Tom Considine's, even with a ridiculous and ubiquitous plastic retractable dagger.

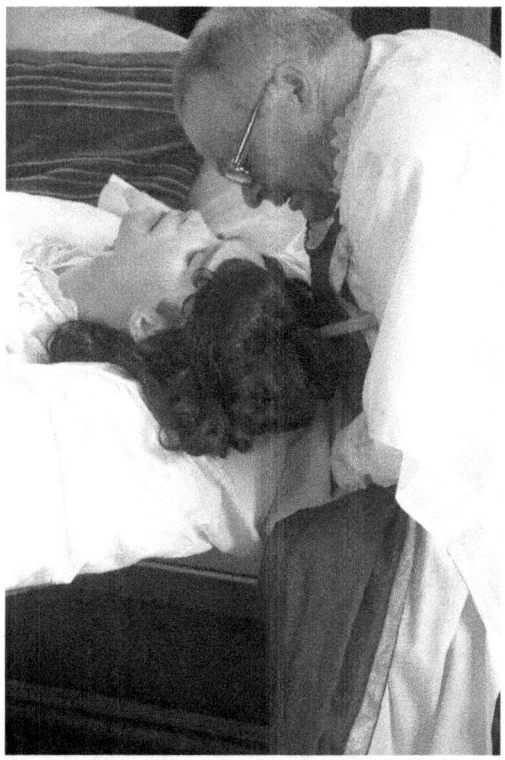

Illustration 9.18: It was very confronting to see this act so close up, both during rehearsals and in front of an audience; the laughter of the earlier scenes gave way to a shocked silence.

(sometimes unintended) comedy that preceded the ending. Here are the photographs of that ending.

The initial drive of this research project/production was to test, with all the limitations we were bringing to it – all-male cast, hastily produced make-up, holding scripts on stage, etc., etc. – whether an audience could still be caught up in the narrative, the tragedy, Iago's web. I wanted to measure this against the audience response recorded by Henry Jackson in 1610. My collaborator on the project, Penelope Woods (representing the Australian Research Council's Centre of Excellence for the History of Emotions, 1100–1800, the body which funded the work), came up with the inspired suggestion of soliciting audience feedback in the form of a letter. The

In 1610 Henry Jackson watched a performance of *Othello* at his University. The King's Men performed the play in Corpus Christi Hall for an audience of students and academics.

A letter that Jackson wrote to a friend, "D. G. P.", survives in the University archives. It describes the performance and his reaction to it – what he particularly noticed and felt.

What would you write to a friend about today's performance?

4 October 2013

Dear Michael,

We have just watched an original practice version of *Othello*. Natural light, thrust stage, and all male cast.

You would have been amused to see the dead Desdomona turn the page of her/his script to keep up. And the actor playing Emilia & Rodeigo, appear on stage with Emelia's wig, but forgot the dress. Not to mention the Duke holding the mad Othello at bay with a butter knife. It was terribly dramatic & I had moments of worry as Othello was smothering Desdomona with a pillow – hoping he wouldn't get carried away. Elisa watched it with me & she liked it very well.

Dear Desdimona,

I'm so sorry for you. You were so pure and beautiful, you chanelled a geisha. Thankyou for sharing the last moments of your life with me.

theatre programme had this on the back page and below, the last word/picture of this photo-essay, are two of the responses.

Rob Conkie is Senior Lecturer in Theatre at La Trobe University. His teaching and research integrates practical and theoretical approaches to Shakespeare in performance. He is the author of *Writing Performative Shakespeares: New Forms for Performance Criticism* (Cambridge University Press, 2016), *The Globe Theatre Project: Shakespeare and Authenticity* (Edwin Mellen, 2006), and numerous journal articles and book chapters. He has twice (2013, 2016) been appointed Associate Investigator of the Australian Research Council Centre of Excellence for the History of Emotions, for which he has produced theatre productions and workshops and related symposia. He has directed about a third of the Shakespeare canon for the stage.

Notes

1. See Tim Fitzpatrick, *Playwright, Space and Place in Early Modern Performance: Shakespeare and Company* (Farnham: Ashgate, 2011).
2. On doubling, Brett Gamboa's *Shakespeare's Double Plays: Dramatic Economy on the Early Modern Stage* (Cambridge: Cambridge University Press, 2018), is the new standard-bearer. See chapter 7 for a discussion of Othello.
3. William Shakespeare, *Othello*, Texts and Contexts, edited by Kim F. Hall (Boston: Bedford/St Martin's, 2007)
4. Rob Conkie, *Writing Performative Shakespeares: New Forms for Performance Criticism* (Cambridge: Cambridge University Press, 2016), 62. For a brilliant account of Othello smudges in the theatre see chapter 2 of Paul Menzer's *Anecdotal Shakespeare: A New Performance History* (London: Bloomsbury, 2015).
5. S.E. Ogude, 'Literature and Racism: The Example of Othello', in Othello, *New Essays from Black Writers*, ed. Mythili Kaul (Washington DC: Howard University Press, 1997), 151–66, 163.
6. Ayanna Thompson, 'The Blackfaced Bard: Returning to Shakespeare or Leaving Him?', *Shakespeare Bulletin* 27, 3 (2009), 437–56, 449–52.
7. Carol Chillington Rutter, 'Unpinning Desdemona (Again) or "Who would be toll'd with Wenches in a shew?"', *Shakespeare Bulletin* 28, 1 (2010), 111–32, 114.

Index

NOTE: Page references with an *f* are figures; page references with an n will be found in Notes.

adaptation, 17, 43–44
   appropriation and, 45
   scholarship on, 45
   The Sonnet Project, 29–32
   of *Sonnets*, 28
   Translating and Rewriting Shakespeare, 29–30
alternate universe (AU) genre
   alternative setting and, 42–43
   revisionary narrative, 42
anapestic, 116
Antony and Cleopatra (Shakespeare), 105
appropriation, of Shakespeare, 45
Arden of Faversham (play), 105
As You Like It (Shakespeare), 103, 109n22
AU genre. *See* alternate universe genre

Bailey, Lucy, 12
Behn, Aphra, 147
Benson, John, 23, 36n6
Brook, Peter, 25–26, 30

Caleo, Bernard, 14–15
Campbell, Mary Baine, 17
canon divergence, 42
Carleton, Dudley, 147

Chamberlain, John, 147, 149, 161n9
   letters of, 161n11
characters, Shakespearean, 6
   actors and, 11
   Angela, 106–7
   Antonio Africanus, 105
   Berowne/Rahere, 103
   Capulet, 103
   Cassio, 168
   Desdemona, 170–72, 174–75
   Duke of Ravenna, 103
   dukes, 103
   Emilia, 172–73
   Garzoni Dentitristi, 104
   Herald, 168
   Hicket, 104
   Holofernes, 106
   Lady Anne, 50
   Lady Rosaline, 106
   Mercutio, 40–41
   nurse, 106–7
   Ophelia, 50
   Othello, 170–71
   Roderigo, 172
   Scruple, 104
   Slapbag, 105–6
   Spedalingo, 103–4
   Squint, 104–5
   Turtle, 106

collaborative writing, 13
The Comedy of Errors (Shakespeare), 106
comedy writing, 8–9
concrete poems, 28
Considine, Tom, 12, 14–15, 169, 171, 175–77
creative engagement, 1–2
creative writing, literary criticism and, 3–6
critical engagement, 1–2
criticism
    fanfiction and, 47–48
    learning from, 3
    literary, 3–6
    Shakespeare, 6–7

Dekker, Thomas, 147, 162n18, 162n33
doubling, of parts, 165–67, 172
Drayton, Michael, 147, 162n23
duke character, 103

Echo and Narcissus, or Man O Man! (play), 119–27
ekphrasis, 11
Eliot, T.S., 6–7
Elizabethan English, 5
'energia,' 6
engagement
    creative, 1–2
    critical, 1–2
    with *Sonnets*, 21
Enter Nurse, 101, 107–18. See also *Love's Labour's Won*
Erasmus, 7
    Ciceronianus, 4–5
Escolme, Bridget, 13

The Faerie Queene (Spenser), 128, 145
The Fair Maid of Alexandria, or The Glass Tower (play), 129–45
fandom
    canon divergence, 42
    gender and, 44, 46, 49–50
    as gift economy, 42
    marginalized readers and, 44
    race and, 44, 46
    revisionary narrative, 42
    scholarship on, 45, 52n16
fanfiction, 16, 38–53
    approach to, 41
    AU, 42–43
    beta or *beta-reader* in, 39–40, 62
    criticism and, 47–48
    defined, 38
    interpretation and, 39–40, 42–43
    King Lear, 45
    The Merchant of Venice, 44
    A Merry Midsummer Labor Merchant's Tempest in King Beatrice's Verona, 54–60
    myth of Shakespeare and, 45
    as pedagogical exercise, 41
    peer review, 39–40
    Richard II, 52n8
    Richard III, 48–49, 61–100
    Romeo and Juliet, 47–48
    scholarship on, 45–46, 52n16
    The Taming of the Shrew, 43, 44
    translations and, 40
    what is, 50
favoured pairings, 53n23
female characters, Shakespearean
    Angela, 106–7
    Desdemona, 170–72, 174–75
    Emilia, 172–73
    Lady Anne, 50
    Lady Rosaline, 106
    Ophelia, 50
films
    Clueless, 52n11
    The New World, 149, 162n34
    The Tempest, 42
    10 Things I Hate about You, 43, 44
    TSP, 29–32
Finn, Kavita Mudan, 61
First Folio, 3. See also *specific plays*
Fletcher, John, 147–48, 161n10, 162n20

Ford, John, 147, 163n44
found-poetry movement, 28

Garzoni, Tomaso, 103–4
gender. *See also* female characters, Shakespearean
 fandom and, 44, 46, 49–50
 same-sex pairings, 53n24
gender-swapped casting, 49, 53n25
General History (Smith), 148, 164n51
The Glass Tower. See The Fair Maid of Alexandria
Globeplayer (website), 30
Greenblatt, Stephen, 6, 119
'gusto,' 6

Hamlet (Shakespeare), 172
 'Hamlet and His Problems,' 6–7
 A Merry Midsummer Labor Merchant's Tempest in King Beatrice's Verona, 54–60
 The Murder of Gonzago in, 5
 Ophelia in, 50
 polysyndeton rhetorical device in, 9–10
 soliloquies, 8–9
'Hamlet and His Problems' (Eliot), 6–7
Hazlitt, William, 6
headcanons, 42, 52n8
Heinemann, Margot, 170–71
Hellekson, Karen, 42
Henderson, John, 102, 104, 106
Henry IV (Shakespeare), 14–15
Henry V (Shakespeare), 102
Herbert, Henry, 146, 149, 163n41
Holderness, Graham, 18
Holland, Peter, 16
L'Hospedale de' pazzi incurabili (Garzoni), 103–4
hospital setting, 102–3
hypertextuality, 22

iambic pentameter, 5, 9–10

anapestic compared with, 116
imitatio, 3
imitation, 6–7
interpretation
 fanfiction and, 39–40, 42–43
 positivism and literary, 47
The Island Princess (Fletcher), 147–48, 161n10, 162n20
Iyengar, Sujata, 43–44, 102

Jewson, Andre, 169, 171–72, 174–77

King, Elizabeth, 2
King Lear (Shakespeare), 10–11, 14, 105
 fanfiction, 45
 A Merry Midsummer Labor Merchant's Tempest in King Beatrice's Verona, 54–60

Lake, David J., 147
L=A=N=G=U=A=G=E poets, 28
Lanier, Douglas, 42
Legault, Paul, 27–30
Lewis, Cynthia, 105
LGBTQIA+ community, fandom and, 44
literary criticism
 creative writing and, 3–6
 judgement and, 6
 of Shakespeare, 6–7
Lopez, Jeremy, 173
 Theatrical Convention and Audience Response, 167
'Love is My Sin' (theatre production), 25–27
Love's Labour's Lost (Shakespeare), 2, 102
 Holofernes in, 106
Love's Labour's Won (Shakespeare), 101–18
 Angela in, 106–7
 Antonio Africanus in, 105
 Autumn in, 107
 Berowne/Rahere in, 103

Capulet in, 103
Duke of Ravenna in, 103
Garzoni Dentitristi in, 104
Hicket in, 104
hospital setting of, 102–4
Lady Rosaline in, 106
roles in, 102–7
Scruple in, 104
Slapbag in, 105–6
Spedalingo in, 103–4
Squint in, 104–5
stage direction, 108
Summer in, 107
textual corruption of, 117
time in, 102, 110
Turtle in, 106

Malick, Terrence, 149, 162n34
Man O Man! (play). See *Echo and Narcissus*
marginalized readers, fandom and, 44
Massey, Gerald, 37n11
material historicism, 24
McCall, Jessica, 54–60
McKellen, Ian, 10–11, 169
McMullan, Gordon, 148
The Merchant of Venice (Shakespeare), 5, 103
fanfiction and, 44
A Merry Midsummer Labor Merchant's Tempest in King Beatrice's Verona (McCall), 54–60
The Merry Wives of Windsor (Shakespeare), 14
Middleton, Thomas, 103
A Midsummer Night's Dream (Shakespeare), 103, 107
Ovid and, 119
Millar, Damien, 168
Morgann, Maurice, 16
Moss, Dan, 17
motive, 6
Much Ado About Nothing (Shakespeare), 54

The Murder of Gonzago (play within *Hamlet*), 5

Nashe, Thomas, 102–4
The New World (film), 149, 162n34
New York (city), TSP and, 29–32
Nicol, David, 16
No Fear Shakespeare, 41
translations, 40
Nunn, Trevor, 11, 169
nurse character, 106–7

Organization for Transformative Works' Archive of Our Own, 46
original practices
doubling, of parts, 165–67
failure and, potential for, 167
Othello, a photographic essay, 11–12, 18, 165–79
Rules of the Game, 165–66
unintended comedy and, 173–74
Othello (Shakespeare), 16, 103
black actors and, 170–71
blackface and, 171
canon divergence, 42
Cassio in, 168
Desdemona in, 170–72, 174–75
doubling, of parts, 165–67, 172
Emilia in, 172–73
Herald in, 168
A Merry Midsummer Labor Merchant's Tempest in King Beatrice's Verona, 54–60
original practices, a photographic essay, 11–12, 18, 165–79
Othello in, 170–71
Othello smudges in, 12, 170–71, 179n4
Roderigo in, 172
'*Othello*, Original Practices: A Photographic Essay,' 11–12, 18, 165–79
Ovid, 119

pairings
  favoured, 53n23
  same-sex, 53n24
Pande, Rukmini, 46
paraphrasing, 12
Pavlich, Bob, 172
Pickled Red Herring; or, CSI: Richard III (Finn), 61
Pocahontas, 161n9
  as Rebecca Rolfe, 161n12
  Smith and, 147–48, 164n56, 164n59
  in *A Tragedy of the Plantation of Virginia*, 148
poetry, 28. *See also* Sonnets
Poly-Olbion (Drayton), 147, 162n23
polysyndeton, 9–10
positivism, 47
presentism, 47
Pugh, Sheenagh, 49–50

Quarshie, Hugh, 170
Quisara, 148

race
  black actors and, 170–71
  blackface and, 171
  fandom and, 44, 46
The Renaissance Hospital: Healing the Body and Healing the Soul (Henderson), 102, 104, 106
revisionary narrative, 42
rhetoric
  polysyndeton, 9–10
  Renaissance, 6
Richard II (Shakespeare), 52n8
Richard III (Shakespeare), 17, 164n54
  fanfiction, 48–49, 61
  Lady Anne, 50
  Pickled Red Herring; or, CSI: Richard III, 61
Rolfe, John, 147–48
Rolfe, Rebecca, 161n12. *See also* Pocahontas
Rollins, Hyder R., 24

Romeo and Juliet (Shakespeare), 2, 105, 108
  canon divergence, 42
  fanfiction, 47–48
  Mercutio in, 40–41
  A Merry Midsummer Labor Merchant's Tempest in King Beatrice's Verona, 54–60
  nurse in, 107
Russo, Rocco, 58
Rutter, Carol Chillington, 172–73

same-sex pairings, 53n24
seasonality, 107
Seinfeld, Jerry, 8
Shakespeare, myth of, 43
  fanfiction and, 45
Shakespearean Scene-Writing seminar, 2
Shakespeare Association of America conference, St Louis, 2014, 1–2
Shakespeare criticism, 6–7
Shakespeare Now!, 18
Shakespeare's Medical Language: A Dictionary (Continuum Press), 102
'shipping,' 53n23
Shmoop, 8
'slash,' 53n24
Smith, John
  General History, 148, 164n51
  Pocahontas and, 147–48, 164n56, 164n59
The Sonnet Project (TSP), 29–32
  location and, 30–31
  methodology, 30
Sonnets (Shakespeare), 17, 21–37
  80, 32–33, 35
  110, 26
  128, 28
  129, 26, 28
  130, 28
  adaptations, of modern English, 28

copy texts, 24
creative responses to, 22–23
editing, 22
editions, 23–24, 36n3
editions, online, 22, 24
engagement with, 21
hypertextuality and, 22
'Love is My Sin' production, 25–27
order of, 23–25, 36n8
reading, 21–22
re-bounding of, 25
1609 quarto (Q) order, 23–24
story of, 37n13
translation, 27–29
The Sonnets: Translating and Rewriting Shakespeare (Cohen, Legault), 27–30
SparkNotes, 8, 41
Spenser, Edmund, 128, 145

The Taming of the Shrew (Shakespeare), 43, 44
Taymor, Julie, 41–42
The Tempest (Shakespeare), 109
  film, 42
  A Tragedy of the Plantation of Virginia and, 162n22
10 Things I Hate about You (film), 43, 44
Theatrical Convention and Audience Response (Lopez), 167
Thompson, Ayanna, 43, 46
Thorpe, Thomas, 36n6, 36n8
time, 102, 110
Tomocomo, 149, 161n15
A Tragedy of the Plantation of Virginia (play), 146–64
  authenticity of, 149
  authorship of, 147, 162n18, 162n33, 163n44
  characterizations in, 148–49
  fictional romance in, 147–48
  Herbert and censorship of, 149, 163n41
  The New World and, 149, 162n34

  Pocahontas in, 148
  sources, 147
  The Tempest and, 162n22
  text, 149–60
  Tomocomo in, 149, 161n15
transcription, 7–8, 12
translations
  fanfiction and, 40
  No Fear Shakespeare, 40
  Sonnets, 27–29
  Troilus and Cressida (Shakespeare), 7–9
  Escolme on, 13
TSP. *See The Sonnet Project*
Turk, Tisha, 42
Twelfth Night (Shakespeare), 107
Two Gentleman of Verona (Shakespeare), 103

The Unfortunate Traveller (Nashe), 102–4

Venus and Adonis (Shakespeare), 108

The Widow Ranter (Behn), 147
Williams, Ross, 29
Wilson, Anna, 41
Wilson, Dover, 5
The Winter's Tale (Shakespeare), 42
works, Shakespeare. *See also Hamlet; Othello; Sonnets*
  Antony and Cleopatra, 105
  As You Like It, 103, 109n22
  The Comedy of Errors, 106
  Henry IV, 14–15
  Henry V, 102
  King Lear, 10–11, 14, 45, 105
  Love's Labour's Lost, 2, 102, 106
  Love's Labour's Won, 101–18
  The Merchant of Venice, 5, 44, 103
  The Merry Wives of Windsor, 14
  A Midsummer Night's Dream, 103, 107, 119
  Much Ado About Nothing, 54

Richard II, 52n8
Richard III, 17, 48–50, 61, 164n54
Romeo and Juliet, 2, 40–42, 47–48, 54, 105, 107, 108
The Taming of the Shrew, 43, 44
The Tempest, 42, 109, 162n22
Troilus and Cressida, 7–9, 13
Twelfth Night, 107
Two Gentleman of Verona, 103

Venus and Adonis, 108
The Winter's Tale, 42
writing
   collaborative, 13
   comedy, 8–9
   creative, 3–6
   'energia' in, 6
writing Shakespeare seminar, 2

YouTube, TSP videos on, 32

www.ingramcontent.com/pod-product-compliance
Lightning Source LLC
Chambersburg PA
CBHW072155100526
44589CB00015B/2234